By Katherine Hall Page

KATHERINE HALL PAGE

SMALL PLATES

Short Fiction

wm

WILLIAM MORROW
An Imprint of HarperCollinsPublishers

"The Proof Is Always in the Pudding" appeared in a slightly different version in the October-January 2010 issue of *The Strand Magazine*. The author's thanks to Andrew Gulli, managing editor.

WILLIAM MORROW
An Imprint of HarperCollins*Publishers*
195 Broadway
New York, New York 10007

With thanks to Dr. Robert E. DeMartino
For his treasured friendship and expertise

One cannot think well, love well,
sleep well, if one has not dined well.

—VIRGINIA WOOLF, *A Room of One's Own*

CONTENTS

INTRODUCTION

"Not that the story need be long, but it will take a long while to make it short," Henry David Thoreau observed to a friend. Edgar Allan Poe, a master of the form, wrote, "A short story must have a single mood and every sentence must build towards it." Taken together, these are a fine summation of the challenge posed by short story writing: that paring-down process, the examination of each word essential for a satisfactory result.

Cheever, O'Connor, Fitzgerald, Carver, Welty, Salinger, Saki, Cather, Joyce—to name a very few favorites I discovered early and have reread often. From time to time, I have published short stories

myself, journeying away from my mystery series
featuring inquisitive amateur sleuth Faith Sibley
Fairchild, a wife, mother, and caterer who is prone
to stumbling across dead bodies. I find the short
stories more difficult to write than the novels—
hard as they are. (I like to go back to that small
1939 gem, *Writing Is Work,* by Mary Roberts
Rinehart, to commiserate.) Yet, I have written a
number of short stories and this volume is a collection of some of them, as well as a few new ones.

The settings for these stories range from coast
to coast in the United States and across the pond.
Although I have set books in other countries, most
of my short stories seem loath to travel, except in
terms of time. One of them takes the reader to a
century still bathed in gaslight.

The characters in these stories are an assorted
lot. A man who longs for widowhood, dreams of
the attention from the casserole brigade—good
women lining up at his door, hopefully presenting
unburnt offerings and perhaps themselves as offerings as well. A newlywed discovers her husband's
ingenious hiding places for objects like spare keys.
One spinster turns to friends for help with the su-
pernatural. Another unmarried lady, who raises
goats on an island off the coast of Maine, finds a
baby named Christopher in her barn on Christmas

eve. In another Maine story, an elderly lobsterman proves to be an extremely acute observer. Faith Fairchild herself appears in most of these stories, though sometimes just as a cameo. She encounters an ideal couple on vacation in Cape Cod and takes an immediate dislike to them. Why? She discovers that a deep-seated superstition of her mother-in-law's is based on fact. Faith and her sister team up to safeguard a bride in peril. And her own culinary prowess is tested as she tries to avoid being "Sliced" in a cutthroat mock reality cooking show.

The title of the collection, *Small Plates*, refers not only to the length of these servings but also to the pleasure that ordering tapas, or two appetizers instead of an entrée, often provides. It is my hope that the tastes here will linger long on the palate.

SMALL PLATES

THE GHOST OF WINTHROP

Prudence Winthrop sat straight up in bed, rigid with fear, her quilt clutched to her chin. There it was again! The sound of the ancient elevator slowly making its way from the basement to the upper floors of the Beacon Hill town house that had served as Prudence's home for twenty of her forty years.

She held her breath and listened. Silence.

The noise had awakened her from an uneasy sleep, and at first she'd thought hazily that it was Aunt Eliza coming to bed after doing the crossword or acrostic that she claimed always guaranteed a good night's rest. "A little brain stimulation just before it shuts down," she was wont to say.

But Aunt Eliza had been sleeping in her sitting room on the ground floor for some time, and, more to the point, the sleep she was sleeping now was not only guaranteed but also did not require any brain stimulation.

Eliza Winthrop was dead.

The sudden screech of metal gears in need of greasing made Prudence jump; then a steady whirring began. The elevator had started up again—inexorably rising closer and closer. Prudence got out of bed and quickly locked her door. Her heart was pounding so loudly, it threatened to drown out the noise. She pressed her ear to the door and listened. The elevator ground to a stop with a gasping shudder. The gate rattled as someone pulled it back; she heard the door to her floor open. Then silence.

"Who's there?" Prudence called out in a quavering voice, summoning all of her courage. There was no answer.

"Who is it?" she asked again. "Nicholas? Nora?" But she knew the queries were in vain. Both the butler and the housekeeper were away until the following morning, an earlier visit to Nora's sister on the South Shore having been postponed by recent events.

The house was completely still. Prudence fancied she could hear the Simon Willard longcase clock purchased by Josiah Winthrop in 1790, placed in the entry hall that year and never moved an inch. Once more she pressed her ear to the solid door. The thick Oriental runner would muffle footsteps, but she strained for a cough, the rustle of a garment—something that would indicate the presence of a human being standing just outside her bedroom. Nothing—and she realized that what she had imagined was the ticking of the clock was really her own rapidly increasing pulse rate.

And then the elevator started up again, descending. Prudence ran for her bed, trembling. She didn't have a phone in her room, and going downstairs to use the one in the library was out of the question even though she knew she must be alone in the house. All the doors and windows were locked. Nicholas would have checked, but she'd still gone around to be sure before retiring. There was no way anyone could have gotten in. She wished Aunt Eliza hadn't been so adamant about not installing an alarm system—"Waste of money. Finicky things too. Most likely you, Nicholas, and Nora would set it off by accident." Someone with a system had given her some window stickers, but she didn't want to put those up either. "An invitation. Might as well put up a sign: VALUABLES INSIDE WORTH PROTECTING."

Prudence heard the elevator stop several floors below.

"I must be going mad," she said out loud.

Faith Sibley Fairchild looked over at Prudence Winthrop, who was sitting in her family pew surrounded by a rather intimidating-looking phalanx of Winthrop relatives that had gathered in full force for Eliza Winthrop's funeral. Pru definitely looked peaked, Faith thought, then gave a small inward start of surprise. Quaint words like *peaked* seemed to be invading her vocabulary with alarming frequency since she'd left the Big Apple for the more bucolic orchards of New England. It had been difficult to abandon her native city, but her first chance meeting in Manhattan and further acquaintance with the young Reverend Thomas Fairchild, parson in Aleford, a small town west of Boston, happily had left her no choice.

She studied Prudence's face more closely. There were tears glistening behind the lenses of the woman's horn-rimmed glasses, but Prudence's aunt had been well over ninety. Could grief alone account for Miss—somehow Ms. seemed inappropriate—Winthrop's extreme pallor and lined brow? It looked as if the woman hadn't slept in months, or had a decent meal. Faith was a caterer, and her thoughts quite naturally turned to food. They also turned to mystery. There was nothing suspicious about Eliza Winthrop's death, though. The wonder was that she'd lived as long as she had with her self-described "delicate heart."

There was nothing else delicate about Aunt Eliza, who had ruled the Winthrops as a not-so-benevolent despot. Never married—self-appointed Keeper of the Flame—she had controlled much of the family fortune and did not suffer fools gladly. Eliza had been known to banish individuals from her Sunday dinners for crimes ranging from voting for the wrong party to planting gladioli, flowers she detested.

There were no gladioli banking the coffin, Faith noted. She turned her head slightly and looked back at the Winthrop pew. Winthrops had been among the founding families of Aleford some three hundred years ago. Since that time, the Winthrops had migrated into town, colonizing Beacon Hill and the Back Bay—when it was filled in. Winthrops did not claim to walk on water, despite what some of their detractors might say.

Yet there had always been some family members who had stayed true to the Aleford congregation, and Eliza Winthrop was one of the most steadfast. At exactly quarter past ten every Sunday, Nicholas, her chauffer and butler, brought her vintage Cadillac to the front of the house on Louisburg Square. At exactly quarter to eleven, Miss Eliza entered her First Parish pew with Prudence scurrying along behind carrying their prayer books. An entire city could safely set its clocks by Eliza's unvarying routines of neighborhood walks, Friday afternoons at the Boston Symphony, and nightly bedtime puzzles accompanied by one small glass of Port—taken for medicinal purposes, she'd told Faith.

Living with Aunt Eliza could scarcely have been one long madcap whirl of pleasure, Faith thought. Perhaps Prudence's tears were tears of joy, although knowing Pru, this was unlikely. She had been devoted to the aunt who'd given her a home when Prudence had been orphaned many years ago. Faith had never heard any mention of a career—Aunt Eliza had plenty for her young niece to do. Nor were there gentlemen callers—not surprising, since they'd have had to get past Eliza first.

Faith continued to scrutinize Pru. There wasn't a whole lot to see. Prudence Winthrop was an ordinary-looking woman with thick auburn hair cut rather unattractively. Yet, she had large, very pretty blue eyes. Faith had a sudden mental image of an old movie in which the Cary Grant–type hero gently removes the heroine's glasses and a bobby pin or two and voilà! She's a raving beauty. Prudence was never going to be that, but Faith itched to get the woman into the hands of a good hairdresser, slap a little makeup on her, and tell her about the wonderful new invention called contact lenses.

Her mind was wandering, as it often did in church, despite having not only a husband but also a father and grandfather in the business. But suddenly Faith's imaginary pictures of a rejuvenated Prudence Winthrop became blurred as she realized there was something much more evident in Pru's blue eyes. There was another reason for her ashen color and the way the woman's hands were gripping the edge of the pew—so hard her knuckles were deathly white. It wasn't grief. It was fear.

Prudence Winthrop was exhibiting all the signs of a woman living in utter terror! And Faith intended to find out why.

It turned out to be easier to start the investigation than Faith anticipated. As they were leaving the church for the cemetery, Prudence herself approached Faith, drawing her aside.

"I need to talk to you and Tom. It's desperately important!" Her eyes looked like a doe's caught by headlights, and she was holding on to Faith's arm as if it were the last gorse bush on a crumbling cliff.

Before Faith could conjure up more similes from nature—something about the woman suggested frightened wildlife and dire mishaps—she proposed lunch instead, gently detaching Prudence's hand before she cut off Faith's circulation.

"Come back with us after the graveside ceremony. I made some butternut squash soup and sandwiches." She knew that there would not be any cold baked meats at the Winthrop town house or elsewhere. Eliza had stipulated no collation after the service. "Don't want everyone having a party at my expense," she'd told her lawyer.

"I hate to be a bother, but that would be wonderful. You see . . ."

"A problem, cousin Prudence?" interrupted Bradford Winthrop IV, looking both elegant and capable in his well-cut black topcoat from Brooks Brothers. Faith hadn't heard him approach. He'd simply oozed his way between them.

Prudence flushed unbecomingly. "No, I was just talking to Mrs. Fairchild about the, uh, service." Unaccustomed to uttering falsehoods, of any color or size, Prudence was stammering.

"Good, good, then let us proceed. Why don't you drive back into town with us afterward?" Although his voice rose, it was clearly not a question but an order.

Bradford was several years younger than his cousin and was known as a highly successful businessman who adhered to the belief that "ruthless" was a complimentary adjective.

He put his arm through Pru's. "I'll send Nicholas back. No need for him to stay and wait for you."

As he ushered her off, Pru looked back at Faith over her shoulder, the proverbial lamb to the slaughter. Faith mouthed, "Call you later" and was heartened to see a slight nod.

Bradford left Prudence briefly and spent several moments in deep conversation with Nicholas before waving the butler-chauffeur away.

It wasn't until lunch the following day that Prudence was able to get to the parsonage. The soup had kept, and Faith had added chicken salad with tarragon and grape sandwiches.

"I hardly know where to begin," Prudence said, dipping her spoon into the soup. "Aunt Eliza was, well, a bit eccentric—and she did like to play games—but she was absolutely of sound mind."

Wondering where this was all going, Faith asked, "Has someone been suggesting otherwise?" Tom had finished his soup and the sandwich would be gone soon too. Her husband was what was known as "a big, hungry boy." Four-year-old Ben was playing with Legos on the floor next to Faith, and Amy, eight months, was enjoying a postprandial snooze. Faith had fed them earlier.

"No, not really. But, you see, it's Aunt Eliza's will. Nobody's actually seen it, and that's the problem. Instead of depositing a copy with her lawyer, Aunt Eliza left a letter to be opened after her death with instructions for the funeral and the information that she'd hidden her Last Will and Testament."

Faith dropped her spoon. Soup splashed on the tablecloth. "Hidden it?"

"Yes." Pru nodded. "Somewhere in the house. And she stated that except for bequests to the servants, the church, and some charities, whoever finds the will inherits everything! She called it 'a treasure hunt.' "

Faith and Tom exchanged surprised glances.

"How incredible," Tom said. "I've heard some odd requests and stipulations in wills, but to play games with a fortune like that!"

And what a fortune it was, Faith reflected. Not simply the house, worth many millions, but also its contents. And then all the other assets, squirreled safely away by Eliza's forebears and guarded by her.

"I get to look first," Pru said. "But I only have a week, starting from the day of her death, when the letter was opened."

"But that only gives you three more days!" Faith said.

"I know—and I've been searching everywhere. I haven't been able to find a thing." It hardly seemed that Pru could look more woebegone, but she did.

"And bright and early Friday morning, you can be sure Bradford and the rest will be at the door with bloodhounds." Faith wasn't quite sure what breed of dog could sniff out documents, but Bradford Winthrop would make certain to find out and acquire one, or several, by Friday.

Prudence put down her spoon and gave up any semblance of eating. "There's something else. I think the house is haunted."

Tom choked, hastily drank some water, and said, "Prudence, you can't be serious."

Even accounting for her unsettled state due to her recent loss, a sudden belief in apparitions was a shock to his clerical sensibility.

"I can't think of any other possible explanation," she said.

She told them about the elevator, adding, "The servants are back now and they swear they have not been using it, yet it comes and goes at the same time—Aunt Eliza's bedtime—every night. I trust them completely; they've been with us since before I came to live in the house. And there's something else. The fire escape ends at my window, and last night I thought I saw something white floating outside. When I went to look, it was gone.

"I have the only key to the house. Aunt Eliza was most insistent that we have only two. Nicholas and Nora don't even have one. Aunt Eliza kept her key in the drawer of the cherry secretary in the front drawing room, and it's there. I checked before I came here. And mine is in my purse."

Faith made a quick decision. Obviously the woman needed help—in more ways than one, but the beauty makeover could come later. Right now they had to save her fortune and find out who was trying to frighten her out of her home. Given the cast of characters Pru had for relations, the "who" wasn't the hard part. It was the "how"—and "where," in the case of the hidden will.

"Why don't Tom and I come in tomorrow to help you search? You can spare the time, can't you, darling?" Faith reached under the table for her husband's hand and gave it a quick squeeze. She knew the stacks of paperwork and reading material in his study had reached near Mount Sinai proportions, but this was an emergency.

"I'd be delighted," Tom said. "Two more pairs of eyes should solve the problem."

Prudence Winthrop smiled.

Phone calls in the middle of the night were not completely out of the ordinary at the parsonage, but at the sound of the first ring, Faith always leaped out of bed prepared for the worst. Although with Tom next to her and both children slumbering down the hallway, it could only be the next worst: her parents, Tom's parents, sisters, brothers. By the time she picked up the phone, reaching it before the reverend did, she had imagined every relation in extremis. It was a positive relief to hear Prudence's voice—until she realized what Pru was saying.

"Faith! Someone just tried to get in my window! I ran out and I'm locked into the library. I don't know what to do! On my way downstairs I screamed for Nicholas and Nora, but they must not have heard me. They aren't answering the bell either! I'm afraid something dreadful has happened to them!"

"Did you call the police?"

"Police?" Prudence seemed to find it a novel thought, and Faith realized that Winthrops did not normally have any dealings with Boston's finest, except perhaps a slight acknowledgment when crossing Beacon Street at rush hour.

"Look, keep the door locked. I'll call the police and Tom or I will be there as soon as we can."

"Oh, Faith, hurry! I'm at wit's end! If someone doesn't come soon, I don't know what I might do!

It was Tom who ended up making the trip to Boston. When he returned a few hours later, Faith was waiting up for him. He'd called to say briefly that all was well but didn't give any details.

"No signs of forced entry," Tom said. "The servants had fallen asleep with the TV on and that's why they didn't hear anything. By the way, Nicholas and Nora must be major couch potatoes. Big screen, surround sound, every fancy remote gadget known to man or woman."

"What did the police say?"

"Not much. I'm afraid our Prudence may not have impressed them as rock-steady. Of course, she was terrified. But she couldn't remember whether it was an actual face or just the outline of a person. She told them about the other events, but conceded that the 'ghost' outside the window could have been an albino pigeon, when one of the officers offered the suggestion."

"Sounds like an inventive guy, but I believe Pru.

And there's only one way to stop this nonsense: find the will. So let's see if we can get an hour or two more of sleep, then head in there."

The last thought Faith had before drifting back to sleep was how odd it was that some people grew up into their names. It was almost predestined. Prudence, indeed! But what about "Faith"? She was asleep before she'd figured that one out.

The next morning the Fairchilds paused to take an appreciative look at the Winthrops' brick town house. A large wisteria vine starting to bloom mingled with English ivy on one side of the doorway. A few panes of the original glass, turned purple by the sun over many years, shone in the morning light. The brass door knocker and handle glittered. Everything about the house proclaimed its long pedigree of careful—and wealthy—inhabitants.

Ben was at nursery school, but baby Amy was securely strapped to Tom in a backpack. The Fairchilds had strolled from their parking place on Commonwealth Avenue through the Public Gardens, pointing excitedly at the swan boats and the bronze statuettes of the mother duck and her offspring from Robert McCloskey's *Make Way for Ducklings*. Amy responded appropriately with a string of nonsense syllables and smiles.

But this was no family outing. They had to find the will, and they had to find it today. So far nothing had happened to Prudence, but tonight she might not be so lucky. Faith was sure the nocturnal visitor was trying to get Prudence to leave in order to search for the will without interference. Faith only hoped that he, or she, hadn't been successful the night before.

They mounted the stone steps and rang the bell. Nicholas, the butler-chauffeur, answered. He looked the part, perfectly groomed down to the moons on his fingernails. He stood ramrod straight as he announced, "Miss Prudence is expecting you in the library."

Faith had visited Eliza Winthrop a number of times, but she was impressed anew by the lovely antiques that filled the spacious room. One wall was lined with bookshelves filled with leather-bound books. A large Canton Blue porcelain bowl, ballast, no doubt, from one of the clipper ships the family had operated during the China Trade years, sat on a Sheraton card table. Prudence was sitting at a large Chippendale secretary at the far end of the room, going through a stack of papers.

"Any luck?" Tom asked.

"No. I started with the books. Don't people usually hide wills between their pages? Aunt Eliza didn't. At least not in here. Now I'm looking through these correspondence boxes, and I'm beginning to think it's impossible. Winthrops have been savers for generations. These are Great-Grandfather Austin Winthrop's receipts from his tailor!"

"I know your aunt didn't get about much these last months," Faith said. "In which rooms did she spend the most time?" It made sense that Eliza would have secreted the will near to hand.

"Well, for almost a year, only two rooms—the library and the front drawing room, which has a little alcove where we moved her bed. We even took our meals in one or the other. She said the dining room depressed her."

Faith had had a rather lugubrious meal in the Winthrop dining room, with its heavy, light-obscuring damask draperies and rows of dour family portraits staring disapprovingly down from the walls as she took each bite. It was no wonder Aunt Eliza had preferred someplace else.

"Why don't we start in the front room, near her bed?"

Nora appeared in the doorway. Like her husband, she could have answered a casting call for any number of productions needing old family retainers—pleasantly plump, crisp white apron, and a kindly look about the eyes and mouth.

"Excuse me, Mrs. Fairchild, but I would be happy to watch the baby if you like."

Like! Faith's diaper bag was stuffed with nourishment and toys for Amy, but Faith had been worried about the effect of Amy's boredom on their hunt. The baby was soon settled in the kitchen, delightedly crowing at Nora's huge orange cat, Aster, as he batted at an elaborate cat teaser.

"My Nicholas made it," Nora said proudly. "He's very mechanical."

Before Faith rejoined Prudence and Tom, she wanted to take a look around—at the elevator and outside, underneath Prudence's window.

There was nothing unusual in the elevator, except for a new-looking panel of controls, perhaps installed by the mechanically adept Nicholas. Faith got in, pulled the ornate metal gate across, and went to the top floor, then down to the basement. She opened the door into the basement and stepped out. Labyrinthine hallways led past a number of rooms. Noting the undisturbed dust on the thresholds, Faith doubted they had been visited lately by anyone, with the possible exception of ghosts. The only two areas that showed signs of recent occupancy were the furnace room and one with a workbench and tools.

Faith left the basement through a door into the

backyard, leaving it unlocked for her return. The trash barrels were set directly to one side, and she lifted the top of the first one, taking a stick to poke around. Nothing incriminating, except some pizza boxes. Perhaps Nora got tired of her own cooking. The other barrel was more interesting. Near the bottom, Faith's stick unearthed two empty Scotch bottles—definitely not the expensive single-malt kind.

She went around to the side of the house and looked at the fire escape that climbed the wall next to a tall pine tree. Last night the police had found no signs of an intruder, but the ground cover in the light of day certainly showed that someone had been straying from the brick path recently. The bright purple myrtle flowers were squashed in several places. Faith peered up at Prudence's window. The ivy appeared intact.

Aunt Eliza's bed was a shock.

Faith had expected something sedate, a pristine white counterpane, but instead it was a riot of color. Aunt Eliza had been a quilter! A vibrant Star of Bethlehem covered the bed with Double Wedding Ring shams on the pillows. A Boston rocker to one side sported a Crazy Quilt hanging over one arm. Quilts were folded across the end of the bed as well.

"This was Aunt Eliza's hobby—ever since she was a young girl," Pru explained. "Her grandmother taught her 'patchwork,' as she called it. The only other thing she really enjoyed was her puzzles."

Faith noted a stack of crossword puzzle and acrostic books next to the bed. A basket filled with quilt squares sat beside them.

"Well, let's get back to work," Tom said with a heartiness he did not appear to feel. They hadn't found so much as a codicil. "It's not as though we're searching for a needle in this quilted haystack. A will is much larger than a needle."

Faith gave him a smile meant to convey appreciation for trying to lift their spirits, and a warning to cool the corny jokes.

An hour later, she would have welcomed any joke, no matter how trite. They'd searched both rooms and their closets from top to bottom. Nothing.

Prudence was sitting on the floor, obviously both tired and discouraged, with the basket of quilt squares in her lap. "This sampler quilt was the last thing Auntie was working on. She never got to put the squares together. Maybe whoever inherits them will let me have them and I can finish it for her." She started to sob, and Faith went over to her.

"There's still plenty of time. Don't give up now."

As she waited for Pru to have her little cry, Faith looked through the stack of quilt squares. Each one was different—she recalled that this was what made the quilt a "sampler"—and each was beautifully done. It was hard to believe someone could make such tiny stitches.

At the bottom of the basket, Faith found a small piece of paper they'd overlooked when they were searching for something bulkier. On it, written in a spidery hand, was a strange-looking formula:

$$\underset{1\ 2}{\_\ \_}\quad \underset{1\ 2\ 3}{\_\ \_\ \_}\quad \underset{1\ 2\ 3\ 4\ 5\ 6}{\_\ \_\ \_\ \_\ \_\ \_}\quad \underset{1\ 2\ 3\ 4\ 5\ 6\ 7\ 8\ 9}{\_\ \_\ \_\ \_\ \_\ \_\ \_\ \_\ \_}$$

"What is that?" Tom asked. "Some kind of code?"

"It looks like one of Aunt Eliza's acrostic puzzles," Pru said. "You know, where you transfer letters to numbered squares and get a phrase."

"Not a phrase! A message!" Faith gasped. "It must be the answer we're looking for—the hiding place!"

Tom scratched his head. "But where are the letters?"

As soon as he spoke, they were all struck by the same thought. Three heads turned toward the quilted squares next to the basket.

"Do you know the names?" Faith asked Prudence. "If not, Pix Miller will." The Millers were members of First Parish, and Pix was an avid quilter.

"I'm pretty sure I know them all." Her voice caught for a moment. "She kept repeating them to me. I haven't mixed them up, have you? I'm sure she left them in order."

Faith shook her head. "I looked at them, but they're just as we found them. Get a piece of paper, Tom, and we'll start listing the names. Before we know it, we'll have the answer as easy as—Boston cream pie!"

Tom handed Faith a pen and took a small notebook from his pocket. "I still don't get it, though."

Prudence's face was flushed—becomingly this time, Faith noted. "It's simple! The number 'one' stands for the first letter of the first name of the first quilt square. 'Two' the second letter of the second square. Then back to 'one,' but it's the first letter of the third square, and so on. When we put the letters over the numbers, we'll know where she hid the will!"

Tom got it. The Fairchild family members were rabid games players from outdoorsy ones like touch football to indoorsy mammoth board game marathons.

The first five squares were: Old Maid's Puzzle, English Ivy, Tall Pine Tree, Boston Puzzle, and Maple Leaf. Starting with the O, they soon spelled out "On top."

"All the names seem to relate to Boston, New England, and Eliza herself," Faith said excitedly.

"She told me the quilt was going to be a memoir. I thought she meant she was using her favorite squares. And now I also know why she kept telling me the names!" Pru said. "Quick, Tom, I mean Reverend Fairchild, here are the next six: City Secrets, Church Steps, Evening Star, Secret Drawer—do you think there is one?—Cherry Basket, and Memory Block."

The third word was *cherry*. Faith could scarcely breathe. One more word and they would have it! She looked about. "*Cherry* could refer to the color, or wood, or a pattern. No shortcuts."

"Here it goes." Pru slowly picked up each of the remaining nine squares and said the names aloud: "Silver and Gold, Beacon Lights, Duck and Ducklings—she loved the statues in the Public Gardens—Hourglass, Aunt Eliza's Star—she said it would be rising soon—Bright Hopes, Fair Play, Brickwork, and Butterfly."

Tom seemed to be taking forever, and Faith almost snatched the notebook from him.

<u>O N</u> <u>T O P</u> <u>C H E R R Y</u> <u>S E C R E T A R Y</u>
1 2   1 2 3   1 2 3 4 5 6   1 2 3 4 5 6 7 8 9

"Secretary," he cried. "On Top Cherry Secretary."

Prudence raced into the library and led them to the Chippendale secretary where she had been seated when they arrived.

Tom, clearly the tallest, dragged a footstool over and stood on top of it. He reached up to the carved scrollwork, then shook his head.

"There's nothing here. We already looked anyway."

"Try the pineapple," Faith urged. The decorative symbol of hospitality extended up. "Twist it. We should have done this before."

Tom did it now, and a small drawer at the bottom of the piece of furniture shot out. Prudence reached inside and squealed, "It's the will!"

"Call your lawyer immediately," Faith advised.

"What about cousin Bradford? Shouldn't I let him know first?"

"Cousin Bradford can wait."

As Pru went toward the phone, the Fairchilds followed. Faith whispered to Tom, "Don't let her—or the will—out of your sight. I'm going downstairs to get Amy and have a little chat with Nicholas."

Tom looked at his wife quizzically. She kissed him and said, "I'll tell you all about it—if I'm right."

Amy greeted her mother with delight, and when Faith told Nicholas and Nora the good news, their relief was apparent.

"Now," said Faith, looking Nicholas squarely in the eye, "how long has Bradford Winthrop been blackmailing you?"

Nicholas winced, and Nora started to cry.

"Oh, Mrs. Fairchild, my Nicholas only takes a drop now and then. We would have been out on the street at our age with no references!"

"You should have come to Miss Winthrop right away. Go upstairs and tell her everything. Leave Bradford to the reverend and me." Sadly, Faith could understand Nicholas and Nora's fear. "You controlled the elevator by remote control, right?"

"Yes," Nicholas said with a touch of pride. "And I rigged up a timer for when we were out of the house. I should have been an engineer," he added wistfully.

"What about the ghost of Aunt Eliza at Miss Winthrop's window? Was that electronic too?"

"No," said Nora, looking guilt stricken. "That was just a rag mop waved in front of the window. In the dark, it looked exactly like the old lady's hair . . ."

That night Pru came out to the parsonage, and they popped a bottle of champagne to celebrate. Tom grinned at them. "Well, Ms. Sherlock and Dr. Watson, what are you going to call this case in your memoirs?"

Faith quickly offered, "How about 'Where's There's a Will, There's a Quilt'?"

Pru shook her head and said, "I think 'A Stitch in Time Saved Mine' is better." She put her hand up to her glasses. "And the first thing I'll spend the money on is a pair of contact lenses . . ."

Prudence indeed!

Death in the Dunes

The moon was waxing in the crystal-clear night. A single gull flew across its face, silhouetted against the light, which was as silver and shimmering as the goddess Diana herself. Tall grasses cast stiletto shadows on the dunes. Nothing was stirring; the air was impossibly still. It was the kind of night when things could be expected to happen and sometimes did.

Inside a small saltbox cottage a fire crackled merrily in a fieldstone fireplace, but not loudly enough to prevent Faith Sibley Fairchild from hearing the waves lapping the Cape Cod shore. She was at The Oceanside Retreat—affectionately shortened to "The Retreat" by the loyal guests who returned like lemmings year after year and, from the look of some, had been on the doorstep when the impressive gates had first opened eight decades ago.

The Oceanside Retreat represented a unique combination of one for all and none for all. The high prices kept it exclusive, but the conferences it hosted diversified the guest population. Situated on over sixty acres of woodlands and fragile dunes fiercely protected by boardwalks, it attracted those with a naturalistic bent—or those who thought it was chic to assume the pose. Thoreaus with thousand-dollar binoculars gazed at the horizon; Carsons with pedicures tiptoed around tide pools. Meals were served "family"-style in a cavernous oak-beamed dining hall, reminiscent of the turn-of-the-century Adirondack retreats built by wealthy New Yorkers similarly in pursuit of the simple life.

Faith was not complaining. Far from it. Her husband, the Reverend Thomas Fairchild, was at The Retreat for a three-day conference, sponsored by the denomination, "Heretics: Heroes and Heroines? Conversations about Sects." Tom was delivering a paper on his specialty, the Albigensians in France, twelfth-century ascetics who rebelled against church and state, losing life, limb, and property in the process.

Besides nonaffiliated guests, The Retreat was playing host to three other groups this week: a footwear sales force, a watercolor society, and the International Association for Human Sexual Response Research and Therapy (IAHSRRT). With sex and sects, it should be a lively and potentially confusing couple of days, Faith had commented to Tom upon reading the welcome board when they checked in.

She gazed into the fireplace, mesmerized by the fire's flames. They'd been extremely lucky to get one of the separate cottages away from the accommodations in the main building and annexes. Tom was out on the beach collecting enough driftwood to prevent the fire from dying down anytime in the near future—say three or four years. He'd already stacked a pile worthy of Paul Bunyan on the deck outside the spacious room. Faith believed fire tending revealed a definite gender difference, like knife sharpening. Not that she didn't keep her kitchen cutlery on the cutting edge—her job as a caterer depended on it. But Tom raised the whole process to new heights with his special Arkansas stone, just the right honing oil, and so on. Sharpening knives could take him hours, and he loved it.

And fires. It was burn, baby, burn all the way— no pleasantly glowing embers, but the equivalent of blazing Yule logs whatever the time of year, in this case summer, the end of June. The weather was typical of the Cape at this time of year: during the day, beach weather—warm, sunny blue skies, once the cold early morning fog lifted. After sunset, the temperature retreated to nights reminiscent of those that were the norm three-quarters of the year in Faith and Tom's Aleford home, west of Boston.

The moment she left the hearth the room was freezing. She pulled on the colorful Missoni sweater sent by her sister, Hope, for Faith's last birthday, a birthday that still put her squarely in her early thirties, and was glad she'd packed it.

Faith got up from her comfortable position and walked over to the sliding glass doors that led to the deck. She drew the drapes back and peered out. The Retreat had tasteful walk lights, but they were unnecessary with the moon's own bright steady beams. A bird cried, or at least Faith thought it was a bird. There was no sign of Tom. She wasn't worried, but she wasn't not worried. Near the window she could hear the waves more clearly. The sound was much less gentle. There were signs everywhere on the beach warning people not to swim—EXTREMELY STRONG CURRENTS.

It was beautiful out and she was tempted to

walk down to the beach to find him. He'd probably need help carrying the forest he'd collected. Plus it was a romantic night, especially since their two children—Ben, five, and Amy, almost two—were many miles away at the parsonage, being totally spoiled by Tom's parents, who seemed to count the days until they could get their hands on the grandchildren—and then perhaps count the days until they could hand them back over again.

Yes, a romantic night, a night of . . .

She was abruptly shaken from her mood by a frantic knocking at the cottage door. Why had Tom decided to come back that way? She ran to let him in.

It wasn't Tom.

"Please, you've got to help me! Please hide me!"

She was a beautiful blonde in her mid- to late twenties with a deep tan that set off her lacy turquoise gown and peignoir. She was barefoot, and the look on her face made Faith instantly reach to pull her inside. This was no joke.

"What is it? Are you in some kind of danger? Do you want me to try to call someone? The police?"

As Faith spoke, she remembered one of the "quaint" customs at The Retreat—no phones in the room, cell use forbidden—which wasn't necessary, as the service was virtually nonexistent. The nearest landline was down by the dining hall, a trek especially at night.

"No, no! Don't tell anyone I'm here!" The woman was getting hysterical. "Just hide me. Hide me quickly!"

As she spoke Faith heard a faint male voice calling, "Carolann! Carolann! Where are you?"

The woman looked as if she was going to faint. Faith pushed her into the bathroom. "Don't worry. The only person coming in will be my husband. You're in safe hands." The woman nodded and silently closed the door.

The voice was getting louder, and after a while Faith heard heavy, deliberate footsteps outside the door. The Fairchilds' was the last cottage in the row. There was plenty of room between them, and whoever it was had been taking his time searching the area. He would call out every once in a while, his voice concerned, loving. What in the world could be happening? A marital spat? He called once more. Faith could hear him clearly. He was on the boardwalk near the deck. The steps stopped, then started again; he was moving away.

Faith suddenly realized she had seen the woman sunbathing at the end of the beach that afternoon. Neither her suit nor her nightwear left much to the imagination, but a great deal to fantasy on the part of some onlookers. She looked more like a California Girl, maybe even a Valley Girl. She'd been alone on the beach, splayed out on her back, her body glistening with oil like some sacrificial offering to the sun god.

The glass door slid open and Faith jumped. "Tom!"

"And you were expecting whom? Brad Pitt, Daniel Craig, given this place, Roger Tory Peterson?" Tom, tall with deep brown eyes and reddish brown hair, windblown and flushed from his exertions, had his own appeal.

"Shhh, there's a young woman in her nightgown hiding in our bathroom. She appeared at the door a few minutes ago, absolutely terrified, begging me to help her."

"You and Pix have been reading her old copy of *The Total Woman* again, haven't you? It's a great shtick, honey, but with Ben and Amy safe and sound at home, I really don't need any inducement to get—"

"Tom! There really *is* a woman in the bathroom. Go see for yourself. She's in some kind of trouble, and we've got to help her."

"Just so long as it's a *live* woman." Faith could tell Tom was humoring her and was starting to feel annoyed.

"Oh, she's very much alive—and I am not hallucinating."

"All right, I'll go look. Meanwhile, why don't you open the cognac and pour me a tad?"

He was back in a flash.

"Faith! There's a woman cowering in our bathtub! What the hell is going on?"

"I told you," Faith said with a justifiable trace of smugness. "She knocked on the door, asked me to hide her, and I did. A man was outside calling for 'Carolann' and that must be her name."

"I heard him when I came up from the beach. He was going down the stairs at the far end."

"That means he's left. If she knows that, she might come out and start talking."

The Fairchilds went to the bathroom door and Faith knocked softly. "He's gone now. Why don't you join us by the fire?" she suggested. When there was no reply, she opened the door.

The room was completely empty, save for the moonlight streaming through the open window. Carolann had seen herself out.

Faith opened her eyes and rolled over. Tom was already gone. The serious business of sects started early, and he'd told her the night before he would be breakfasting at seven if she cared to join him. She did not, but noting that it was after eight and there would be no food after nine, she jumped out of bed, showered, dressed, and headed off for sustenance.

Tom and she had talked about the mysterious woman in turquoise until well after midnight, but the only explanation seemed to be a quarrel, which her husband soon regretted. Faith wondered whether she'd be on the beach again.

Breakfast was semi-cafeteria-style. You chose what you wanted, and then someone brought it piping hot to your table. Apparently neither flab nor cholesterol worried anyone at The Retreat. Offerings included eggs in many guises, sausages, bacon, ham, home fries, pancakes, muffins, toast, and huge pecan sticky buns—and as a sop to the health conscious, chunks of melon and mounds of strawberries. Faith chose fruit and a bun, planning to walk it off.

There were few late risers and she was seated in solitary splendor at one of the big, round tables with the whole lazy Susan to herself. It was crowded with fresh Odwalla orange juice, coffee, milk, cream, and an endless variety of jams and jellies. Occupied with the serious business of food, Faith didn't see the woman from the previous night until the woman passed her table with a man who matched her in age, tan, and hair color.

"Hello," said Faith, weighing her next words. It might not be so tactful to say "Everything patched up between you two?" or "Have any trouble getting out of my bathroom window?" Before she could decide, the couple had moved toward the kitchen, the woman returning the greeting—without even a flicker of recognition on her face.

Faith had a good view of them when they came back and sat a few tables away. Whatever was wrong the night before *had* been resolved. They could have been honeymooners—and maybe were. Both wore wedding bands. He kissed her hand when she passed him the salt, and Faith was sure there were kneesies going on under the chaste, white tablecloth while they ate.

When the man rose to go toward the servers at the end of the room, Faith seized her chance and made her way over to their table.

"Is everything all right? You were so distressed last night, then when you disappeared, we didn't know what to think."

The woman was startled and answered hastily, "Yes, yes, everything's fine." Faith was struck by the confusion on her face. Was it a question of Faith's knowing too much? The way a friend who has unburdened him- or herself of some problem often becomes a mere acquaintance afterward?

The man was walking toward the table now and Faith stayed put. It would have been awkward to leave.

"I couldn't help myself. I ordered more of those pancakes. The food here is fantastic." It was the same voice that had called "Carolann"—a hearty, used-car-salesman-type voice.

While Faith's sticky bun had been edible, she wouldn't go so far as to call it "fantastic," and she'd had no trouble in leaving it unfinished. Maybe lunch would show the chef's true colors.

"Hi, I'm Jim Hadley. My wife, Carolann, and I stay at The Retreat whenever we're up here. Been coming for years." He put out his hand, and Faith shook it. He had a strong grip.

"Hello, I'm Faith Fairchild. This is my first visit. My husband is attending a conference."

"Which one?" Jim sniggered slightly.

"The one on heretics," Faith said, forgoing the temptation to satisfy his prurient interest by declaring Tom one of the world's leading authorities on participatory sexual research.

Jim was not disappointed. "Oh the sects, not sex." His self-congratulatory grin indicated he'd obviously been waiting for the opportunity to get that off since his arrival.

"Oh, darling, you are terrible! What will

Mrs. Fairchild think?" Carolann said with mock severity—and absolutely no fear.

Faith said good-bye. She had serious beach plans for the rest of the morning.

Soon she was slathering herself with the highest numerical SPF in existence, pondering the absurdity of lying in the sun while doing everything possible to avoid a tan. The sound of the waves, and the sun's warm, gentle rays began to work on her senses, and her eyelids drooped.

"Now, don't go falling asleep. That's a sure way to get a burn, especially with your complexion." A shadow fell across her.

Faith sat up. It was Carolann. And from the tone of her voice, the world's leading authority on tanning.

"You have to do this gradually." She spread her towel companionably close, Faith noted in dismay. She was treasuring solitude on this vacation—a rare thing in her everyday life. Still, with Jim nowhere in sight, Carolann might talk about the previous evening.

But she didn't. What she did do was talk about everything else under the sun. Their starter apartment in New York City that was on the market for ten million five, because they wanted to move to Westchester.

"It's more normal up there," Carolann confided. "You don't see so many homeless people." She also managed to work in their Mercedes and an account of a second home they had looked at the week before in the Hamptons, a steal at eight million—"just a cottage really. But of course it's a teardown."

"Of course," Faith murmured, looking surreptitiously at her watch. It wasn't lunchtime.

When Nan Tucker, one of the other clerical wives, came along with children and sand pails in tow, Faith positively leapt at her, insisting she join them. Mrs. Tucker, slightly bewildered by the intensity of Faith's invitation, nevertheless spread out a blanket and began to unpack. The sight of all those juice boxes, kites, shovels, small hats, flip-flops, and granola bars gave Faith a fleeting pang of guilt—guilt for not missing the kids more. It really was wonderful to be able simply to get up and leave a beach without the frantic cries to stay just a little longer and the accompanying tears. Nor did she miss the dump truck loads of sand that invariably accumulated on various parts of a child's body or the role of mother as packhorse—a child on each hip and a fifty-pound sack of toys on one's back.

"Perhaps I'll see you at lunch," she said, turning

away from Carolann and toward Nan. Her plan was to steer the conversation to tanning, allowing Carolann to give her lecture to a new victim, who— if Faith remembered correctly from the barbecue dinner of the night before—had a few lectures of her own up her sleeve. Mrs. Tucker was one of those women who ask extremely detailed questions—in the hopes of catching you out in a lie, or worse. Before Faith could bring up the topic, the clerical helpmate said in an accusatory tone, "We didn't see you at breakfast. Where were you?" As a method of information gathering it was unsubtle but effective, Faith realized, as she struggled for a more impressive excuse than "sleeping in"—something like a dawn ten-mile run or early morning bird-watching. She left the two women to each other's devices and made her escape.

At lunch she regaled Tom with an account of her morning, complete with a description of the sex researchers on the beach. The Japanese and many of the Europeans wore suits and ties with their IAHSRRT name tags prominently displayed on neat lapels. They'd spent a great deal of time taking photographs of each other in front of the ocean, looking completely incongruous among the sunbathers. Their colleagues were a bit more relaxed—flip-flops, khakis, and open-necked shirts.

Tom was relieved to hear that all was well with "the toothsome morsel in our shower."

"I'd be happy to risk skin cancer if you like, Tom, and maybe there's a Victoria's Secret at the Sagamore Outlet Mall." Faith was slightly miffed. "Anyway, my blond hair isn't out of a bottle." She tossed her shoulder-length locks, glad she had decided not to cut them before the trip.

" 'Toothsome' as in cotton candy, fluff. You, my love, are the real thing—the *mousse au chocolat,* the soufflé Grand Marnier, the—"

"I get it." Faith was appeased. "But please stop talking about food!" She was pushing runny turkey potpie and broccoli steamed to a pulp around on her plate. The Retreat was obviously not acquainted with New American cuisine. All Faith's hopes for the use of local ingredients fresh from the sea and garden had been dashed by the menu that greeted them at the dining room door. Pineapple tapioca was listed for dessert. "We have got to go somewhere else for dinner, honey."

Tom nodded vehemently and then said loudly, "What a terrific place this is."

A voice at Faith's shoulder said firmly, "Is something wrong with your lunch? You do not like the food?"

It was Elsa Whittemore, The Retreat's formidable director. She had delivered a short speech of welcome to their group at the opening-night barbecue before marching off to more important things like reclaiming the dunes single-handedly. She had reminded Faith of the woman in one of those James Bond movies with the knives in the toes of her shoes. Click, click. She could almost hear Elsa's heels. The knives were out and aimed at Faith.

"Actually, I had such a big breakfast, I'm not very hungry," Faith lied shamelessly. She was starving. For some reason, doing nothing all morning had given her quite an appetite.

Tom was slavishly cleaning his plate. Faith glowered at him. Elsa left, shoulders back, chest out. Her graying Dutch bob did not dare to move a strand.

"Yum yum. Yes, sweetheart, I agree. We have to get out of here for dinner," Tom said.

"You are such a fraud."

"First of all, as you well know, I eat everything, and second, I can't let down the troops. We may want to meet here again. You have to admit, it is an ideal spot. And I hear Elsa pretty much controls who comes and who doesn't."

On the way out, Faith noticed that the shoe people, as she had come to call them, had what looked like Baked Alaska for dessert and wine with their meal. The watercolorists had received garden salads in addition to their potpies. It was an interesting pecking order.

"What are you going to do this afternoon?" Tom asked as he kissed her before leaving for the next intriguing lecture, "Martin Luther at the Schlosskirche Doors: Did He Really Want In?" "I'll be finished by four, then there's a social hour from five to six and after that we can slip away." He hadn't eaten the tapioca.

"Perfect. I can make reservations at that fish restaurant we heard about in Falmouth. Or the Belfry Inne and Bistro in Sandwich—I'm heading for the Sandwich Glass Museum this afternoon. I heard someone say the Bistro had been converted from an abbey, so that's right up your alley, Tom. And everyone says the food is divine, as one would expect."

"I'm sure it is, but maybe the Falmouth place. I think by dinner I'll want something stronger than a Virgin Mary, although there are bound to be plenty of loaves and fishes."

An hour later Faith was standing in front of a glassblower watching in fascination as she deftly handled the molten globule, spinning it and pressing it into a mold to create a beaker, using the same techniques that had made Sandwich, the oldest town on the Cape, synonymous with American glass. She wished Ben were at her side. He would have loved it. But the face next to hers was Jim Hadley's, not Ben's. Carolann was seated on the bench on his other side. The moment she had sat down, they had appeared.

"Great place, isn't it? You've got to be sure not to skip the Levine Lighting Gallery—it covers the whole history from candles to the first lightbulb— although there's so much in the permanent collection, you could run out of time," Jim enthused.

"Thank you, I'll try not to miss it," Faith said. She hadn't pegged the couple as history buffs of any sort, except for what an object might be worth, but she was obviously wrong.

Ten minutes later, as Faith was examining a case filled with rows of lamps, she heard a voice that was becoming much too familiar. "Must have given off a stink. The whale oil, I mean. Carolann's off powdering her nose." It was Jim, moving to her side.

Faith looked him squarely in the face. The Hadleys' ubiquitous presence, starting with Carolann's dramatic appearance the night before, was developing into quite a string of coincidences. Maybe they thought the Fairchilds were swingers. Maybe they were embarrassed about the scene Carolann had made and didn't know how to introduce the subject. Maybe it was just her dumb luck.

"So, what do you do, Jim?" Faith asked, and strolled to the next exhibit. The case was filled with candlesticks, some shaped like dolphins in cobalt blue glass.

"I'm in insurance, supervise branch offices, do some sales. I'm on the road a lot," he replied. She was not surprised. He had the handshake and the voice—confident, with undertones of genuine, money-back-guaranteed interest. He demonstrated it by asking in turn, "And what about you, Mrs. Fairchild? I know your husband's line of work, but not yours. Domestic engineer?" The sneer in his voice was palpable. And she hated the euphemism. Why couldn't he just say "housewife" and be done with it?

"In a way," she said. "I'm a caterer. I started my business, Have Faith, in Manhattan before my marriage and it moved with me." She hoped he wouldn't start asking her about her coverage—or worse, start figuring the exact minute, hour, and date of her demise as a prelude to a life insurance pitch. Death was a fact she hoped would come as a pleasant, far distant, surprise.

Carolann's face appeared reflected among the blue glass dolphins, her face a sea creature framed by her curls like tentacles.

"I have to be going," Faith said. "I want to get my children something in the gift shop." She had also noted that there was a poster advertising Penrose glass jewelry for sale. She could use a gift herself. "Do you have kids?" Faith wasn't sure why she asked. After the letdown of last night's potential drama, the Hadleys, busy clawing their way to the top with all their shallow symbols, held ever-decreasing interest for her.

"None—yet, but we're looking forward to working on it," Jim responded and put his arm around his wife. She was wearing a backless sundress and there wasn't a trace of a tan mark anywhere. His hand moved from her shoulder to the nape of her neck and continued down. Faith didn't wait to see where it ended up.

Tom was in the cottage when Faith returned.

"I could get very used to this way of life," Faith told him. "If only you didn't have to go to all these talks."

"How about we skip the social? I hear Walter Wade, a worthy reverend from someplace in North

Dakota, plans to entertain us with a medley of sing-along songs."

"But you love 'Michael Row the Boat Ashore'!"

"I know, but it might not be in his repertoire . . . and besides, I can think of a better activity for the time, an activity decidedly not antisocial."

So could Faith.

The fish restaurant was jammed, and Faith was glad she'd made reservations. Even so they had to wait on the pleasant, flower-filled patio. They were sipping martinis—a very off-the-leash drink, she'd thought—and helping themselves to the tasty crackers spread liberally with smoked bluefish pâté proffered by a waiter when Faith suddenly grabbed Tom's arm, nearly spilling his drink.

"I can't believe it! They're here! No, don't turn around. Maybe they won't see us."

It was the Hadleys, of course, and at that very moment a smiling young woman came walking through the crowd calling, "Fairchild, party of two. Your table is ready. Fairchild, party . . ." Faith quickly waved to her and dragged Tom to the table before the Hadleys could suggest a foursome.

"Honey, I think you're getting a little paranoid about all this," Tom said as they sat down. "These are simply chance meetings. Obviously they were not up for Swiss steak either—why it is called that I hope you will explain to me someday—and this is one of the closest restaurants."

"I know, I know. It doesn't make any sense. It's just the way they look at me. They seem to be measuring me for something—and Carolann doesn't strike me as the type who is handy with a needle."

"Well, neither are you. If they have any interest in us, it's probably to sell us insurance. Now why don't you forget about them and concentrate on more important things, like the menu and your husband? I'm going to start with stuffed quahogs and then have the baked scrod. What are you going to have?"

Knowing that her husband was the kind who shared, Faith ordered Wellfleet oysters and cherrystones. The bread had already arrived, and it was a promising-looking crusty Portuguese whole half. She decided to go for a linguica-and-mussel pasta special—when in Lisbon . . . The arrival of their food pushed all thoughts of the Hadleys, and much of anything else, from their minds. Faith was in such a good mood that even the Hadleys' appearance at their table near the end of the meal did not dampen her spirits.

"You had a great meal, right?" Jim boomed,

his red face indicating that his voice's increase in decibels was probably due to more than one drink. "They do everything well here, even steak—God forgive you order it so close to the ocean. We really love this place—come every year—don't we, Carolann?"

The server arrived with the check, but still the couple did not move away from the table. Faith stood up. It was time for the ladies' room. She hadn't counted on Carolann joining her, but then, she seemed to need to powder her nose often. Faith stepped back to let her lead the way and they soon found themselves in the kitchen.

"I have such a poor sense of direction," Carolann apologized. "And I'm a little tiddly! It's over there, of course." Back on track, they soon found the right door, the one labeled GULLS. Carolann did spend some time refreshing her makeup, and as Faith washed her hands, she thought the woman painstakingly applying eyeliner in the mirror looked anxious again. Another fight brewing? Should she offer their shower again?

"Have you and Jim been married long?" Faith asked.

"Four years. Why do you ask?" There was no mistaking the coolness in her tone.

"Oh, you seem a bit like newlyweds, that's all,"

Faith commented, then added an oblique allusion to the previous night: "It's nice to see people so much in love they can straighten out any difficulties that come up." She hoped Carolann would take the bait, but all she said was "Uh-huh," and applied a second coating of lip gloss.

The Fairchilds drove back to The Retreat by way of Woods Hole for a look at the Vineyard in the distance. Tom's conversation with Jim had been only marginally more scintillating than Faith's with Carolann. The men had talked baseball.

"I may be getting as bad as you," Tom said, "but one thing was funny. He said something about it being a shame that we weren't staying longer. Did you tell them when we were leaving?"

"No, but the conference dates are probably posted somewhere." Faith was devil's advocate now. It had been such a nice evening. She didn't want to think about the Hadleys.

"True, but many of the participants are staying on. Remember, we could have done that, but decided to go home instead."

Faith had forgotten the option. Tom's parents had always been great about taking first Ben and now both kids, but she didn't want to impose on them—plus she wanted to save up some days for another trip.

They drove through The Oceanside Retreat gate, defined by stone pillars topped with faintly oriental-looking iron pagoda shapes, and started down the scrub-pine-lined drive. This part of the Cape did not lend itself to majestic trees. They were almost to the reception center when a figure popped out in front of their car and firmly gestured them to stop. Tom hit the brakes, the tires squealed, and the car narrowly avoided slamming into the imperious hand raised in front of them. It was Elsa.

"Jumping Jehoshaphat! What does *she* want?" Faith had never heard her husband use this expression. He must be as shaken as she was, but the words leaping to her mind were a great deal pithier.

Tom rolled down the window. "Good evening, Miss Whittemore. Is there something I can do for you?"

"Just checking, Reverend Fairchild. We did not see you, or your wife," she added pointedly, "at dinner, and no one seemed to know of your whereabouts. We had some concern. That is all." Her voice managed to suggest that the police from several counties were searching the area with helicopters, bloodhounds were sniffing the grounds, and divers were combing the ocean floor for the Fairchilds' lifeless bodies.

"I'm sorry you were troubled. We took the op-portunity to see a bit more of this lovely area." It was the wrong thing for Tom to say. Clearly for Elsa, nothing matched The Retreat.

"In case you're concerned about the Hadleys, we saw them at dinner," Faith said, driven by some flashback to childhood. Maybe she wouldn't have to miss recess after all.

"The *Hadleys* informed us of their plans this afternoon." No need to ask who would be get-ting blackberries and milk and who would be sent straight to bed.

After that there wasn't a whole lot to add but "good night." Elsa stepped back and motioned them on with her powerful flashlight.

"I feel like I just got caught sneaking a girl, or a beer, into my room!" Tom laughed. Faith tried to laugh too, but discovered that she was extremely annoyed.

"What ever happened to good old-fashioned pri-vacy? We are paying to stay here, aren't we? Every time I turn around someone's following me!"

They parked, got out of the car, and walked toward the cottage.

Two deer, a doe and a fawn, were feeding a few yards from their deck and the night air was still warm. Faith was partly appeased. "I guess she's annoyed because we don't like the food. She's probably been waiting for us there since dinner." The thought further lifted her spirits and by the time, pleasantly much later, they were drifting to sleep, she had conceded that she would come back to The Retreat again for the setting and facilities—if allowed.

"I think I'll do one of those crafty things tomorrow." The Oceanside Retreat had an energetic activities director, Sal Pedrone, who was constantly pushing everything from aquatic aerobics in the pool to enamel jewelry making.

"This is so unlike you," Tom mumbled, already half-asleep.

"Maybe you just don't know me as well as you think," Faith retorted, equally sleepy. Her last conscious thought was that it *was* unlike her but seemed to go with the whole camp atmosphere of the place. She'd like to have at least one thing to bring home to Mother.

Something woke her at three o'clock in the morning. A bird again? It sounded a little like a baby crying, but she hadn't seen any babies at The Retreat. It wasn't her baby, at any rate, but she found that she could not get back to sleep, and after fifteen minutes of tossing, she got out of bed, put Tom's jacket on, and slid open the door to the deck.

The night air hit her full in the face. It was cold

and damp. She went back and got one of the extra blankets. The moon was a bit more full than the night before, so again there was enough light to see outlines. She couldn't see the beach or the main buildings because of the fog, but some of the other cabins were visible, dark shapes scattered about the dunes. There were apparently no other insomniacs. She wound the blanket around herself and sat on a bench, leaning up against the side of the cabin.

So far the vacation had been only intermittently the one she'd hoped for. Like a sore tooth, the Hadleys kept appearing to remind her that something was wrong. Very wrong. It was a thought she'd kept in the back of her mind since the night before, unwilling to take it out for closer examination, but there was no way to avoid it.

The woman the night before—Carolann—had been terrified. It wasn't a squeezing-the-toothpaste-tube-in-the-middle-or-from-the-end kind of spat; it was fear. Fear for her own safety. When she had begged for help, begged to be hidden, her face had been filled with terror. At the sound of Jim's voice—and now Faith knew it had been Jim—the woman had almost passed out.

After every encounter with the Hadleys, Faith had tried to erase the memory of Carolann's frightened face. But nothing was wrong. No crime had been committed, or none that was visible. Maybe Jim was skimming some off the top. Maybe their apartment, up for sale in Manhattan, had bedbugs. Maybe . . . Maybe what? Faith shook her head. It was freezing and she was getting stiff. Stiff. Stiffs. No stiffs in sight. Carolann was as hale and hearty as Miss June.

Faith got up and went inside. It felt as warm as a sauna in contrast, and she crawled next to Tom gratefully. She was getting drowsy. Tomorrow afternoon they'd head off for home and would stop for one last dinner in Boston before getting to Aleford. She'd eat a gargantuan breakfast and tell Elsa how yummy every last mouthful tasted. Tom's was the last scheduled talk of the conference. She hoped not too many participants were planning to cut out early, but men and women of the cloth tended to be charitable—or perhaps might have memories of how they felt when parishioners slipped from the pews in the middle of the sermon.

And then they'd leave the material Hadleys far behind. "Material Girl"—and boy. The words to the song kept repeating until she was sound asleep.

Faith got up early with Tom the next morning. She didn't feel much like facing either the Hadleys or that inquisitive clerical spouse over breakfast. But she picked Mrs. Tucker—who'd be eating well before Jim and Carolann—as the lesser of two evils, fully prepared to hear "We didn't see you at dinner?" and so forth until Faith's entire sinful life would be laid bare.

Secure in the knowledge that their reservations at the top of the Prudential Center were not until nine o'clock, Faith ordered two eggs over easy, Canadian bacon, and English muffins plus fruit. Tom had the same plus waffles. They were rewarded by a slight nod from the director. There was, as she'd thought, no sign of the Hadleys.

"I have to go now, sweetheart." Tom, finishing quickly, gave her a kiss. "Have fun at your basket weaving or whatever."

"Sand casting," Faith corrected him. "I'll meet you in the cottage. I'm going to pack now, so we can leave right away." He nodded and walked off in the wrong direction, recollected himself, and went the right way. He wasn't nervous about his talk later, just preoccupied.

The wrong direction. It reminded Faith of Carolann heading for the kitchen instead of the bathroom in that restaurant she knew so well. Faith shoved the Hadleys firmly and figuratively away as she returned to the weathered gray saltbox. She concentrated instead on the heathers and grasses growing on the dunes to either side of the board-walks. Her favorite was something she'd learned was called Poverty Grass, which looked like a skinny broom, one that had been used for a long time but could still sweep. There was a patch just by the door, swaying in the morning breeze. The fog was starting to lift, and Faith could see the deep teal color of the ocean. Later it would take on a greenish hue, just as the sky would be clear blue and empty of anything save brightly colored kites anchored in the sand, stretched to the length of their strings.

She packed quickly and changed from jeans to shorts. The class started at nine thirty and lasted two hours. She pulled her hair back—it wouldn't do to get it mixed up in the plaster—put her keys in her pocket, and set off. When she came to the conference center where the group was to gather, she saw Carolann absorbed in conversation with Elsa. As they parted, Carolann actually patted the other woman on the arm affectionately. Not the sort of thing Faith was used to seeing in New England. Maybe Carolann *was* a California Girl. No matter the young woman's native home, Elsa did not seem eminently pattable, and what was this all about? A reduced rate for a return visit? The older woman moved off purposefully. Dragons to slay.

"Well, good morning. What are you up to to-day?" Carolann was approaching Faith now. She hadn't had to hide in a shower last night evidently.

Faith couldn't think of an escape. She'd already signed up for the class and Sal Pedrone was coming toward her, his "welcome, crafty lady" smile firmly in place.

"I'm taking a workshop this morning, then I'm afraid we have to be off."

"The sand casting one?"

Faith nodded. She knew what was coming.

"Me too." Carolann looped her arm through Faith's. "I know whatever I make is going to look awful, but it's fun to try new things."

Sal introduced them to their teacher, who looked to be nineteen and dedicated to her art. She was wearing sand-cast jewelry and had a display table with objects she'd made. Her name, she told them with a straight face, was Sandy. Which came first? Faith wondered.

Soon the participants, all female, were ready to start. Everything was set out under the trees. Faith headed for a spot at one of the long tables that had been set up, Carolann at her heels. It was inevitable.

"It's sad you have to leave so early," Carolann commiserated. "You just got here." Faith realized it was true. They'd been at The Retreat less than three days. It seemed much longer.

"You're sure you have to go?" she added.

"Yes, we have to get back home to our kids," Faith said.

Wild horses wouldn't drag the name of Aleford from Faith's lips. She glanced over at Carolann and was surprised to see that the woman definitely looked relieved. There was no mistake.

Faith was startled. As Tom had said that first night upon discovering the woman in the bath—what the hell was going on?

Sandy clapped her hands together. "Now, ladies, the first thing I'm going to ask you to do is take off your rings, watches, bracelets, anything that might get in the sand or plaster. Believe me, it will be too late after you get all gooky." She sounded as excited as a child.

Faith slipped off her wedding band and engagement ring, putting them securely in her pocket. She watched Carolann do the same. First the rock on her right ring finger, too large to fit with her wedding band. Then the band. She wiggled her fingers in the air.

"I can't believe I'm doing this. I just had my nails done!"

Sandy was bringing each person a basin of wet

sand. Carolann held her hands above hers. She seemed to regard the prospect of molding the grains with as much enthusiasm as if she were molding cow patties. Faith wondered why she was doing it. Faith wondered—and then Faith knew.

She turned to her neighbor. "I'll be right back. I should have stopped at the bathroom before I left the cabin."

"Don't worry," Carolann said. "I'll tell Sandy you'll be back in a minute."

But it wasn't a minute. It was over an hour later and the class was winding down when Faith Fairchild returned, accompanied by several members of the local police force, who walked up to Faith's sometime shadow and partner in crafts, read her her rights, and arrested her for the murder of her twin sister, Carolann Hadley.

Here's looking at you, kid." Tom Fairchild raised his glass to his wife, who was sitting opposite him at the Top of the Hub with the lights of Boston spread like a bejeweled flying carpet behind her.

Faith sighed with pleasure—and fatigue. It *had* been a rather tumultuous day, starting with her desperate attempts to convince the police that she was not a lunatic and that in all probability a woman had been murdered. Finally they had agreed to call Faith's old friend—and, she liked to think, partner—Detective Lieutenant John Dunne of the Massachusetts State Police. She'd decided against Aleford's Chief MacIsaac as possibly too small-town, besides possessing an anathema toward the phone that sometimes led to dire miscommunications. Dunne had vouched for her—quickly, to her passing surprise—and they were off and running.

The crime was so obvious it had almost worked, and Faith was annoyed that she hadn't considered it earlier. "Twins," Faith said to Tom later, "that desperate ploy of mystery writers everywhere."

Once the police established that Carolann Hadley did in fact have a twin sister, Carolee Reese, living not too far from the Cape in New Bedford, Massachusetts, events accelerated. Two discreet officers were dispatched to The Oceanside Retreat to make sure the Hadleys stayed put. The authorities in New Bedford were notified and, sure enough, found a very dead woman wearing a turquoise nightgown lying in bed at Carolee Reese's address. The house had been ransacked and a window broken to create the appearance of a robbery. Neighbors said that Carolee Reese had told them she would be on vacation for a few weeks. It was not unusual for her to take trips, one woman added. The New Bedford police even obtained a description of Jim Hadley, a frequent guest. "I'm on the road a lot"—his words at the museum rang in Faith's ears.

And the two must have been on the road the night before last. Carolann had been strangled, probably shortly after leaving the Fairchilds, trapped in the dunes as she tried to escape once more. Carolee and Jim would have put the body in the trunk or propped it in the backseat, then made a quick trip across the Bourne Bridge and onto the highway to New Bedford and back to The Oceanside Retreat for Mr. and "Mrs." Hadley's grand performance.

Faith took a sip of the Kir Royale she'd ordered and shuddered slightly. "Her own sister, that's what keeps coming back to me!" Faith and Hope had had their differences, but even as kids, nothing remotely murderous.

"I keep imagining Carolann's last moments. She knew her husband was after her, but what a horror it would have been to see her twin sister's face!"

Tom nodded. "Evidently Carolee had purchased a large life insurance policy with Carolann as sole beneficiary. Carolee—or rather, she and Jim— were smart enough to have done it over a year ago and not used his company. The girls had no other siblings, and their parents are dead, as are Jim's.

It was almost the perfect crime—the discovery of the tragic murder, the inheritance, and all the Mercedes and 'teardowns' they wanted—except somehow Carolann got away from them and came to our cottage."

"And they *have* been watching us, especially me. To see if they were pulling it off. That must have been a tense moment at breakfast when I asked Carolee—really these names are so confusing, why do parents of twins do that?—if she was all right."

Breakfast reminded Faith of Elsa Whittemore, who had practically started the Fairchilds' car for them, so eager was she to hurry them off the grounds. Murders didn't happen at The Retreat. And if they did, they weren't committed by nice people like the Hadleys who had been coming for years, except the Hadleys weren't nice and weren't the Hadleys, at least not both of them.

"You know, honey, I can't believe this, but I keep forgetting to ask you how you knew Carolann Hadley was her sister, Carolee Reese? Did she let something slip at that class?"

"In a way." Faith smiled. "When she took her wedding band off her left hand, there was no mark. There should have been a stripe as white as snow, given her tan. There was no way they could have been married for as long as they said. I think she was so busy keeping an eye on me she got sloppy. Agree?"

Tom reached for his wife's left hand, raised his glass once again, and said, "I do."

The Would-Be Widower

Mr. Carter wanted to be a widower. And since he already had a wife, he figured he was halfway there.

The idea of bereavement was irresistible. At meals, sitting across the table from his wife, he would indulge in rosy reverie, picturing especially those first days—the steady stream of comfort flowing into his house in the form of sympathetic friends bearing casseroles and baked goods. He would be stoic, breaking down only occasionally to shed some tears and whisper, "Why? Why?"

His new status would confer instant membership into the club that he knew from careful observation yielded invitations to dinner, parties, plays, concerts, cruises, and bed from widows, divorcées, the never-marrieds. An unattached man of his age in decent health, still with his own teeth, was a rarity. He was his own best capital and he longed to spend it. Mourning beckoned with all the promise of a new day. Besides, he loathed his wife.

Mabel had been a secretary at the small family-owned insurance agency where Mr. Carter, not part of the family, had worked his entire adult life. Two years ago he'd been forced to retire by the grandson of the founder, a kid he used to entertain by pulling nickels from his ears. Apparently Mr. Carter's inability to master the new technology, go with the flow on the information highway, made him a liability instead of an asset. The fact that most of his accounts had gone to the great big actuarial table in the sky had also hastened his departure. Mabel hadn't been a family member either. She'd come in off the street to apply for the position after Mr. Carter had been working there ten years or so. She was a cute little thing then. "Petite," not "short"—she was quick to correct anyone who made the mistake. She was quick to correct any mistakes, Mr. Carter discovered shortly, not petitely, after their marriage. She was quick to learn new things too. She'd had no trouble moving first from a manual to electric typewriter, then to a word processor. She tossed words like *gigabyte* and *RAM* around with aplomb. "It's so simple, Charles. Children four and five years old, younger even, use computers all the time. I should think a man in his sixties would have no trouble." He'd give it a shot and after a while hit a key plunging the screen into darkness or producing ominous messages with fused bomb icons.

It was following one of these episodes, which took one of the younger agents in the office an hour to rectify, that retirement was strongly suggested. Forty years. No gold watch. No testimonial dinner. Squat. Mabel, who'd decided to retire at the same time over the protests of her boss, got a dozen long-stemmed American Beauty roses and a cut glass Waterford vase. "Very tasteful," she'd pronounced.

Yes, she'd been a cute little thing, but as the years went by, only "little" remained. She had always been plagued with allergies, and as a consequence her nose was red, her face pinched, and her eyes watery. She kept tissues stuffed up her sleeves. It drove Mr. Carter crazy to see them sticking out from her cuffs, bits of white—wet with mucus. After Mabel stopped working, she stopped dressing up and replaced the suits and high heels she'd favored with sweats and athletic shoes. "Why not be comfortable?" she said and ridiculed the way he kept his closetful of suits brushed, his wing tips polished. He wore the khakis and plaid sports shirts previously reserved for weekends every day now, but each Sunday he put on one of his suits for church, rotating it to the end of the row when he took it off. Mabel had stopped going to church. "I can talk to God anywhere." She used the time for her daily power walk. She was constantly urging him to join her and do something other than sit indoors and read. "If not walking, then go to a gym. Anything but vegetate. You don't even have a hobby!"

Mabel's hobby was her garden. She grew flowers and more produce than they could ever eat, crowding the chest freezer in the basement—next to the pails of mushrooms she tended—with lima beans, stewed tomatoes, and other things Mr. Carter disliked eating.

Mr. Carter didn't feel the need of a gym. He weighed the same as he had the day he was married. And he *did* get out of the house. He walked to the library. And sometimes he took the bus and went to one of the museums in Boston. His hobbies were reading, he told Mabel, and art. She would snort at his answer. "You're supposed to produce something with a hobby. Besides, reading doesn't count. Anybody can read."

Maybe he wouldn't hate her so much if they'd had children, but Mabel hadn't been too keen on the idea, and then when she'd grudgingly given in, they couldn't. "It wasn't meant to be," she told anyone bold enough to inquire. He supposed he could have divorced her, but he'd been busy at work and their nightly interactions had been brief, limited to a quick dinner before he settled in with his book and she with her seed catalogues. And what would have been the grounds? Drippy nose? Bossiness? Lima beans? More important, "divorced" was not as desirable as "widowed." Divorced meant something had been wrong with your marriage, that maybe you had done something wrong. It wasn't the image he wanted for himself. And it wasn't true.

Maybe he wouldn't hate her so much if she'd kept working. It was her constant presence that was driving him mad. He'd suggested she think about taking a part-time job, not let her skills go to waste. "Why on earth would I want to go back to work?" she'd said. "I've worked all my life. Now it's my time." She sounded like a television commercial: "Now It's My Time." It was after the third repetition of the phrase that he decided to kill her.

It felt good to have a goal. He was happier than he'd been in many years. He was glad now that they hadn't had a family. He wouldn't have been able to deprive children of a mother or grandchildren of a grandmother. And their own families posed no problems. Both his and her parents had died years ago. Mr. Carter was an only child, and Mabel had an older sister living in Canada. The two had never been close and Mabel didn't even know whether the woman was still alive. So there would be no relatives to question the sudden death of a beloved family member.

It would have to be a perfect crime. That went without saying. He would immediately be the prime suspect. It's always the husband. He'd read enough mysteries and true crime books to know that. Well, maybe not always, but usually. There was no point in going through with it if he wasn't going to be able to reap the benefits of being a widower. Much as he disliked living with Mabel, it was preferable to prison. He knew there was a risk, but oh, the rewards!

After the food and the calls tapered off, he saw himself joining one of those grief support groups, basking in the pathos of others like himself. He would go on Elderhostels to Tuscany and Prague—places he had only read about. Places Mabel had never cared to visit. "If you want greasy Italian food, you can get all you want in the North End. Besides, you have to bring your own water and toilet paper. Who needs that?" He would date attractive women with beautifully coifed silver hair. Women who wore scent and took the trouble to apply flawless makeup. He would get subscription tickets for the symphony. His own seats. He would nod to those around him, careful not to be too familiar. He would maintain his aura, his dignity. They would nod back, commenting to one another in low voices about the well-dressed elderly gentleman, retired businessman no doubt—or perhaps an academic. After the concert, he and his lady friend—he liked the sound of that—would have supper at the Brasserie Jo, cosmopolitan places, and when he took her home, she would invite him in for coffee. She'd offer decaf, but he'd smile and say he could handle the real thing. She'd laugh and he would kiss her. He could close his eyes even now and feel the warmth and softness of her skin on his lips. They would go to bed and she would protest that her body was not what it had been when she was young. He would whisper that if anything she must be more beautiful. They would make love. And sleep long and dreamlessly, waking in each other's arms. She would not blow her nose. She would not say they were too old for such nonsense. She would not laugh at Mr. Carter's naked body nor comment that his skin seemed to have grown too large for his bones. She would not move into the guest room and call it hers.

Mr. Carter didn't own a gun or a weapon of any kind, although Mabel kept her clippers and some of her other garden tools razor sharp. But he couldn't shoot her—the police would see through the "I thought she was a burglar" story in a flash—nor could he fake her suicide. There was the whole problem of powder burns. They'd have to be on her hand, not his, and he didn't think he could get Mabel to hold a gun and pull the trigger. Possibly he could drug her and then, using gloves, put the weapon in her hand and maneuver her finger to fire the shot. This might just do the trick, but the gun would of course be traced back to him. He'd have to buy one at a gun shop or from a pawnbroker, since he didn't have any street connections. He supposed he could go into Boston at night and try to purchase one, but he might also get himself mugged or even killed, which would spoil everything.

As for the garden tools, it was highly unlikely that Mabel could be induced to decapitate herself. She could, however, have an accident with her chipper, getting her hand stuck as she fed in leaves and branches, bleeding to death. He filed the notion away for further thought.

After reviewing his options over some weeks,

Mr. Carter came to the conclusion that the simpler the method the better. No weapons, poisons, lethal machinery. He'd take Mabel to the mountains and push her off a cliff. Hikers had accidents all the time. Especially novices, which they were. He'd have no trouble convincing her to go. She wanted him to exercise and she wanted him to have a hobby. Hiking would be his new love, and he wasted no time in preparing the groundwork.

"Mabel," he told her at dinner, one of her more inspired efforts—scrod baked in canned cream of mushroom soup, the current crop of her own mushrooms still in a state of immaturity. "You're right. I do need to get out more, but walking would bore me. I'd rather look at the beauty of nature than rows of houses and passing cars. I'm going to take up hiking."

He had expected an enthusiastic response, but this was Mabel.

"It's not as easy as you think. You'll need to get proper hiking boots, for a start."

"Already in my closet. I went to Eastern Mountain Sports this afternoon. And I took out a membership in the Appalachian Mountain Club. I should be getting maps and guides soon. Meanwhile I'll start with some of the little hills around here. If you'd care to join me, I'd be delighted."

"I'll get some boots."

He took a large bite of the fish. Whatever firmness of flesh it had possessed in the wild had been destroyed in Mabel's preparation and it was almost as liquid as the sauce. He smacked his lips. His heart was full and he gazed at his wife gratefully. "Wonderful," he said. "Absolutely wonderful."

It had been a mild winter, hardly any snow. Global warming, Mr. Carter supposed, but it provided excellent hiking weather, and in the following weeks he and his spouse attempted ever-hardier climbs with frequent day trips to the mountains in New Hampshire. He was surprised to find himself enjoying the exercise, noting the first signs of spring, and gradually adopting Mabel's hunter-gatherer habits. She was a firm disciple of Euell Gibbons, masticating sassafras leaves, pouncing on acorns to grind for bread and muffins, and scooping wintergreen leaves for tea into one of the Ziploc bags she always carried in her rucksack. Knowing she would soon be gone granted him tolerance and the odd moment of affection for his wife. It would all be put to good use when he played the part of the lonely, grieving widower.

When spring began to give way to summer, they tackled the White Mountains. Mr. Carter had studied the AMC guides and maps until he knew every trail, every outcropping, every precipice with the precision of blind fingers over Braille. At last he decided they were ready—his goal: the top of the headwall on the Tuckerman Ravine Trail on Mount Washington. Ever since he'd read in the guide that Mount Washington had claimed more lives than any other peak in North America, the trail had beckoned like Shangri-la, its image a haunting melody during every hike, a coda to his footfalls. He booked a room, twin beds, at an inn in nearby Jackson for five days. It would be their anniversary gift to each other he told Mabel. A sentimental gesture.

Their anniversary fell on Thursday and if luck was with him, so would Mabel. It wouldn't do to arrive and kill her immediately. He would need to establish themselves as an affable—and devoted—couple. Two people enjoying retirement and each other. Two people with a new hobby. Two people who might get into trouble in the mountains.

When the day came, it was perfect. At breakfast some of the other guests remarked on the weather and hastened away to prepare for their own outings. It would seem that the paths would be crowded; not a moment of privacy, but Mr. Carter wasn't worried. He'd checked the conditions carefully. The ski season, which continued well into the spring at this elevation, had ended. School was still in session, so no intrepid Von Trapp–type families to get in the way. And he'd avoided the weekend, which would bring more people to the popular trail. A moment was all he needed, and he was sure he would get it.

"Shall we, my dear?" he asked playfully as his wife finished her stewed prunes.

Soon they were on the trail, a more difficult one than they had attempted before. A challenge. He was positively giddy with joy. The sky was blue. Not a single cloud. The hours passed swiftly and then, unless he was wrong, five more minutes would bring them to the spot he'd selected. A fabulous view. He owed her that at least. They were above the timberline. No trees to grab on the way down.

And it all went according to plan.

"Why don't we stop a moment? The footing's a little tricky here and I want to rest," he told her. "Besides, it's spectacular." He swept his arm out, encompassing the surrounding peaks—the Wildcat Range opposite—and the valley, far, far below. Then swept his arm back, neatly knocking her off her small feet and sending her hurtling over the edge, crying, "Watch out!" at the same time for her sake—and the sake of others on the trail out of sight but not earshot.

It was done. He was free.

He was falling.

She had grabbed him by the ankle. She was taking him with her. His fury knew no bounds. Then, nothing.

The next thing he knew he was strapped to a stretcher and a ranger was telling him to lie still, that he'd be all right. "Looks like you broke a leg, but you're a very lucky man."

"My wife, what about my wife?" Mr. Carter asked.

"She's fine, a bit bruised and shaken up of course. You landed on a small projection thirty feet down. It's a miracle. We lost a hiker from that very spot a year ago. Your wife's just ahead of us. Didn't hit her head the way you did; still, they'll want to check her out at the hospital."

A second ranger broke in, admonishing him, "I hope you understand you folks could have been killed. Your wife mentioned you've just started climbing. It's treacherous up here, especially with all the loose rock after the snow's melted." She repeated the other ranger's words: "You're a very lucky man."

Mr. Carter groaned and let himself slip back into unconsciousness.

He hadn't broken a leg. Just his ankle. His recovery gave him plenty of time to think. Maybe simple hadn't been such a good idea. He'd have to come up with something a bit more complicated than a shove—something a bit more sure. His wife was busy in the garden from morning to night, so there was that to be thankful for. While she was out at the nursery getting more manure, he hobbled to the shed in the backyard and looked at the assortment of things she used to keep weeds and garden pests away. Virtually every preparation carried the skull-and-crossbones logo he'd been conjuring up as he sat indoors reading. Then there was the chipper. It was tucked in a corner with her small rototiller. The good old chipper.

He gazed longingly at the poisons again. LAST MEAL FOR SLUGS read one. Last meal for Mabel. But unless he could convince the police she was suicidal, the use of any of these goodies would immediately be traced back to him. He felt like a kid in a candy store with empty pockets. He turned and went back to the house. His ankle was throbbing.

The whole thing would be much easier if he were less of a gentleman, he thought bitterly. He wanted to kill his wife, but he didn't want her to know he had. Let her go to her grave firm in the belief that she'd had a good marriage. It would be unspeakably boorish to behave otherwise. If he hadn't cared about protecting her, he could simply have smothered her with a pillow and arranged the whole thing to look like an allergy attack. She'd certainly had some severe ones and was allergic to everything from dust to bee stings.

Day after day he turned the problem over and over in his mind. He couldn't arrange a car accident. Mabel had never learned to drive, and besides, he hadn't the faintest notion of how to cut brake cables or whatever it was they were always doing in books. It got to the point where he couldn't sleep at night. His ankle bothered him. It had been a nasty break and the pain matched the pain in his aching brain.

After the fourth night in a row with scant rest, Mr. Carter called the doctor and that afternoon the drugstore delivered some chloral hydrate. He opened the bottle and sniffed. It smelled like cherry syrup. Not unpleasant at all. Then he read the lengthy printout—from a computer, of course— that listed the recommended dosage and all the side effects. He supposed the drug companies covered themselves this way. Terrify the consumer with a smorgasbord of alarming symptoms; cover themselves, so no one could sue. He read through the "Do not combine with alcohol" and "Do not

operate heavy machinery" warnings, getting to the
"May cause skin rash, mental confusion, ataxia"—
he'd have to look that up—"headache, nausea, diz-
ziness, drowsiness"—well, wasn't that the whole
point?—"stupor, depression, irritability, poor
judgment, neglect of personal appearance"—they
were really covering themselves here, and then a
catchall—"central nervous system depression." He
went to the bookshelves and took down *Webster's*.
Ataxia—loss of the ability to control muscle movement.

He put the book in its place and went back to
his armchair, wending his way through the jungle
of Mabel's plants that filled the room. He picked
up the bottle and held it to the light, watching the
way the sun made a bright red blotch on the morning paper. Chloral hydrate. Just what the doctor
ordered.

Mr. Carter hadn't mentioned his sleeplessness
to his wife, nor his subsequent call to the doctor.
Now he congratulated himself on his discretion. It
was almost as if his unconscious mind was taking
over and charting the right course. His conscious
mind had simply not wanted to talk to Mabel. She
wasn't a drinker, but she liked to indulge herself
every now and then with a liqueur after dinner. He
found the peppermint schnapps, melon liqueurs,

and cherry brandies she favored nauseatingly sweet. If he kept her company, which he seldom did, he sipped a small snifter of cognac. Mabel made herself concoctions poured over crushed ice, drinking them from their everyday tumblers. "It's the same drink in a jelly glass or your precious crystal," she pointed out. They hadn't received many wedding gifts when they'd married and the crystal had been from his parents. Mabel had managed to break most of it over the years and he washed it himself now. Maybe if it had been from her parents, she'd have felt differently. They'd given the newlyweds a check—a rather small one.

He bided his time. Each night he measured out his dose—and didn't take it. When he had accumulated what would surely be enough, he put his plan into action.

"You've worked hard all day, my dear," he said after dinner—Mabel's famous "Vegetable Stew," a mélange of whatever was ripe dumped into the pressure cooker. "Why don't I make you a drink? I'm going to have one myself."

Mabel said that would be nice. She was still in her gardening clothes, although her hands were clean, scrubbed raw, the nails chipped. Gloves were a bother and got in her way.

He went to the kitchen, thinking paradoxically

that a truly thoughtful wife would offer to fetch the libations herself rather than be waited on by her handicapped husband. She had been typically unsympathetic about the injury and had expressed her opinion several times too often that he needed to walk more or his muscles would be even limper. He reached for the glass she liked and using the ice maker on the refrigerator door, filled it. He took the chloral hydrate from behind the flour canister, where he'd placed it earlier in the day, and poured it, filling half the tumbler. The dose the doctor had prescribed was two teaspoons before bedtime. Mr. Carter was both taller and heavier than his wife; most people were. With the addition of the cherry brandy, the drink should send her swiftly to sleep and then with any luck into a deadly coma. He planned to put her to bed, inhaler on the floor by her side, apparently knocked out of reach.

Unlike the pillow method, she'd never know what hit her. The perfect crime. He'd be certain to mention the brandy to whomever responded to the 911 call he'd make in the morning after failing to rouse her and noting with horror the absence of all vital signs. No one would suspect the chloral, but if it was found, he'd been taking his medicine as ordered each night and there was his name on the half-empty bottle to prove it. But he doubted it would come to that. If Mabel and he had been younger, perhaps there would be some suspicions, but at their age people did die, especially people with severe allergy-induced asthma.

He topped off her drink with the sweet brandy and poured himself a more generous than usual amount of Rémy Martin. He had heard that it was the cognac connoisseurs drank. It was expensive enough, certainly. Carrying the two glasses, he made his way back into the living room, emphasizing the awkwardness of his cast as he approached Mabel's chair. She was reading *The Encyclopedia of Plant Lore,* a gift from him several Christmases ago. She snapped it shut and took her drink. "Yum." She smiled appreciatively, and by the time he reached his own chair and turned around to face her, she'd quaffed more than half of it. He started to chide her. Really, it was most unbecoming to watch a woman swill alcohol that way, but stopped himself. The quicker the better. The quicker the deader.

"Cheers," he said and lifted his glass. She set hers down and picked up the book again. Was it his imagination or did she seem unusually flushed? He held his breath and put his cognac down. Tonight of all nights he needed a clear head. Tonight! His blood raced. It would be tonight. Probably the first person he'd call after the emergency number would be Mrs. Parsons, who lived next door. They had been neighbors for thirty years, and when Mr. Parsons had been alive, the two couples occasionally played bridge. They were pleasant enough but fully occupied in bringing up their four children. Mrs. Parsons had put on considerable weight since the death of her husband, and an endless stream of children and grandchildren were in and out of the house. She was a good cook, judging from the Christmas cookies and Fourth of July blueberry pie she bestowed upon them each year. He could count on her for any number of meals and other forms of sustenance.

He let his mind drift to the next few days. Tomorrow would be the worst—or the best, depending on one's viewpoint. There would be the police rescue squad, then when it became apparent that it was, alas, too late, he'd have to deal with the medical examiner, or perhaps it would be their own doctor? He'd be finding out soon. Then arrangements with the funeral home, and he had no doubt that the Reverend Dobbins would arrive with words of comfort immediately. Mr. Carter thought "For the Beauty of the Earth" would be an appropriate hymn for Mabel's service. He'd leave the rest to Reverend Dobbins.

Interment was no problem. They had a plot, purchased years ago. He'd have his own name carved on the headstone too with his birth date and the rest blank. Although, if he remarried, that might hurt his next wife's feelings. Just Mabel's then, with an appropriate epitaph. Best not to burn one's bridges.

Word would get around. The phone, which seldom rang, would ring off the hook. He'd ask one of the women in the church to help him plan a suitable collation for after the service. Lilies, not gladioli.

"I think I'll go to bed. Kinda tired." Mabel's speech was definitely slurred. She stood up and knocked into the Benjamin's fig tree next to her chair as she stepped toward the stairs.

"Are you all right, my dear?"

"Fine. Need to sleep, that's all."

Mr. Carter lingered for a moment, enjoying the emptiness of the room and the prospect of the continued void in his future, then went to bed himself. He set the alarm for three o'clock—enough time for the lethal cocktail to have worked and time to set the stage. When it sounded, he walked soundlessly down the carpeted hall and opened the door to his wife's room. For a moment he felt a twinge of regret as he gazed at the still figure in the bed, but it passed quickly and he found he had a sudden desire to laugh with glee. But that would be unseemly. He composed his face into a proper widower's expression and approached Mabel's corpse. The inhaler was on her bedside table within arm's reach. He reached to move it, and fling the bedclothes about a bit, then froze.

"What do you think you're doing?" Mabel sat up in bed, her face an angry mask. "I thought I made it clear, we're past that sort of thing."

Fright turned to stunned surprise, and he gulped for words, unable to utter the ones racing through his head. How could she possibly have drunk the mixture and be alive? And awake!

"Thought I heard you call, my dear," he mumbled. "Must have been dreaming." He hastened out of the room, pulling the door firmly shut. Yes, he had been dreaming and awakened to a nightmare.

Mr. Carter was a persistent man. He had been successful at his job not because of hard or soft sell, but persistent sell. He possessed the ability to wait. Rebuffed by prospective clients, he'd call two years later and like as not sign them as new customers, dissatisfied with the coverage they'd purchased instead. Most of the population regarded insurance companies as potential adversaries, and it wasn't difficult to get them to switch loyalties with a few well-chosen aspersions. Therefore, when he awoke the next morning, he was calm. True, he had expected to be widowed by the end of the summer, but these things took time. He'd taken to reading the obituaries and news reports of fatal accidents for ideas. Most involved automobiles, but one day he happened upon a column describing, with some humor, what a death trap one's home was.

He read eagerly, eliminating household poisons, ladders, and carbon monoxide as unsuitable for his purpose. The section his eyes lingered lovingly over involved electrical appliances and water. He should have thought of it before. It wasn't as kind as the other approaches, but Mabel was making things difficult. However, there was always the chance that it would be so quick, she wouldn't realize what was happening. Several years ago they had indulged themselves with a whirlpool tub, or rather Mabel had. Mr. Carter never used it, finding the jets of water disconcerting and the noise it made annoying. All he had to do was plug in a radio and drop it into the tub. She wouldn't hear him come into the bathroom, and by the time she noticed, it would be too late. When the rescue squad came, he'd lament his wife's foolhardy habit of listening to music while she bathed and regret that he hadn't thought to give her one safe for such use. According to the newspaper, countless Americans died just this way each year.

He folded the newspaper, put it in the recycle bin, and went out to the kitchen, where Mabel was putting lunch on the table. The garden was at its height and lately they seemed to have become vegetarians. He promised himself a thick steak after a suitable period of absence of appetite was observed.

A cold cream soup and salad awaited. Recently some of Mabel's efforts had not gone down so well and he was relieved to see plain fare. She was slicing some zucchini bread, warm from the oven.

"Looks delicious. Fruits of your labor. You've been hard at it, I can see. You should treat yourself to a long soak in the whirlpool, my dear."

Mabel said she thought that was a good idea and sat down.

Mr. Carter was spooning the last drops of the soup, leek, he thought, when he felt himself breaking out in a cold sweat. He looked at his wife in alarm. His heart suddenly seemed to have stopped beating, and he was terribly dizzy. He tried to get up and a wave of nausea passed over him. The vomit rose in his throat, but he managed to gasp, "What was it?"

"Oleander. Mimics a heart attack. Sorry it had to be this way, but nothing else was working."

His gaze was clouding over, yet he still managed a smile. A big smile. A wasp had landed unnoticed on Mabel's arm, bare in her sleeveless shirt. Another joined it, drawn by the smell of the bread on the table. He closed his eyes, faintly hearing her startled cries.

Early on he'd replaced the epinephrine in her syringes with saline.

Luck had been with him after all.

ACROSS THE POND

Three women were having a late lunch high above New York City's Madison Avenue at Fred's, the upscale eatery at Barneys. Two of the women had come in together first and bore enough of a resemblance to make the guess they were sisters a sure thing. Height, weight, carriage, and facial expressions were the same. The main difference was in their coloring—a blue-eyed honey blonde and a brunette with startling emerald eyes. They were laughing as they took their places.

The third woman didn't keep them waiting long. The maître d' escorted her to the table minutes after the others were seated. She was blond as well, but the hue was almost platinum and her hair fell in soft waves just to her chin. The three had hugged and kissed—European-style, on either side of the face—but not air kisses. These particular ladies about to lunch were obviously good friends.

When the food arrived, a casual observer may have been surprised at their menu choices. No salads minus everything but the greens and perhaps a cucumber slice or a single string bean, no dressing at all, not even on the side, and horrors of horrors—bread! No thank you! Against expectations, all three had ordered Fred's justly famous Dietzler Farms burger—rare and of course on a bun—with Belgian *frites*, and somehow one sensed they had plans for dessert as well. Two were drinking Chardonnay—so often the choice of a certain kind of woman that blood types in the Big Apple needed AOCs, Appellations of Origin—and the third was enjoying a glass of Vino Nobile from Montepulciano. Calories, carbs galore—yet no sign of them on the women themselves. They had shed their winter coats, and all three were wearing fitted, chic little black dresses, prompting an observer to conclude that often life wasn't fair. All metabolisms were *not* created equal.

There was a lull in the conversation as the women consumed the meal with obvious enjoyment. Inveterate eavesdroppers such as ourselves surely would have felt a twinge of disappointment at this interruption to what had earlier been a juicy conversation indeed.

Coffee arrived and a trio of desserts: mascarpone cheesecake, white-chocolate bread pudding, and a seasonal caramelized apple tart. There was much tasting and sharing before the conversation returned to the matter at hand: a wedding.

Curtain up.

I'm extremely touched that you would want me as . . . what would you call it—not a bridesmaid, an attendant?—and I'm sure Hope is too, but don't you Brits usually have adorable small children accompany you?" Faith Fairchild said.

Faith's sister, Hope, was not only an Anglophile but also a Royalist and quickly concurred, citing notable examples back to Princess Anne. She added, "I do think Faith is right, Polly. Lovely that you want us by your side on your big day—well, second big day—but what about Tess and Fiona?"

Polly Ackroyd had gone back to her maiden name after her first, very brief, marriage—the first "big day"—had gone down the drain. Quite literally, as it happened. She had returned to their London flat early from a trip to her parents' estate in Scotland intending to surprise her newly minted husband. Under her well-cut Highland tweeds she was wearing some very naughty knickers and not much else. Instead the surprise was all hers when she discovered hubby David enjoying a rumpy-pumpy in the Jacuzzi with one of her best friends. "Such a cliché," she had later moaned to Faith and Hope, whom she'd met as a teenager when they were all at the Dalton School during the years Polly's father, Godfrey, did "something diplomatic" in New York. Polly had pulled the plug on the tub and the marriage, tossing her husband's bespoke wardrobe into the street and changing the locks.

Faith was delighted that Polly had found someone to erase the memory of that first matrimony. She did agree with Hope, however, about Polly's attendants. "If you don't want the little ones, then shouldn't you ask your sisters? One or both?"

Technically Tess and Fiona were Polly's stepsisters, added to the family in a genealogically challenging way. Godfrey Ackroyd married a widow with two small daughters, and she died before they had any offspring. He then married again. Since Tess and Fiona's late biological father was a kind of cousin to their adoptive one, Tess and Fiona became Ackroyds. It was generally thought to have worked out well, blood will tell. Possibly Polly's mother may have blanched a bit at taking on two small children before producing her own, but that was why God had created nannies.

Tess and Fiona had both been at university when Godfrey Ackroyd accepted the New York posting, but they had spent enough time in Manhattan for Faith and Hope to get to know them. Accomplished, attractive, and extremely self-confident, Faith, for one, had always found them more than a little scary. Unlike Polly, they were keen on sports, especially riding—younger versions of Camilla Parker Bowles.

Polly was sitting up very straight. "Aside from the fact that I consider you two my sisters more than either of them, there's a bit of a hiccup just now with Fiona."

"A hiccup?" Hope asked, wondering whether this was a British medical euphemism or simply a bump in the road.

"You see, I met darling Ian at Fiona's engagement party."

"And that's a problem, because . . . ?" Faith said

"Because it was his and Fiona's."

"I think we need more coffee—or maybe a drink," Hope said.

Definitely a bump.

They ordered three of Fred's St. Germain cocktails, elderflower liqueur with white wine and a splash of soda.

"It was a coup de foudre for both of us," Polly said. "I know, I know, terribly awkward, but what could we do?"

Polly's posh BBC-announcer accent ordinarily made even a remark about the weather sound both charming and important. It turned these two sentences into memorable lines—like something straight from a drawing room comedy by Noël Coward.

"I hadn't met him before, just heard Fiona go on about him. Did something terribly important in the City, old family, always a horse at Ascot. All the things that matter a great deal to her and not at all to me, so I never really paid attention. How was I to know how perfectly scrumptious he was?"

Although this sounded as though she were describing a slice of Victoria sponge cake, both Hope's and Faith's expressions signaled agreement. The first thing Polly had done after greeting them earlier was show them photos of Ian on her phone and her ring, in that order. Ian made Colin Firth look rather plain, and the ring would have made a fine addition to the Crown Jewels.

"I gather Fiona is cutting up rather rough about

it all?" When Faith was with Polly, or other British people, she tended to adopt the language and struggled not to unwittingly imitate the accent as well.

"Yes, actually, she is. It's why I'm here. Mummy thought it best for me to leave the country for a while. Ian, poor dear, has to work and in any case, he would never turn tail and run." Polly's voice was filled with pride, suggesting the kind of hero unafraid to stare down a tiger.

Faith still hoped Ian was being vigilant. Fiona, and Tess, who must be beyond furious on her sister's behalf, would be formidable foes. He wouldn't be showing his face much around town, she supposed, but he could always hole up at White's, the venerable gentlemen's club in St. James that still had a "men only" policy, breaking it just once, for a visit from the queen. Ian was bound to be a member, given the pedigree Polly had hinted at and Fiona would have required.

"When did all this happen?" Hope said.

"The wedding was supposed to be at Christmas and they got engaged in June, but you know how everyone is always away on holiday in the summer, so the big official party was two weeks ago." She looked a bit sheepish. "We feel terrible, of course, but think how awful it would have been if we'd first met at the wedding. Ian is such a kind person. He doesn't even like to swat a mosquito, so you know how difficult this was for him."

Silently noting that ditching one's fiancée two and a half months prior to the nuptials was a bit more than slapping at an annoying pest, Faith said, "Wouldn't it be better to slip away to Gretna Green or wherever it is people go these days to elope, get married quietly, and then take an extremely long honeymoon? India? The Amazon?" Tigers and mosquitoes were getting mixed up in her thoughts.

Polly emphatically shook her head no.

"Ian has never been married before, and I'm not going to deny him a real wedding. It won't be Saint Margaret's. That would be salt in the wounds, since he and Fiona were to have been married there. Besides, that's where David and I were married. Possible bad karma. No, the sweet vicar at Saint Michael's has said he will marry us there in June. That should give Fiona—and Tess, she's quite *fâchée* too—time to calm down, plus Mummy and I need to work out all the details. Wedding breakfast not at the Savoy as last time, but someplace nice. And I nipped over to Beauchamp Place before I left. Suzanne Neville has my measurements and is sending some sketches for my dress, which reminds me she'll need yours. I'm thinking sapphire. Something bright like stained glass. The church has a gorgeous Evie Hone rose window that replaced the one the Nazis bombed. Horrible Huns."

Noting that Polly was beginning to sound like a character from a Nancy Mitford novel, Faith reconsidered her initial objection to being Polly's attendant. It really couldn't be one or both of Polly's stepsisters. Even though June was many months away—and surely Fiona wouldn't want to marry someone who didn't want to marry her—it was her pride that had taken the bad fall. Fiona's was on a scale with Everest, hence a long way down.

The thought of Polly's wedding was enticing—and a dress from the noted British designer Suzanne Neville! Heaven!

Being eight and a half months pregnant with Ben, who was now in second grade, Faith had missed Polly's first wedding. Hope's description of it had left her feeling very envious, especially as about the time when the couple were exchanging their vows, Faith was in the throes of delivery, wondering why the ordeal was called a blessed event. While "labor" was aptly named, "easy childbirth" was definitely an oxymoron.

St. Margaret's Westminster, right next to the Abbey, was *the* place for society weddings, many of them royal. It had been especially popular among the 1920s Bright Young Things, wealthy Bohemians who ran around London between the wars, stealing bobbies' helmets and drinking champagne from slippers—precursors to the set haunting Annabel's in the 1960s and '70s. Same elite class, same tony addresses—streets and titles. Which reminded Faith that Polly was able to get married at St. Michael's in Highgate because, among other holdings, her parents had an extremely beautiful house there. She and Hope had spent time as guests on several occasions before each of them had gotten married themselves. It all seemed ages ago, even if it wasn't, strictly speaking.

Marriage and motherhood had fast-forwarded the years for Faith. Ben had been joined by Amy, and now that Amy was in kindergarten, both were blessedly in school. She adored her children, but God had not dropped a Mary Poppins into her household. Hope, a financial lawyer, had married Quentin after much synchronizing of BlackBerrys to find a moment both wouldn't be working. No progeny yet, but Hope had mentioned it would be coming up on the agenda in the near future. Despite their closeness in age—Faith was a year older—and closeness as sisters, the two former Sibleys were as different as two siblings could be. Faith had found her calling in the kitchen as a caterer; Hope skipped *My Weekly Reader* and went straight to the *Wall Street Journal*. Her life was an agenda, whereas Faith's was a to-do list.

London in June. Could she possibly get away? One look across the table at her sister hinted that the same thought was running through Hope's mind and her next words confirmed it: "I suppose we'll have to organize a hen party for you."

Polly squealed, "I knew you'd do it! Now, let's get squiffy," and ordered another round.

Polly's first accident occurred two days after the lunch at Fred's. Faith was still in the city, ostensibly there for early Christmas shopping and a visit to her parents. Faith and Hope had grown up as PKs—Preacher's Kids—in a duplex apartment on the Upper East Side of Manhattan. Although not exactly a traditional parsonage, it had been a fishbowl existence nonetheless. This had led to a pact between the sisters to avoid it, but Faith had had her own coup de foudre, meeting the Reverend Thomas Fairchild at a wedding she was catering and falling head over heels before realizing he was at the reception because he had just performed the ceremony. Now ensconced in a New England parish, she regarded these periodic trips back to her hometown as lifelines.

She was at her parents' apartment when Hope called with the news.

"Polly got jostled on the subway platform— why she was there, she never takes the subway, I do not know—and would have fallen onto the tracks in front of the oncoming train, if a man hadn't grabbed her in time. Unfortunately in the process, he had to push her down on the concrete and landed on top of her. Nothing is broken, but she's badly bruised and of course shaken. I can't leave work. Could you go get her? She's at Mount Sinai. Stay with her at the apartment? I'll come as soon as I can."

"Of course. I'll leave now. Terrible! But thank God it wasn't worse."

After picking her up at the hospital, Faith bundled a frightened and pale Polly into a cab and they headed downtown. The Ackroyds kept a pied-à-terre on Gramercy Park. Faith tucked Polly into bed with one of the Percocets the hospital had prescribed and went into the kitchen to make some mint tea, among the young woman's favorite tipples, so there was sure to be some in the larder. There was, also bread and jam. Faith made toast and arranged everything on a tray. There was Marmite too in the Ackroyd pantry, but lines must be drawn.

"Well done, you," Polly murmured muzzily. The Percocet was working.

Faith plumped the pillows and Polly sat up. Her room was classic Colefax and Fowler. All that was needed was a Corgi or two. Faith glanced out at the private park that gave Gramercy Park its name and exclusive reputation. It was barren now as fall was ending and could have been any one of London's similar squares. She half expected to see a double-decker red bus go by.

As Polly nibbled the toast and sipped her tea, Faith decided that the patient was doing better, so she began with gently quizzing her about what had happened, starting with the obvious.

"Why were you in the subway? Where were you going?"

"Oh, you mean the Underground. But don't you know? I got your text on my mobile telling me exactly which tube to take at Grand Central station and get off, oh dear, I can't remember where, but you said it was the best way to get to Bloomies and we'd have a jolly time trying new makeup. Although, Faith, you do know that I am positively wedded to MAC and absolutely everything Molton Brown for skin . . ."

Her voice trailed off at the end, and Faith knew

she had to let Polly sleep, but she had one last question.

"Did they take your purse for safekeeping at the hospital?"

She had to ask, even though she was quite sure what the answer was going to be.

"They must have, mustn't they? And you have it now? You are an angel, Faith. You and Hope. What would I do without my Yankee sisters? I just thought of that. 'Yankee sisters.' Sounds like a pop group. Quite funny, yes? Must remember to tell Ian." And with that Polly went out like a light.

The hospital had given Faith a small clear plastic bag with the jewelry Polly had been wearing—her watch, a string of pearls, and plain gold hoop earrings. No purse. It must have been snatched when she went down. By someone seizing the opportunity—or someone who was part of a plan?

She drew the drapes, closed the door, and went into the living room to wait for Hope. The cell phone was gone. No way to trace who had texted Polly.

Only one thing was sure. It hadn't been Faith.

Polly woke up shortly after Hope arrived bearing several loaded shopping bags from E.A.T. She'd ordered what she'd considered Polly's comfort food plus one of her own: scones, cucumber and other assorted sandwiches, salads, and a large container of Eli's chicken soup. Soon the three women were once again sharing a late lunch. Polly had declared herself ravenous and was having the soup plus an "egg mayonnaise" sandwich. She had switched from mint to Earl Grey tea. Faith and Hope were drinking martinis from the Ackroyds' well-stocked liquor cabinet and eating smoked salmon on thin slices of E.A.T.'s Health bread—a crunchy whole wheat loaf.

Surprisingly Polly didn't seem upset at the news that the text hadn't been from Faith.

"I've been expecting something of the sort. If it wasn't Fiona, it was Tess. Rather Tess-like now that I think of it. She does like to organize, and her firm has a branch here, so easy to get someone to do it, although clever girl, she would get the time difference right as I wouldn't and probably did it herself. She has been very much against what she calls my 'jumping the queue.' I think that bothers her even more than it's being Ian. She's the eldest, got married first, now it's Fiona's turn, then it will be mine."

"But you were married before, and anyway, it's not like taking numbers in a shop," Faith said, stopping before adding, "in the High Street" or some other Anglicism.

"They don't count that one apparently. Nor do I really. Anyway, it's still not my turn."

Hope was holding up her glass. She'd opened the drapes and the last light was making its way into the room, catching the rim. Baccarat, she thought, putting it down to face Polly.

"You could have been *killed*," she said. "Whether it was Tess or Fiona, the intent was, well, evil."

Polly laughed. "Too Agatha Christie, darling. Whichever one it was—Tess or Fiona—simply meant to send me on a wild goose chase and an extremely unpleasant one at that—really your Underground! The push was a coincidence, and I don't know why hundreds of you aren't perishing all the time."

While glad that Polly wasn't scarred by the experience, save for her now indelible view of New York's subterranean world, Faith was inclined toward Hope's interpretation. Revenge might be a dish best served cold, but this particular menu item had most certainly stayed piping hot despite being served up across the pond.

Faith had to get back home to Massachusetts and considered taking Polly with her, but Hope thought it best to get their friend to a location where neither stepsister could find her. They knew, or could easily discover, Faith's address. With Hope back to her usual routine of working round the clock and Faith leaving, Polly was amenable to being packed off, "rather like a parcel," especially as it was to Nassau, where a friend of Hope and Quentin's had a house currently unoccupied except for staff. Polly was welcome to stay as long as she wished, and when she told Ian about the move, he told her he'd be able to join her for part of the time.

The second accident occurred the day after he arrived a week later. Like the first, Polly dismissed it as a coincidence, but she did call Hope to report it, and once more the Sibley sisters found themselves on the phone worrying about their friend.

"That house is kept in perfect shape," Hope said. "Lionel and Vicky are extremely meticulous. There's no way one of the boards in the stairs to the beach would have been rotten. And besides, Polly has been using them for more than a week without noticing anything wrong."

"Good thing she was able to grab hold of a sea grape tree to break her fall. You've been there. Is it steep?"

"Very, and before you get to the white sandy beach there's a rather jagged rocky outcropping. Faith, this was no accident. A sprained wrist may hurt for a bit, but the wicked stepsisters have struck again. I'm sure they intended our bride to suffer far worse! It was stupid to send her to a member of the Commonwealth, where, of course, they'd have plenty of contacts, dubious ones included!"

"Ian is there now. They aren't likely to try anything with him around. But what's going to happen at Christmas? She wants to go home. I wish she would take all this more seriously." Faith sighed. "We could talk to Ian, but never having even laid eyes on him except in a photo makes it awkward. Polly said she did tell him about the subway, so hopefully he's keeping a close watch. He couldn't be as clueless as she is."

"Trusting, not clueless. Our Polly isn't stupid. Just much too nice." Hope sighed as well, more heavily. "We have to hope that having their parents around will keep Fiona and Tess in check. Maybe Fiona will meet someone over the holidays and then everything will be all right. If all else fails, don't they have Match.com there too? We could sign her up."

"It would have to be a very exclusive sort of site, but I do wish we could get Fiona back in the saddle again, so to speak."

Both sisters began to laugh so hard they could barely say good-bye.

A happy Christmas was had by all and January passed without incident. Polly was back in her London flat, flooding the Sibley sisters' in-boxes with e-mails about wedding plans. *Tact,* it appeared, was the watchword of the day—no over-the-top nuptial display—yet there was to be no scrimping. The designer Suzanne Neville was altering the "Lucia" model, described by Polly as "Brilliant!—ivory corded lace, fitted bodice, lace cap sleeves, column skirt, and low-cut back with a million tiny buttons all the way down over my bum. We're altering the design, shortening the train to a 'Sweep,' one barely touching the floor."

It amused Faith that in Britain there were so many different kinds of trains that a whole vocabulary existed to describe them. The big question was veil or no veil. Polly was leaning toward a Juliet cap with perhaps a single posy. "Granny" was lending jewelry—a diamond necklace and earrings—currently nestled in velvet cases at the bank.

Suzanne Neville's workshop had done toiles, cotton replicas of Hope's and Faith's dresses, for them to try on. They were to go to their own dressmakers and have them write down any alterations. No problem for Hope in New York, but Faith did not have anyone who whipped up gowns for her. Pix Miller, her next-door neighbor, was handy with a needle, and between the two of them they made notes of what needed to be done, fortunately not much. The final sleeveless dresses would be sapphire silk-faced satin with a simple draped bodice. They'd have column skirts similar to the bride's, but stopping midcalf. "And Manolo stilettos in sapphire—I already ordered them for you, not another word," Polly told Faith.

"Perhaps Polly is right and the text was a prank, the rest coincidence," Hope said to Faith in one of their increasingly frequent phone consultations. Hope had cleared enough time for the wedding and arranged a discreet hen party at the five-star spa at the Dorchester Hotel. Faith had begun to make her own arrangements, relying on her husband, but even more on the seemingly endless kindness not of strangers but of Pix again and the built-in babysitters her teens had become. Both sisters had booked flights and would stay with the bride at her parents' Highgate house.

Valentine's Day put paid to any notion that the rejected fiancée had decided to forgive and forget.

"Too, too sick-making," Polly said when she called Faith to tell her about the gorgeous box from Prestat, the chocolatier, she'd found at her flat that proved to contain an animal heart—"a sheep, I believe"—crawling with maggots. "It's Fiona. She knows I adore Prestat's truffles and not just because of *Charlie and the Chocolate Factory*. I'd planned on boxes of them as wedding favors, but now I'm not sure I can look at them without seeing that bloody mess."

Faith assumed she was using both meanings of the adjective, and her own heart sank. The assault was still being waged. Things were only bound to escalate the closer they got to the wedding day.

"Can't your parents talk to Fiona—and Tess?"

"I told Mummy about the horrid valentine, but she just said, 'Poor old Fiona. Not the thing to do, of course, but do admit, she has cause.'"

Faith could hear Mrs. Ackroyd saying this, especially as Polly had altered her tone of voice in an exact mimicry of her mother.

"How about Ian?"

"Oh, I don't think that would fly at all." Polly sounded shocked. "He can't very well ring up the woman he jilted and scold her for being mean to his new love!"

"No, I meant that perhaps he could talk to your father or to Tess's husband. Man to man." Faith held the notion that Britain still operated as an Old Boys Club. Ian was bound to have gone to the same public, meaning private, school or was some connection of one of the two men, probably both.

"Mmm." Polly paused. "I suppose I *could* suggest it. His father and Daddy were in the same college at Oxford."

There it was. Old school tie. Faith was sure it would stanch the flow of whatever bloody-minded effort the stepsisters were planning next.

It didn't.

Yet once more Polly viewed what happened as an annoying and yes, malicious, prank—but nothing further—and concentrated on her wedding plans.

Having decided to get the business of stating their intentions at the Register Office out of the way, the couple went to file, as required, with the fee and proper documents, including proof of Polly's divorce from David. The notice of intent was duly posted on the office's public notice board for the scheduled fifteen days. Polly had almost forgotten about it when Ian called to say that their particular form had been defaced.

"They wouldn't tell me how specifically, just asked that we come down and do a new one for the remaining week. Who would do such a thing? You don't think it's Fiona, do you?"

Polly did think it was Fiona, but no need to fuss.

They'd fill out a new form and it would be nice to see Ian in the middle of the day. "It's a busy place and no doubt someone was cheesed off about a parking citation and decided to take it out on the notices," she'd said.

There could be no mistake about who was responsible for the cock-up in the reading of the banns, however. Since they were getting married in St. Michael's, the Ackroyds' parish church, on June twenty-third, the banns had to be read on three Sundays in the three months prior. The first go was perfect. Ian's family, as well as his best man and his wife were all there, along with Polly's parents and several of her close friends. Her stepsisters were notably absent, but that was generally felt to be a good thing and tactful of them. Afterward, Godfrey Ackroyd hosted a luncheon at The Vine, a gastropub on Highgate Road. The sun had broken through the clouds, and it was nice enough for the party to sit outside. The weather had been the first thing Polly had mentioned to Faith, as was usual among the English when it wasn't raining—and when it was, as well.

Diabolical ingenuity was employed at the second reading of the banns. The vicar had finished up with ". . . If any of you know cause or just impediment why these two persons should not be joined together in Holy Matrimony, ye are to declare it," and was moving right along when a well-dressed young woman rose from one of the rear pews and declared in a firm voice, "I do. Mr. Howard is already married."

Straight from the pages of *Jane Eyre*.

The vicar's expression indicated that this had never happened to him before, but he handled the moment with aplomb. "We will discuss the matter in my study following the rest of the service."

Fiona had planned well. Only Polly was in church. Ian was, in fact, out of the country, in Switzerland on business. Her parents were in Spain on holiday, her mother having declared herself exhausted by all the wedding arrangements, which so far had not entailed much on her part save her dress fittings. She had informed Polly early on that the entire "do" was her show. "I did the first one, pet. Surely it's your turn." She had graciously offered to send out the invitations eight weeks prior to the big day, but in an uncharacteristic fit of caution, Polly said she would do it, posting them from Highgate so no one would twig to the fact that the parents of the bride had not actually posted them themselves.

Later, on the phone with both her friends at once, Polly told them she knew the woman was an actress the moment she spoke. "Too, too rehearsed."

Rehearsed or not, the woman was carrying a sheaf of very official-looking documents that attested to the civil, and very legal, marriage of one Ian George Howard to her sister, one Penelope Hardwick, in Ottawa, Canada, five months ago.

"Trust Fiona not to get herself dumped twice, since this was after we'd announced," Polly said. "Except obviously it was all bosh. I called Ian right away, and just as he was faxing his passport pages to the church office to prove he hadn't been to Canada at that time, the woman excused herself to 'wash her hands' and promptly disappeared. She must have slipped out through the cemetery."

Highgate Cemetery behind St. Michael's was one of Faith's favorite places in London. Walking through its thirty-seven beautifully verdant acres was always a nostalgic visit to the final resting places of so many of her much beloved writers, actors, and artists—Stella Gibbons, George Eliot, the Rossettis, Sir Ralph Richardson, Lucian Freud, and so many others. And then there was the imposing tomb of Karl Marx, which made her think, in turn, of *Morgan!,* one of her favorite classic movies containing a scene shot in the cemetery. She also thought of another scene from the film, the one where Morgan disrupts his very beloved ex-wife's wedding. Faith would keep an eye out for anyone dressed in a gorilla costume during Polly's nuptials.

The vicar assured Polly that the couple was still betrothed in his and God's eyes, so not to worry. The incident did have one happy issue out of the misfortune, however. Godfrey Ackroyd, upon hearing of it, called Fiona and Tess and told them in no uncertain words to "suck it up." The incident in the church had been public and veered close to reflecting on him.

Polly's final brush with injury, or worse, occurred at the hen party. She entered the spa looking drawn and confessed to Faith that she had not been sleeping well.

"I'm not superstitious, but it does seem that I keep having to walk around ladders and this morning I noticed the mirror in the bath has a large crack in it. I asked Mummy to get it replaced, and she told me I was being silly and it would have to wait until after the wedding. She couldn't have 'people' in now doing things. Plus it's not simply raining but coming down in chunks, and someone is bound to leave an open umbrella indoors to dry. I just have to get past Saturday and then I can take a real breath."

The couple hadn't told anyone where they were going for the honeymoon, but Polly mentioned she'd cleaned out the swimsuit department at Harvey Nichols, so Faith assumed the destination was tropical. She wasn't superstitious either, nor was Hope, but both were wishing time away. That it could skip ahead to the reception with Polly well and truly wed. Until then, ladders, mirrors, open brollies—whatever the British regarded as bad luck—were to be avoided.

"Start with a massage before the rest of the guests arrive. I promise you no male strippers dressed as Beefeaters and no crashers, male or female," Hope said to Polly, recalling the prank Fergie and the late Princess Diana had tried to pull many years ago at Prince Andrew's bachelor party. Hope had also cautioned all the ladies not to breathe a word of the party's locale lest Fiona or Tess find out. They were *not* on the guest list.

Forty minutes later everyone had arrived. There was a cheery buzz as the guests, sipping Kir Royales, chatted while indulging in manis and pedis. The bride was still enjoying her massage. Meeting Polly's friends was like seeing an issue of *Tatler* come to life, and Faith was having a good time.

A staff member entered the room and quietly said something to Hope, who got up immediately and followed her out. When Hope returned some minutes later, she announced, "Polly is happily going to bliss out for a bit longer and said to tell everyone to drink up!"

A fresh tray of flutes and Bento boxes containing delectable-looking sushi and sashimi appeared. As the rest of the guests moved toward them, Hope drew Faith to her side.

"Fiona or some minion has struck again. One of the attendants went to check on Polly, found the door locked, and went for help. When they got inside, they found her almost unconscious. Someone had applied a facial mask—bright red—filling Polly's nostrils and virtually sealing her mouth. She was fine once they peeled it off. They're applying something that will get rid of the worst effects of the color, but from now on I'm not leaving her side until she and Ian say 'I will.' "

A half hour later Polly, rather pink, but otherwise appearing none the worse for wear, joined the group and cried out rather frantically, "Let's get this party started!"

Like sentries outside Buckingham Palace, Faith flanked Polly on one side, Hope the other. At the spa, during the rehearsal at the church—easy, as they were supposed to stand close—and afterward at the dinner at the Ackroyds'. They got up early Saturday morning and, like the handmaidens they were, helped Polly into her Lucia gown, managing the tiny buttons with the buttonhook she had thought to supply. The dress was perfect and she looked a dream. They donned their own Neville posh frocks in her room—chary about letting her out of their sight for even that long.

The church was full, sun streamed through the stained glass, and the flowers—all roses in soft shades—filled the air with their scent. Faith listened intently as the familiar service progressed, taking an occasional glance back over her shoulder to be sure nothing was amiss among the pews, especially the one occupied by Polly's family. Mrs. Ackroyd was resplendent in silver satin. Fiona and Tess, contrary to Faith's expectations, were not wearing black, but navy blue. Near enough. And hats. All the women were wearing those tea tray hats so dear to the British female.

"Those whom God has joined together let no one put asunder," the vicar proclaimed. And it was over. Polly was safely married, emphasis on *safe*.

The radiant couple emerged from the church and stepped into a Victorian horse-drawn open carriage for the short ride to Lauderdale House, the site of the wedding breakfast. Truly the heavens were smiling. There wasn't a cloud in the bright blue sky.

Faith had learned enough about the difference in names for things—England and America being two countries divided by a common language—to know that "wedding breakfast" meant a dinner, not eggs and streaky bacon. The venue for the event was perfect too.

Lauderdale House in Waterlow Park on Highgate Hill had been built in 1582 for the Lord Mayor of London and had a long, colorful history—Nell Gwynne lived in it for a time. The gardens and house were soon overflowing with guests. The afternoon spiraled on through the starter of smoked salmon terrine, main course—Beef Wellington, Ian was a traditionalist—and finally the cake, four delectable tiers covered with edible flowers. Only the toasts were left, and shortly it would all come to an end. It couldn't be soon enough for Faith and Hope.

Three women were eating large slices of cake and drinking champagne high above Central London. The bride and her two matrons of honour had left the head table and slipped off to a smaller one, momentarily empty, to the side. They were laughing.

"Oh, my darlings, how could I ever have gotten through all this without you?"

There was nothing either Faith or Hope could say to that and instead, in turn, gave Polly a hug. She'd be slipping off soon—after the toasts and then one dance with Daddy, one with Ian.

Ian was standing up now, moving toward the head table, where Godfrey Ackroyd already held a glass high, about to begin his toasts to the groom's family and the happy couple. Ian caught his bride's eye and raised his full glass to her. She stood and paused, caught in his loving gaze. They could have been the only two people in the room.

"To you, my one and only," he called out and drank.

"To you," Polly started to reply in kind when suddenly her words became incoherent screams as she watched her groom fall to the floor clutching wildly at his throat.

Faith dashed across the room, passing Fiona, who was sitting alone. Fiona's complacent smile stopped Faith.

"More fool, her."

Curtain down.

A PERFECT MAINE DAY

I knew Myra Peters was dead the moment I saw her. She was wedged into the rocks, the outgoing tide dragging seaweed and a few periwinkles across her poor body. A crab skittered across her forehead. I dipped my hand in the water and flicked it away. There was no point in trying mouth-to-mouth. No point in trying anything at all.

She hadn't been in the water all that long. Her husband had radioed for help the moment he'd realized Myra had gone over the side while hauling. She'd been his sternman. Had been ever since they got married, must be almost two years ago. Remember the wedding well. Myra's people put on a dandy reception at the Legion Hall, spared no expense for their only daughter. Only child. Jim Gordon, her dad, had a nice business on the island, third-generation lobstering company. At the end of the shindig, when the whole lot of us, feeling no pain, were actively saying good-bye to the bride and groom, Jim handed Myra and Brian a framed photograph and some keys. A brand-new boat. Brian had been a sternman himself. Now he was his own boss. He'd grabbed his father-in-law in a big bear hug and christened the boat *My Myra* right then and there. Now being on the *My Myra* had killed her.

The beach was almost deserted. Summer people have their own private beaches, and most tourists never find this one. Island mothers like to bring their kids later in the day after chores are done. Course it gets crowded on weekends. It is just about the only place we can use, since people from away started buying up every foot of shorefront. Bert Elkins owns it and he says he'll eat worms before he'll sell. Hope he doesn't have to.

Cynthia Stoddard was sitting under a big umbrella at the far end and I went over to her, careful not to let Hector get too close to the pictures she was painting. Hector's a good mutt and provides me with an occupation now that the doctor says I can't fish anymore. I can walk Hector, though, and that's what we do every day about this time, so

Mother can get my dinner ready and do everything else that wants doing without me underfoot. Or that's what she says, anyway.

I came straight to the point.

"Myra Peters went over the side of Brian's boat early this morning and drowned. Heard it on the CB. Body's come to shore at the other end of the beach. I'm going to go back and keep an eye on her. Think you can go to my truck and call Arnold?"

Her face went as white as the paper in her lap.

"But that's terrible! How could it happen? Couldn't Brian do something?"

"Probably didn't see it happen. Engine's pretty noisy and the radio would've been on."

"Wasn't she wearing a life jacket? Isn't it the law that you have to wear a life jacket?" Seemed like Cynthia was wanting to turn time back and buckle Myra into her vest.

I nodded. It is the law, but a lot of fishermen don't bother. Even the new jackets get in the way. We don't have a swimming pool on the island. At least none of us who really live here. I never learned to swim. Doubted Myra had—or Brian. Most of us can't. No time, and the water is too damned cold. Cynthia was a swimmer, though. Told me once she'd learned to swim here from her grandmother, who went in every day like clockwork. I could see damp marks from her wet bathing suit on the tee shirt Cynthia had on. Her long hair was wet too. When it was dry, it looked like the silk on the corn we plant every spring, hoping to have a few ears by Labor Day. Myra's hair was wet now too. Dry it was short and dark—like a cap. Working hair.

Cynthia was a summer girl. Her great-grand-parents built one of those big old places out on The Point and the family's been coming to the island ever since. Swimming every day is the type of thing these people do. Also sail, cut their own brush, and generally make sure they don't waste any time while they're on vacation. They don't take the steamer from Boston anymore; have to drive five hours. In some ways the old days were better. Things took longer, but you had more time. Cynthia didn't go back to Boston at the end of last summer but decided to live here year-round. There's a few who try that. Most don't last more than a year or two. Winters can get kind of long around February. Cynthia's an artist. Sells her pictures up and down the coast—a lot here on the island at Jean Marshall's shop, The Clamshell. I could see Cynthia had had a busy morning. There was a bunch of watercolor paintings lined up against a log. I have to admire anyone with a talent like this. The only thing I could ever draw was a waterline on a boat.

"Think you could do that? Call Arnold?"

She jumped up and almost spilled the water her brushes were in.

"Of course!" The color was back in her face, but it was all scrunched up now. "Horrible. It's horrible. Her poor family!"

Cynthia took off down the beach. She had long legs—a pretty girl if you like the skinny type. Mother isn't. Better than an electric blanket on a cold night, and that's just fine with me.

I trudged on back to Myra. She hadn't moved. Didn't think she would. Not with the tide going out. I was tempted to pull her out onto dry land, but knew enough not to. We don't have a police force on the island. Too small. What we have is Arnold, Deputy Sheriff Bates, from the county sheriff's office on the mainland, who patrols here pretty regular. Plus the selectmen appoint a few of us to act as constables, which mainly means that we direct traffic on the Fourth of July, keep an eye on things during hunting season, and try to stop the kids from getting too rowdy and foolish.

The tide was going fast and the pool where Myra had come to rest was emptying out. I could smell the bait on her gloves. She was a small woman, but strong. She'd worked alongside her dad all her life, then her husband. It was a break for Brian and the

Fosters that she'd washed up here so soon. I've seen some that have been in the water longer, and it's nothing kin should have to deal with—plus there's all those who never get found at all. Just a stone over an empty grave.

She was in her fishing gear of course. Only things missing were her boots and socks. Her feet looked pearly white under the water, two tiny pieces of flesh sticking out from her bright orange oil pants. In her journey through the waves, a piece of rope and some kelp had tangled themselves around her ankles. Her eyes were open. Always thought they were the prettiest thing about her. Deep blue. Everything else was fine, where it was supposed to be and all, but nothing special. A plain woman, starting to get a little plump like her mother.

I sat down on the ledge next to Myra. She and Brian hadn't got around to having any kids yet. Still kids themselves and they were saving for a house. Meanwhile they'd been living in Brian's trailer up on the quarry road. But fishing had been good this year. I'd seen Brian at the store last week and he'd kidded me some about it. Said we old-timers was wrong to say there couldn't be two such good years in a row. I was tempted to tell him that when I'd started fishing all we had was a line and a lead plus a box compass so's we could find our traps in the fog. With all the fancy equipment now, if there was a lobster anywhere in Penobscot Bay, the fishermen knew it. Instead I teased him back about the paint job he'd given *My Myra* over the winter—bright yellow with turquoise trim. He'd gotten the paint on special, and anyway, Myra's favorite color was yellow, he'd told me. I could tell he'd been getting a lot of ribbing about his "lemon," so I shut up. Fishermen are pretty sensitive about their boats. Same with their territory. Put traps even a hair over in someone else's and they'll be gone, lines cut, before you're back at your mooring.

I knew it would take Arnold a while to get here. Cynthia was back and I could tell she was hesitating. Trying to decide whether she should come on over. I walked back and thanked her. Told her to stay where she was. She said she'd been just about to go home and I told her that was fine. I looked at her pictures again and complimented her. We stood for a minute staring at the water. The beach faces Eggemoggin Reach and across to the mainland. It was so clear you could see Mount Desert Island in the distance. The sky was as blue as a robin's egg and filled with puffy white clouds. A few sailboats made their way down toward Camden.

It was a perfect Maine day.

The funeral was a sad affair. I knew Myra's par-

ents would be cut up, but in her own quiet way
she'd been popular with the whole island, and everybody turned out. Brian looked like someone
half-dead himself. Didn't cry. Just sat in the front
row of the church, his eyes locked on the coffin.
Saw him shake his head a few times. He was holding his mother-in-law's hand. She wasn't crying
either, but Jim Gordon made up for both of them.
Tears just ran down his face, making puddles in his
neck until Mother passed him some Kleenex. We
were in the front row too on account of my finding
her and because I'm Jim's cousin.

Then life went back to normal for most people.
There was an article and an obit in our paper and
one of those fool guest opinions about the impor-
tance of wearing life jackets. Thought that could
have waited and told the editor when I saw him at
the post office.

"Someone sends me something, have to print it.
That's freedom of the press."

"That's bullshit," I told him. I can get a little
ornery.

Mother noticed that I was sort of quiet and I
imagine she must have thought it was because of
the hot spell we'd been having. Tuesday she asked
me if I'd drop off a casserole she'd made at Brian's
before I went to the Odd Fellows meeting that

night. It wasn't much out of my way and I said I didn't mind. Although, to my way of thinking, Brian probably had enough casseroles to last him until Christmas by now, because this is what the women on this island do. Casseroles and pies.

I took Hector to the beach. Cynthia wasn't there, but the mothers had come early and the kids were running in and out of the water. Hector joined them and they had a fine old time. On the way home I stopped at The Clamshell and talked to Jean for a while. Mother and I weeded the garden. Corn was looking good. Then I took a rest. Doctor's orders.

It was about five o'clock when I pulled into Brian's. There was another car there, one of those BMWs. You see them here in the summertime. See them more and more.

It was Cynthia's car and she was sitting at the kitchen table. There was a casserole in front of her. It looked a little fancier than the tuna one Mother had made, but not by much. They were drinking beer. Cynthia had poured hers into a glass. Brian offered me one, but I said no.

"What did you use to weigh her down?" I asked and pulled up a chair.

Brian stood up, knocking Cynthia's beer over. "What the hell are you talking about?"

"Myra. What did you use to keep her from com-

ing to the surface and floating away before Cynthia
could swim out and drag her to shore? You must
have tied her to a trap. By her feet, I expect, when
she was busy baiting. Then pitched her over."

Cynthia started to cry. "I knew something like
this would happen!"

"Shut up!" Brian yelled and slapped her. She
looked stunned and ran for the door. The trailer, in
Myra's absence, was a mess, and Cynthia tripped
over a pile of pot buoys Brian had been painting.
I helped her up and told her she had better just sit
down.

"I'm hoping you didn't plan this out before you
married the poor girl. I'm hoping she had a few
happy days."

Brian crushed his beer can, threw it, and reached
for another.

"Keep talking, you crazy old coot," he sneered.
"Even if one word of this was true, you couldn't
prove a thing."

I smiled and decided to have a beer after all.

"You couldn't take the chance that she wouldn't
be found. Knew I'd be coming along later with
Hector as usual and if I didn't, there was Cynthia
here. Except it was better to have someone else.
Someone who wasn't tied into the whole business.
Assume you had a good policy on her and those

insurance people are most probably dragging their heels as it is. No body and you might have had to wait until you're gray-haired like me. Plus how long in the state of Maine before you two could get married? Before Myra'd be legally dead? Six, seven years? Something like that."

Arnold, from the doorway, supplied the answer: "Seven years."

Then he read them their rights and Brian started in swearing. Arnold's a big man and I'm no runt, so there wasn't any more than that. Cynthia sat with her mouth shut tight in one thin line. The mark from Brian's hand was tattooed deep red right across her cheek.

I went out to the pickup and came back with the framed picture I'd borrowed from Jean. It was one of Cynthia's, signed and dated on the back. One of the ones I'd seen propped against the log on the beach. I held it up, so they could both have a good look. There was the Reach, the clouds, the sky—and the *My Myra*, Brian's bright-yellow-and-turquoise lobster boat, dead center.

"Myra must have wondered why you were stopping. She'd have known like everybody else you don't have any traps in that part of the Reach."

HIDING PLACES

The Wyndhams were an ideal match. Everybody said so. Normally this would not mean much—a convenient phrase—but in this case, it happened to be true.

Felicity Wyndham was sitting in a large wicker chair. She'd covered its overstuffed cushions with a crisp blue-and-white windowpane check that matched the blue stripe of the paper that lined the walls not covered with bookshelves. The room, a small library and her favorite, was in the front of the house—a large Victorian in Ridgewood, New Jersey. She'd placed the chair directly in front of the bow window that faced the lawn across the porch.

The snow was finally melting. Soon she would

take a walk and see if the snowdrops were up.
Meanwhile, it was heaven to sit in the sunshine that
streamed through the glass, its warm rays streak-
ing across her face making her feel even lazier than
she had when she'd dropped into it to take a break.
Being pregnant had produced a pleasant lethargy
once her mercifully brief bout of morning sickness
had passed. She put her hand across her stomach,
feeling the bump that she still found hard to believe was a human being.

A boy. Their son. She hadn't wanted to know
the sex, but Geoff had convinced her that knowing would mean an even closer bonding. Besides,
her doctor knew. It wasn't one of the universe's secrets. Yet that's exactly how the whole pregnancy
had struck her from the beginning. Miraculously
secret or secretly miraculous? Both? She smiled to
herself. No name for the baby so far. More fun
to toss suggestions around. Geoff was open to all;
adamantly opposed only to "Brendan." No reason,
he said, just didn't like the name. Still, Felicity suspected it must have belonged to someone in his
past. She'd nixed "Patricia"—"Patty"—recalling
the mean girl who had bullied her so relentlessly in
second grade for no reason Felicity could fathom
then or now.

A slight kick, a flutter. Not enough yet to make

her wince. But enough to make her feel an intense well-being she had never experienced before. A kind of floating—floating on a warm sea with no thoughts at all save one. She'd lined one of those French baby baskets with leftover fabric from the chair and imagined herself sitting in this same spot, watching their child sleep as the seasons changed outside the window.

Geoff had given her free rein with the house. He'd spotted it during their search, online, and then called the Realtor, arranging to see it that very day. She'd known it was perfect even before she walked through the front door. A wisteria vine in full bloom shaded one half of the porch and climbed high up the side of the house. There were old-fashioned flower beds—hydrangea with flowers as large as bowling balls, roses, lilies. Ridgewood was only twenty miles from Manhattan, close enough for an easy commute to Geoff's office, but it felt many more miles away. The house had been built in 1900, and Felicity liked to think about the families who had lived here, the children who had run up and down the stairs—formal ones in the front, the servants' stairs in the back. Another child would go up and down them in the not-too-distant future.

Decorating the house had been a labor of love.

She'd wanted to stay true to the period, but not make it feel as if they were living in a museum. Before her marriage, she had been an interior designer and enjoyed mixing periods—a Midcentury Modern accent like a George Nelson clock in an otherwise Arts and Crafts interior. She'd done the same with the Victoriana here: bright, contemporary fabrics paired with walls painted in the dark reds, ochers, and greens of the period. Eastlake meets Marimekko, she'd told Geoff. He'd told her she was a genius. That he was a lucky man.

And she was a lucky woman. Felicity got up and walked closer to the window. A year ago she was struggling to make ends meet. The downturn in the economy had meant a sharp decline in her business. There had been no reduction in her rent, however. She had been thinking about moving out of her West Side apartment to someplace more affordable—although no place in the city was, and forget about Brooklyn these days!—when Geoff walked into her life. Things hadn't been going all that well in the romance department either. Predictably Felicity and her college boyfriend had broken up a month after graduation, and then she went through a series of relationships that she'd known weren't going to work. Even so, each time she'd hung on too long in the belief that things would change. Suddenly she was twenty-six, turning heads with her long legs, slim figure, blond hair from her mother's Scandinavian heritage, and big brown eyes, her skin slightly tan as well from her Tuscan grandparents. But no Prince Charming or Happily Ever After in sight. That is until the benefit cocktail party one of her loyal clients gave for City Harvest, inviting Felicity and suggesting she bring cards, as everyone would adore what she had done to the apartment.

Geoff Wyndham, whose coloring so closely matched Felicity's they could have been siblings, but thank goodness weren't, she later reflected, was a venture capitalist in his early thirties who had made a great deal of money and was making more. He had an office in Manhattan and one in San Francisco. He was ready to settle down if he could only meet the right woman. By the end of the evening over a late dinner at Jean-Georges, he told Felicity he was pretty sure he had.

Flowers arrived. Small gifts, thoughtful ones—a new CD she'd mentioned was out, hummingbird cupcakes from the Magnolia Bakery, a William Morris scarf and umbrella from the Metropolitan Museum after she'd told Geoff of her lifelong love of the designs. They took a vacation to Anguilla, missing a huge snowstorm that crippled the East

Coast. He proposed in the airport as they sat waiting for the next possible flight out. An emerald-cut diamond ring from Cartier had been in his pocket; he'd been waiting for the right moment, and that one—that sitting in a crowded airport lounge with people milling about, most of them angry—was it. He realized he didn't want to be anywhere else or with anyone else. Ever. She said yes. Yes, yes, yes.

Felicity's parents had married late and she had been a bit of a surprise. Her father had died when she was still in high school, a chronic heart condition, and then her mother the year after college—a cancer so swift Felicity had barely time to get to Ohio and say good-bye. Geoff had no siblings either and only his father was alive—remarried, living in Florida, interested in golf, the ponies, the new wife a little, Geoff not at all. So Felicity and Geoff tied the knot in Manhattan at City Hall.

The client who had given the fortuitous party and Geoff's college roommate who happened to be in town from Chicago stood up with them. Afterward, they all had a riotous lunch with much wine nearby at City Hall Restaurant, because Geoff said it was too apt a name to pass up, and besides, he wanted oysters plus a Delmonico steak.

A few hours later the newlyweds caught a night flight to Paris. Each was eager to show the other "their" Paris, but Geoff's turned out to be far different from Felicity's—even now the memory of walking into the suite at the George V took her breath away. And the Michelin three-star meals! Still, Geoff had loved the bistro—amazingly still there on the Île Saint-Louis—that she had discovered one spring break and always came back to on her too-infrequent visits to Paris since.

Geoff had had to go to the West Coast almost as soon as they returned, but they'd already found the house, and she was busy moving. He had been up front about the amount of traveling he had to do, but while she missed him when he was away, Felicity had always been content to be on her own and never more so than now when she was truly nesting. He'd be back from this current trip in two days. She pictured him when she opened the door, the smile that would light up his face—and she could almost feel his embrace. The sex had been a revelation from the start, even better now than when they had just been getting to know what each other liked. She flushed at the thought. Two days was beginning to feel like a long time.

Get going, she chided herself. Take your walk, or finish dusting the books. Felicity and Geoff's combined library had revealed their eclectic tastes, and the arrangement on the shelves revealed what

Geoff called his "slight OCDness." He arranged books alphabetically within fiction and nonfiction, with further categories for art, biography, and so forth. He had described himself to her early on as a would-be librarian. She'd been excited to discover that a passion for books was just another of the things they had in common.

Felicity disliked disorder as well. Her designs had always focused on de-cluttering a space. She'd assigned herself the job of dusting the books while Geoff was on this trip. She knew she wouldn't be doing it once the baby arrived. She'd finished the nonfiction, including the coffee table books, which were stacked on the broad bottom shelves. She was up to the *D*'s in fiction. She'd dust to *M*, then go outdoors. Dante, Danticat, Delafield, Dickens.

A Tale of Two Cities. Not her copy, if she'd ever had one. She hadn't read it since high school. This one had a fancy binding, leather embossed with gold. Where had Geoff picked it up? But it wasn't a book at all! It was a fake one sold for hiding valuables with a compartment carved from the pages in the middle! She'd have fun teasing him about this. Especially since what he'd hidden was his spare set of keys. What was with men and their keys? Why did they need so many? She had two—car and house. Period.

Geoff's spares were on the same kind of key ring
that was in his pocket right now. A simple loop from
Tiffany with small knobs on each end, nothing dan-
gling except the keys. It was so like him to put these
spares in the fake book. Very precise. Very safe. Her
spare house key had been in one of the planters by
the front stoop until she'd happened to mention it
to him. The next day he'd presented her with a fake
rock, suggesting she put it *behind* the house.

Felicity worked her way to Mann, Marquis,
Melville, Mitford, called it quits at Morrison, put
on a jacket, and went to look for signs of spring.
As she left the house she was slightly disappointed
that the hiding place hadn't revealed anything
more interesting. Like love letters—although did
she really want to find any of those? She'd tossed
everything from her own past when she'd moved
out of her apartment, and it had felt great. Nothing
for a future tenant to stumble across. Once when
she was finishing staging an apartment going on
the market, she had found a leather bag containing
handcuffs and a small whip stuffed in the bottom
of the owner's majolica umbrella stand. It had
creeped her out more than a bit, and she'd put it
back, then doused herself liberally with Purell.

She was rewarded for making the effort to leave
the house. The snowdrops were up in the rear of

the back garden, a mass of them peeking through the snow. Next year she'd show little not-named-Brendan.

Two weeks later Geoff was away again and Felicity found a wad of cash in what looked like a can of WD-40 on a shelf in the basement near his workbench. She'd gone to get a hammer to hang some framed vintage Mother Goose illustrations from the local thrift store. She wasn't superstitious and neither was Geoff, so the baby's room was almost ready—the walls pale green like the crocus shoots coming up now, a toile frieze of Mother Goose characters along the top. The prints were a find.

All Geoff's hammers hung outlined on a Peg-Board, so there was no mistaking where each belonged. She grabbed a small one and went to find the Plexiglas box with picture hooks. Reaching for it, she knocked the can of lubricant off. Geoff had this sort of thing organized too, like the books. Alphabetized within a category. For a moment Felicity hoped the inevitable disarray a baby—and child—meant wouldn't be too hard for the dad. As quickly as the thought entered her mind, it vanished. Geoff was over the moon about the baby—especially the prospect of teaching a son how to fly-fish, a passion of his, indulged with a yearly trip to Montana with a group of like-minded men.

She picked up the can. It was very light. She'd tell him he needed more. Then she noticed that the label said "WD-20" and the container had a screw top. Another hiding place! She opened it and almost laughed aloud. An enormous wad of bills was tightly rolled and filled the interior. She didn't want to disturb it, but she could see Ben Franklin's face. A friend had told her that after 9/11, when it had been impossible to get to ATMs or banks, a lot of people in the New York area hid cash in their homes. It made her feel very secure to think that Geoff was looking out for his family.

If I was sure my skin would look like yours, I'd get pregnant tomorrow," Adele said.

Felicity was having a ladies lunch with Adele and Lucy, friends from her design days, at Robert, the Museum of Arts and Design's restaurant overlooking Columbus Circle. Adele had beautiful skin, the result of periodic trips to Canyon Ranch as well as Georgette Klinger in the city—the day it reopened was probably still circled in red on Adele's calendar. The last thing she wanted was a baby. She and her husband, Henry, traveled the world shopping for their clients and lived an admittedly hedonistic, childfree life.

"You know you don't mean that," Felicity said.

"She's right, though," Lucy said. "You do look wonderful, and I'm not sure it's only due to that Madonna glow. Marriage agrees with you. And how could you miss, with someone like Geoff? You two make an ideal couple."

"I don't know how ideal we are, but we *are* happy. I thought I'd miss working and maybe I will someday, but not now. I'm just enjoying being Sadie, Sadie Married Lady."

The food arrived. Felicity found that she was hungry all the time but wasn't putting on too much baby weight, so had ordered *frites* with her steak— she'd craved this kind of big, juicy protein from the start. Her friends had both ordered entrée salads and left the breadbasket untouched.

Lucy took one *frite* from Felicity's plate. "I do plan to get pregnant. Forget the glow. I just want to be able to eat carbs! I'll be thirty in June, so the clock is ticking."

"Oh, don't wait!" Felicity said. "Think of the playdates we could have together."

Adele shook her head. "Isn't that what nannies are for?"

"Geoff suggested we get a nanny, especially for

the first months, but I don't want anyone else sharing my baby, and he understood. I think he feels the same way. He didn't want a nanny who would live in."

After talking about the Milan Furniture Fair—both women had been there in April—and some good dish about people they knew in common, Felicity told them about Geoff's hiding places.

"I was going to tell him I'd discovered them, but let him keep his little secrets."

"I think it's adorable," Lucy said. "Besides, all couples have stashes like this. I always have a bag of M and M's tucked away in my Tampax box."

Adele nodded in agreement. "I had an aunt who used to keep ten-dollar bills in between her good china. Service for twelve—the whole shebang, dinner, salad, luncheon, and dessert plates. She left it to my mother, and when we went to pack it up, there was almost five hundred bucks!"

"You're always reading about people who buy things at auction and find money," Felicity said. "Although sadly I never did." She almost added "and after I married Geoff, I didn't have to worry about money." His knack for predicting the next big thing in his area of expertise—pharmaceuticals—provided her with a standard of living she had never imagined attaining.

"True confessions—now that we know about your M and M habit, Lucy. I've never been able to get rid of the letters my first boyfriend sent me," Adele said. "We went to different colleges and thought our love would last forever. I really don't have to hide them—Henry wouldn't care—but they're in an empty muesli box, he hates the stuff, in one of the kitchen cabinets. I read them about once a year to remind me of my much younger, much different self." She gave a slight sigh.

Felicity reached across the table and patted her hand. "I think it's dear. And we know you're a total softie under that highly polished exterior."

Three weeks later on a sweltering foretaste of summer, Felicity found a third hiding place. Although she wasn't sure it counted, since it wasn't disguised as something else. The cleaners had come, and as usual everything was slightly off-kilter. She was putting Geoff's Florentine leather jewelry box back in place when she thought she'd better open it and make sure nothing had shifted—he wouldn't appreciate the contents askew. He kept the gold pocket watch that had belonged to his great-grandfather and his cuff links in it. He favored French cuffs, which she found delightful. The first gift she'd given him was a pair of vintage ones from Georg Jensen. She realigned the cuff links in the holder on the top tray and lifted it to check the watch and fob in the bottom. When she replaced the tray she noticed that the box was much deeper than the two compartments. She took the top velvet-lined tray out again and removed the watch pieces as well, then shook the box gently. A slight rattle. There was another compartment and something was in it. Turning the box over, she noticed a tiny brass button, flush with the leather. She pushed it. Nothing. She pulled it and, voilà, another compartment was released—narrower than the others. There were more cuff links inside plus several gold coins in thin plastic cases.

Felicity was beginning to think of all this as a kind of scavenger hunt. It was like her favorite book from childhood, *The Secret Garden,* except the secrets were all in her house! The cuff links—gifts from old flames? He'd told her he'd started wearing cuff links at Harvard as an undergraduate—"I was terribly affected"—and Geoff wasn't the type to sell things on eBay. These, and the coins, were obviously too valuable to toss—hence another hiding place. Could her husband be any more fascinating? She put everything back exactly as it had been and, thinking of Adele's muesli hidey-hole, went downstairs to the kitchen. The thrill of the chase!

While the kitchen had been remodeled many times over before they bought the house, the pantry had not. Felicity hadn't wanted to change a thing either, the glass-fronted cabinets for china, the silver safe, the sink—which she used when she arranged flowers, the vases close to hand—and especially the wide shelves for spices, canned goods, and all sorts of other groceries. She regarded them appraisingly. What did Geoff eat that she never touched? Tate & Lyle's Black Treacle and Cap'n Crunch to start. Not together, thankfully. The man did have some taste. She'd tried his treacle on an English muffin—it was his favorite weekend breakfast paired with coddled eggs. One bite had been enough for a lifetime. Very sticky and with a slightly bitter aftertaste despite the sweetness. And as for the cereal, so sweet, her mouth puckered. It had been his go-to comfort food during exams in college and later law school and still was—plain by the handfuls or late at night with milk. "You never have to worry about cooking something for me."

There were always two or three boxes of the breakfast cereal on hand, and Geoff bought large tins of the British "delicacy" whenever he saw that size for sale. Felicity started with these, hoping for another false bottom. The search proved fruitless, however. No phony fronts, or hidden compart-

ments. No doubloons hidden in the Cap'n's oats
and corn. No gems buried in the very thick dark
syrup. At least in the one that was opened. The
others had a tight seal.

When he got back next week, she intended to
relate her adventures, gently teasing this husband
of hers, who still obviously had part of a foot in
childhood. He and his son could make a secret
fort in the backyard, one with a big NO GIRLS AL-
LOWED sign. (Except Mom, she'd add.) They could
hide out there and munch cereal.

But the day Geoff was due back, Felicity went
into labor. All thoughts of hiding places rapidly
vanished, replaced instead with the very visible arrival of Alexander Ashton Wyndham.

"Such a long moniker for such a tiny little boy,"
Geoff murmured in his wife's ear, softly stroking
the pale down on his son's head as he nursed greedily at his mother's breast. Felicity had been en-
chanted by the increase in her bosom and planned
to nurse long enough to expose plenty of the cleav-
age she'd never had.

"Too long?" she asked, worrying suddenly at their
choice. "Ashton" was her maiden name. "Maybe no
middle name, or something short like 'John'?"

Geoff moved his hand to stroke his wife—and
not her head.

"He's a product of the two of us and needs both our names. Plus it sounds good—even with just the initial. Maybe he'll write books. Picture it on a front cover. If there *are* books with covers by the time he's old enough to write one."

"Or be in one," Felicity said. She was deliriously happy, and what all her woman friends who had had babies told her was true: once it was over, you couldn't remember the pain, the sweat, the everything. (That is until you went through it again, one had pointed out.) She moved Alexander to her other breast, her nipple popping from his mouth like a champagne cork. As she did she looked at her engagement ring. Arriving in time to go with her to the hospital, Geoff, who thought of everything, had her remove all her jewelry. When he'd brought her rings back, her engagement diamond had been joined by a diamond on either side, because "Now we are three."

In the late spring Geoff had presented Felicity with what he called a "mommy car," but one he said was for a "very classy mommy"—a Mercedes-Benz GL. Now, months later, she was almost finished packing it with what seemed like an entire department store of baby accoutrements and her own modest bags, leaving room for Geoff's, which he liked to do himself. As a man always on the go, he could pack in a flash. They'd be leaving for the Hamptons shortly after he got home. Alexander was napping. She'd feed him just before they left. His first real car trip!

A girl could get used to this, Felicity thought to herself. Geoff had found a rental on the beach with plenty of privacy and had arranged for someone to come in and leave meals for them as well as clean. A resort vacation without the hassle of being with other people. Just the three of them walking on the beach, reading on the deck—and just the two of them for hours and hours in bed. He was taking a whole two weeks off to make up, he said, for the two weeks he'd had to be away in July.

She looked at her watch—he should be home soon—and consulted the list she'd made. Felicity had always been a list maker. Everything was crossed off except "cameras."

She got hers and checked the Memory Stick. It was full. She'd been afraid of that. Alexander was already on his way to being the most photographed baby of the year. She wanted to record every expression, every movement. Geoff's camera was the same brand, and he kept extra sticks in the pocket of the camera case, which she kept meaning to do as well. He'd taken the case down and it was next to the bags he'd be packing. She took his camera out and flicked through some of the recent photos he'd taken, getting slightly choked up at the series from last Saturday. He'd shot the three of them at the front door, using the camera's timer and a tripod. He'd told her he wanted to take one in the same spot on the same date every month for the first year and after that every other month—but, he'd laughed at himself, "OCD again—you know it will be every month."

Felicity loved him so much it hurt.

She tucked the full stick from her camera in her pocket and took the one with the highest GBs from the others in Geoff's case. She was putting it into her camera when she thought she'd better check and make sure it didn't have anything on it.

There *were* photos—many. It took a moment before she could make any sense out of them. And even then, it didn't make sense. No sense at all.

Three people at a front door. The same pose as she'd stood in just last weekend. At first glance it looked like the same house. A Victorian, but the trim was more Painted Lady. The sky above was bluer, cloudless. A San Francisco sky? And at first glance, it looked like the same people, she realized with mounting panic. Definitely one of them was.

There was Geoff dressed as he'd been standing

beside Felicity in a Paul Stuart short-sleeved linen striped shirt and pima cotton khaki pants, his casual wear.

She felt dizzy; her throat choked with the start of a scream. The woman in the shot was Felicity's double. Same age, same appearance, same pose. The baby . . . THE BABY! She tore through the photos. More of the baby. More of the woman.

Of course they weren't Alexander and Felicity.

But they could have been. The woman's hair was the exact color as hers—and the style! She could hear Geoff's voice, "Such beautiful hair. Like spun gold. Maybe try bangs. They're very mysterious." She'd been cloned, Felicity thought, or vice versa?

She stopped at a close-up of the woman. She was wearing Felicity's ring! Felicity checked her finger to make sure it was still there. For an instant she thought it had been spirited away—or it had never been on her finger. His voice once more, "Now we are three." Three? Or more?

She heard Geoff's voice again. But he was here—in the bedroom, footsteps muffled by the carpet—leaning over closer and closer, murmuring in her ear in a tone she'd never heard before. She froze.

The keys—spares—but, she realized now, a duplicate to the doors of both houses. His "OCDness." The ready cash, alternate cuff links—all tucked away in his hiding places. And now here was one more. The final one.

"It's really too bad you found these."

THE PROOF IS ALWAYS IN THE PUDDING

I need a man."

Faith Fairchild looked at her mother-in-law, Marian, in surprise. With three sons and a husband, one would have thought men were not in short supply. And after some forty years of marriage with no detours down the primrose path, her needs apparently having been met by Faith's father-in-law, it was odd that Marian would choose this time in her life for an amorous adventure. However, it was just before Christmas, and the holidays had been known to dredge up all sorts of feelings. Faith's own main feeling was fatigue. Although not sculpting Chartres Cathedral in gingerbread or assuming any of the other over-the-top projects that women insanely tended to take on during the holidays, she was extremely busy with her catering business.

As a minister's wife, however, she also knew that the season gave rise to all sorts of emotions, some long repressed. Was this the case with Marian? Or could it just be that she was tired of going to the Boston Symphony on Fridays unescorted? Dick Fairchild had a lifelong aversion to classical music.

While Faith was framing a discreet inquiry, Marian continued, "Otherwise there will be thirteen at Christmas dinner—seven women, six men."

So that was it. Yet, still puzzling. Marian Fairchild was one of the least superstitious, most down-to-earth women Faith had ever met.

Faith decided to make light of it all. "While I'm grateful to Noah for his two-by-two choice, I don't think Miss Manners objects to non-Ark seating arrangements these days. And considering you've had black cats as long as I've known you, thirteen shouldn't be a problem."

Marian shook her head vigorously. "It's *Christmas* dinner, Faith!"

"Why should that matter in particular?"

Her mother-in-law looked shocked. "Surely Tom has told you about the Fairchild Christmas Dinner Curse."

It was Faith's turn to shake her head, and she did so slowly. Another instance of the Reverend Thomas Preston Fairchild's failure to pass on the juicy stuff. She could understand his inability to convey the secrets of what would have been a confessional (had the First Parish church in Aleford, Massachusetts, had one), but this was family lore.

Meanwhile Marian was doing a count on her fingers out loud: "Dick and me, you and Tom, Betsey and her new beau, Robert and Michael, Craig and Jessie, Auntie Maude, and Auntie Ann."

"I make that an even dozen, not thirteen," Faith said. "It's six male and six female, perfectly matched."

"Yes, so convenient that Robert has Michael, which normally balances the aunts. Everything was all set, but then Ann called this morning to ask whether she could bring a friend, Margaret McKeen, from her librarian days. Margaret will be spending the holidays with them. How could I say no? She and Ann are the last in that tombola thing, so that makes it even worse."

Anxiety was making normally clearheaded and clear-spoken Marian difficult to comprehend. Auntie Maude and Auntie Ann were Dick Fairchild's older sisters. Maude was widowed—Faith had noted the move from black to gray and now pale violet over the years—and Ann had never married. They lived together in neighboring Duxbury. Games of chance did not come to mind when thinking of the two silver-haired sisters.

"Tombola?"

"Years ago when they retired, Ann and four of her librarian friends named each other as beneficiaries in their wills. When one died, everything rolled over to the others. None of them had anyone else to leave it to—Maude, as you know, is comfortable and has no children."

"Comfortable" in New England parlance meant many pennies saved. Dick and Marian were comfy too.

"Sort of a 'Last Man Standing,' or rather woman, notion?"

"Exactly. Anyway, it's quite a sizable amount now, and there are just the two of them left— Ann and her friend Margaret. If anything were to happen to Margaret at Christmas dinner, or Ann, well, I can't even think about it. No, we have to come up with someone. Otherwise it's foolishly tempting fate, and don't suggest having the children at the table. They'd hate it. And besides, the cousins table has always been in the kitchen."

Faith knew Marian was right. The cousins, including her two children, Ben and Amy, would be happier making noise and dispensing with company manners in the kitchen.

"But why should you think either lady might need the Heimlich, or keel over from too much plum pudding?"

"There now, Tom *has* told you! You know about the pudding!"

Marian Fairchild had been pacing about her kitchen. Faith had arrived a few minutes earlier to help with Marian's holiday baking. She'd known something was amiss when her mother-in-law hadn't offered coffee the moment Faith stepped across the threshold. It was Marian's custom, as well as that of every other woman Faith had met after moving to Aleford from Manhattan after her marriage. She took her mother-in-law's hand, led her toward the large round kitchen table, and pulled out a chair for her before starting the percolator. No French press or Keurig nonsense here.

"You need to start from the beginning and tell me the whole story. The whole Christmas Dinner Curse story."

Marian sighed. "There are some Fig Newtons in the tin on the counter." Fig Newtons and Lorna Doones were Fairchild Family panaceas. It appeared Marian was rousing. Soon there was a steaming mug of Maxwell House in her hand and she started talking.

"It was before the Fairchilds moved to Norwell. They lived in Boston on Beacon Hill. Quite a good address—Mount Vernon Street. I remember Dick's grandfather speaking of it with pride."

This was going to be a day of surprises, Faith thought. She'd assumed the Fairchilds had been on the South Shore since one of their forbearers came down the *Mayflower*'s plank, jumped off the rock, and landed up the road from Plymouth in Norwell more or less by accident.

"Great-Grandfather was in real estate, most of it in the Back Bay, after it was filled."

"When would this have been?"

"In the late eighteen hundreds." Marian's voice took on a slightly dreamlike character, or perhaps it was the soothing nature of the figgy cookie and fragrant coffee. She put the cup down and her tone changed abruptly. "It happened, of course, at this time of year . . ."

Victoria Fairchild looked out at the snow that had begun to fall. Some of the panes in the front parlor's bowed window were amethyst, a badge of authenticity on Beacon Hill that meant one's home dated back to the time when the glass had been imported from England. Slight impurities reacted with sunlight over time to produce the violet hue. Victoria's mother had been from England, hence her name and subsequent affection for all things British.

She viewed the pine and holly swags that graced the Adam fireplace and other parts of the room with complacency. Christmas was her favorite holiday, and it was kept in a manner that Mr. Pickwick, as well as his creator, would have recognized. There would be goose for Christmas dinner, and a turkey, since her husband, Elliot, always insisted on the national bird. The kitchen had been preparing for weeks now and the desserts alone would cover the gleaming mahogany dining room table.

It had been a good year for Fairchild Properties, and she'd had Mr. Sargent paint her portrait as a Christmas gift for Elliot. Of course he'd have to pay the bill. She'd originally thought Sargent could paint her with Franny—mother and daughter—but she'd been more than a little angry with Frances all fall and in a fit of pique decided not to include her. She'd never considered the boys, although they were nice-looking, especially Will. And they never gave her the worry Franny did, still they were young yet.

Victoria sighed and turned away from the window. She'd done everything she could. Sent Franny to Winsor, had a lovely dance to introduce her to Boston society, and saw that she made calls properly. Now all the silly girl had to do was accept Sumner Cabot's proposal and everything would be set. He came from a good family, had graduated from Harvard—perhaps not brilliantly, but he'd made it—and was working in the family firm now. She pictured them in one of Elliot's new town houses on Commonwealth Avenue or maybe out in Brookline if they wanted the country, although she herself could never abide the thought of rural life. All those farmers.

"Excuse me, ma'am." It was the maid, and she looked agitated.

"What is it, Molly?"

"That man is here again."

Victoria struggled to maintain her composure. It wouldn't do to lose control in front of one of the servants.

"Tell him if he calls again, Mr. Fairchild will summon the authorities."

A look of apprehension crossed Molly's face and she gasped slightly before saying, "Very good, ma'am."

Victoria started toward the wing chair by the fire where she'd left her needlework, but stopped, turning back toward the maid.

"No, on second thought, show Mr. O'Hara in."

When the door closed, she went over to the chair and sat, carefully arranging her skirt. She arranged her face, as well, and when Molly opened the door, ushering the caller in, Victoria might as well have been chiseled from marble.

"I won't ask you to sit down, because you won't be staying long," she said. "I don't know why you are persisting in your unwanted and possibly illegal attentions toward my daughter, but I warn you, you will be very sorry if you continue."

"Unwanted? Is that what she says? Call Franny down here and let me hear it from her lips, not yours."

Patrick O'Hara was a large man—tall and muscular. He was regarding Victoria with irritation, but any anger he felt toward the woman seemed well under control.

"It doesn't matter what Miss Fairchild says, your attentions are unwanted by her parents. Any decent man would acknowledge this and desist."

"Apart from the land of my birth, what objections do you have? I'll be able to keep Franny in the style to which she's accustomed—even better. I've worked hard all my life, don't drink overmuch, smoke rarely, and am a regular churchgoer. I'll even leave my church for yours if that will help."

Victoria gave a small cry. The idea of this, this Irishman in a pew near hers!

"I love Franny and she loves me. Isn't that what counts?" he said. His face softened.

"Love! What has that got to do with mar . . ." Victoria didn't finish. What she'd been about to reveal was none of this insufferable young man's business. She had a sudden thought—and needing a moment to consider it fully, invited him to take a seat.

Now O'Hara's expression clearly revealed his bewilderment. What was this Boston Brahmin up to with this sudden display of politeness to a lace-curtain Irish lad?

"Perhaps I've been a bit hasty, Mr. O'Hara. In the spirit of the season, will you join us for Christmas dinner? Just the family and a few close friends—the Winthrops and the Cabots."

Patrick laughed aloud and stood up. "Sure and it's a rare treat for a clod from the Old County to be included in such company." His accent thickened, and Victoria flushed. She knew he was doing it deliberately. "Many's the time I've heard the saying:

"*And here's to good old Boston*
The Land of the bean and the cod
Where Lowells talk only to Cabots
And Cabots talk only to God.

"So I accept with pleasure the chance to break bread with some Cabots at best," he said.

Victoria Fairchild rang for Molly to show the impertinent O'Hara out. Despite her irritation with what she termed "his performance," she was pleased with her plan and allowed a slight smile to cross her lips. The sparkle in her eyes, always almost unnaturally bright, grew. Franny was her daughter, after all. And you can take that to the bank, Mr. O'Hara, because you won't be taking her. The table would be unbalanced with thirteen, but it would be Patrick O'Hara's last meal with the Fairchilds or anyone . . . she pushed the thought to the dark recesses of her mind, and her smile broadened.

Now, Bridget, I know it won't have aged as much as it should, but I want you to make a special plum pudding. A very large one. Here are the charms and a sixpence. Mind you don't lose them. I'll pour the brandy on myself."

The cook gave a slight curtsy and nodded. She knew her mistress didn't trust her with spirits. Mrs. Fairchild should be keeping a closer eye on those two scamps Master William and Master Albert. Bridget just hoped the brandy would light, given how much water those two had put in the decanters to hide what they'd drunk.

There was a knock on the back door. Bridget looked through the glass, then gave a quick glance around to be sure Mrs. Fairchild had gone back upstairs before opening it.

"Aren't you a fine sight with flour on your cheek!"

"Well, give your sister a quick kiss and be on your way. The mistress wants a whole 'nother pudding."

"Hmmm—tell you what. I'll come by with a special charm for you to put in at the end."

Bridget opened her mouth and closed it. She'd have to add more fruit or it would be all metal bits.

"Do you serve it out yourself or does your mistress?"

The question puzzled her. Patrick had never been much interested in household details when they were growing up, but she told him.

"She comes down here and douses it with the brandy. Molly brings it to her in the dining room, where she lights it at the table and everyone oohs and aahs, then Molly takes it back down and I cut it up before it's back up again on the plates. Molly's fair wore out by the time it's over."

He helped himself to one of the molasses cookies cooling on a rack. She slapped his hand—and he was gone.

The guests had returned to the table after an interval in which the ladies repaired to Victoria Fairchild's bedroom to titivate and the men to Elliot Fairchild's library to smoke cigars. All had need of a breather before dessert, after the meal that had started with oysters and romped through Mock Turtle Soup, stuffed flounder, and the roasted birds with accompanying side dishes before finishing up with cheeses and water crackers from England by way of S. S. Pierce.

Patrick O'Hara caught Franny Fairchild's eye, causing the young lady to blush becomingly. What a fine woman she was, he thought, and how could her people think of saddling her with that sorry excuse for a man, Sumner Cabot? Well, it would soon be over. He grinned at his hostess at the foot of the table.

"A fine spread you're giving us, Mrs. Fairchild!"

She acknowledged his compliment with a slight nod. Despite her instructions to the servants—and Elliot—to offer him drink, he had consumed only one glass of claret. He'd listened politely to Martha Cabot's description of her new greenhouse and Oliver Winthrop's diatribe against Mayor O'Brien. "Don't you worry—we'll make sure he gets only one term. Don't know how we slipped up." Yet Victoria wasn't worried.

"If you'll excuse me, I'll just see to the pudding," she said.

Her husband beamed. Maybe she wasn't the easiest woman to live with, but he could count on her to keep up the Fairchilds' celebrated reputation for hospitality. Wish she'd consulted him before she'd hired Sargent, though. Could have gotten someone cheaper.

Franny surveyed the table. She wished she were sitting next to Patrick. They could hold hands under their large white damask napkins. His handsome face was so alive, a marked contrast to the pale, undistinguished men surrounding him. Boring. The meal was boring. Her life was boring, but she'd soon be free of it all.

The pudding on its silver salver was enormous, and when Victoria set it alight, the blue flames threatened to set the table on fire. Molly quickly took it back downstairs to serve while the table had to content themselves with mince and cranberry pies, Nesselrode pudding, sweetmeats, and fruit.

Victoria slipped out again, returned, and then it was Franny's turn to vanish briefly and discreetly. No one would have been rude enough to inquire about their whereabouts. It was well known that the Fairchilds had lavatories on each floor!

Molly was surprised when Bridget followed her

upstairs carrying the rest of the dessert and even more surprised when Bridget instructed her to give Miss Franny a particular piece. And then after the ladies were served, Bridget handed her two plates, saying, "The one on the left is to go to the young Mr. Cabot, the right to Mr. O'Hara."

As Molly passed Albert Fairchild, he looked quickly around the table, saw the attention of the adults otherwise engaged, and grabbed the large slice of pudding from Molly's left hand. He was a favorite downstairs and she let him take it, giving Sumner Cabot the slightly smaller one Bridget had said was for Patrick O'Hara. It must have to do with the charms, some sort of joke. But she couldn't very well snatch the plate away from the young master, could she?

Bridget was tired. She'd done as her brother Patrick and her mistress had asked and that was that. Bunch of tomfoolery. Back in the kitchen she put her feet up and dozed off. It seemed only seconds before Molly came flying through the door, shrieking, "You've poisoned the child for sure! Come quickly!"

Upstairs young Albert Fairchild was clutching his stomach and crying out in pain. His mother was by his side and, seeing Bridget, screamed at her, "Which plate did he get?"

"Same as everyone," Bridget said firmly. Molly grabbed her arm and started to say something. Bridget hushed her.

Victoria picked up Albert's plate and examined the charm. It was a button. In a frenzy, she ran around the table, snatching forks from her startled guests.

"The shoe, Bridget! The one I told you had the horseshoe! Where is it?"

"We must send for Dr. Shaw," Martha Cabot said to Elliot Fairchild. "Your son is obviously very ill and Victoria has gone mad."

"Molly, send Amos for the doctor," Elliot Fairchild ordered. "And, everyone, please go into the drawing room. I'm sure Albert merely overdid himself at the table."

Sumner Cabot, well known as a trencherman, had cleaned his plate as soon as he'd been served—as well as all the plates earlier. He looked concerned, worried about his own digestion no doubt, and started to make his way from the room. He had no sooner taken a few steps when he too began to cry out, collapsing onto the floor. Everyone rushed back.

Victoria ran to where he had been sitting and seized his plate, empty save for traces of the thick powdered sugar that had covered the portion, sending two little charms flying, a wishbone and a horseshoe. She covered her mouth, stifling a scream, and fainted dead away.

Franny Fairchild looked at Patrick O'Hara in alarm. She had carefully removed the ring he'd had his sister place in her plum pudding and was waiting. But why was Albert sick? And what was the matter with Sumner? She gave her beloved a despairing glance and moved toward her mother. She knew Victoria always kept smelling salts in the small reticule she was carrying.

Dr. Shaw lived a few doors away and left his Christmas dinner immediately. He went first to Albert, now vomiting copiously into a large Rose Medallion bowl his brother had fetched from the sideboard. A moment later, the doctor announced, "The boy has no fever and his eyes are clear. Where's his plate?" Molly handed it to him and he sniffed the crumbs, "Ipecac. A nasty joke. Soaking his pudding that way!"

All eyes turned toward brother Will.

"I never did!" Further protestations were drowned out by the room's relieved comments. Ipecac! It was in every household. Sumner must have gotten a dose too, and the doctor turned his attention to the figure writhing on the carpet in agony. Relief would soon turn to horror.

"We must get this man to a bed. It is ipecac from the odor, but it's something else as well. Where's his plate?"

When it was produced, Dr. Shaw looked at the crusted sugar left and dipped his finger into it, tasting a minuscule amount. "He's been poisoned. I suspect arsenic."

Victoria Fairchild had regained consciousness, aided by her smelling salts. She appeared not to have heard the doctor's words and asked, "Albert, my Albert, is he all right? And Mr. O'Hara, is he sick too?"

Franny had been holding her mother's hand. She dropped it.

"Albert will be fine and Mr. O'Hara isn't sick at all. Sumner is the one who is gravely ill."

Victoria moaned.

"Please get my mother a glass of water, Molly," Franny said.

The men were carrying Sumner to one of the bedrooms upstairs and Albert to his own. Patrick hadn't been asked to help. Frances Fairchild went over to him.

"Is it good-bye, then?" he said.

"It almost was, but no, it's not good-bye."

Faith Fairchild's coffee was stone cold, but she took a gulp. Enthralled, she'd forgotten to drink it. "So it *was* arsenic and Sumner Cabot died?"

Marian nodded. "Arsenic mixed with the powdered sugar sprinkled onto just that portion of pudding."

"The question is was it Franny or Victoria—or maybe both?" Faith added this last reflectively.

"No one was ever charged, and the death was ruled accidental, but the cook swore her mistress pushed a horseshoe charm into one portion instructing her to give it to Molly for Mr. O'Hara—Bridget's own brother! Victoria denied it. And there was arsenic in the house, not just in the shed for pests. Both Victoria and Franny used it to make their eyes look brighter, as many women did then."

"Arsenic trioxide was easily confused with flour or sugar," Faith said. "The Victorians called it 'Inheritance Powder.' In this case, the goal was different, a marriage to be avoided at all costs, but the outcome—a painful death—was the same. Yet, why the ipecac?"

Amid these speculations, the thought uppermost in Faith's mind was: How could Tom have neglected to mention what was undoubtedly one and possibly two Borgia ancestresses?

"The Fairchilds moved to Norwell immediately

afterward," Marian said. "Franny ran off and married Patrick O'Hara. I believe they lived in Jamaica Plain."

Real estate—the Fairchilds, who had immediately established what were now Fairchild Properties, as well as other named endeavors on the South Shore, seemed to be uppermost in her mother-in-law's mind. "To return to the matter at hand," Faith said, getting up for fresh coffee. "This was all a very long time ago. I think we can leave the Christmas dinner table as is."

"That's what my mother-in-law thought one year. The year her husband fell facedown at Christmas dinner into his mince pie—Fairchilds never served plum pudding again—dead of a massive coronary at only age sixty-eight."

Faith almost dropped her mug. Clearly she had to try to find out what had really happened or generations to come, including her own two children, would be saddled with the Christmas Dinner Curse ad infinitum.

What did they know for sure?

Two lovers who wanted to elope, hoping to slip away in the confusion—did one or both also want to eliminate Cabot, admittedly a roadblock, as well? Poisoning one serving made the victim too obvious, but they—or Franny alone—must not have wanted two to die. So, ipecac—a harmless substitute. The same could be said for Victoria. Her goal was to eliminate Patrick O'Hara, someone she considered a nonperson—it wasn't really murder, if the victim wasn't a human being. She'd have to have someone else get sick so that ipecac would be assumed the culprit for both—how sad that Mr. O'Hara reacted so severely to it! She'd marked Mr. O'Hara's piece by pushing a horseshoe charm into the top, but Sumner Cabot had gotten it instead.

Or were both women guilty? Did Franny pour ipecac over the pudding at random, planning only to create a disturbance to cover her escape with Patrick? Meanwhile had her mother launched a deadlier plan?

Marian had said the Fairchilds had moved to Norwell immediately afterward. If Faith had learned one thing about her in-laws—and every other New Englander she'd met—it was that nothing that came into the family's possession ever left, including those proverbial boxes of "String Too Short to Be Saved." There were stacks of correspondence boxes in the barn that had long ago been converted to a garage. No Fairchild cars had ever been housed there since it was filled to the rafters with "stuff." The boxes containing papers were in the old hayloft.

It took Faith several visits to finally come across

the answer. In the meantime she'd learned that her father-in-law had apparently been unable to toss a single empty bleach bottle (cut a piece out and they made excellent boat bailers), that Fairchilds also never threw away a single map—the kind from AAA and the kinds from the *National Geographic* (there were piles of the magazine itself too), and happily, every once in a while she'd come across a real treasure—Marian's childhood books, which Amy would love—and a mammoth Erector set in the original metal box for Ben. While she had hoped for a written confession, what she found in an old hatbox was close: a bundle of letters, tied with a faded blue ribbon, written to Victoria from her daughter, Frances O'Hara.

She took them to the house to read aloud with Marian. The first one was dated a year after the fateful Christmas with an address in Jamaica Plain written below the date.

> Dearest Mother and Father,
>   I trust this missive finds you well and I am writing to send greetings of the season to all. I am also writing to tell you some news. Tuesday last I was safely delivered of a daughter, whom we have named Louisa, after dear Grandmother. With

your permission, we would like to give the
baby, who is blessedly healthy, Victoria as a
middle name.

Mr. O'Hara is now the foreman at
work. The owner of the company has no
children and has told him that he will make
him a partner soon. They have almost
more jobs than they can handle and will
be breaking ground for a grand new house
here for the mayor soon.

I am very happy save for the regret
that my hasty departure and subsequent
marriage have caused this rift between us.
As I have written before, I would like to
come to Norwell to see you—especially
now to introduce your new granddaughter.
Please grant me this Christmas wish.

I remain your loving daughter,
Franny

The rest of the letters spanned a number of years
and told of the reconciliation; Patrick O'Hara's ad-
vancement leading to his own big home in Jamaica
Plain to house his growing family—another girl
and two boys; Albert's and Will's inevitable Harvard degrees and Will's surprising match with the

daughter of an English earl that meant moving to a castle in Yorkshire; the death of Elliot Fairchild; and then a last letter in a different hand. Victoria's. It was in an envelope addressed to "Mrs. Patrick O'Hara, 114 The Jamaicaway, Boston, Massachusetts." It had never been mailed.

Dear Franny,

As I am about to pass onto a better world and will soon be facing my Maker, it is time to unburden my conscience after so many years.

What I did was wicked and I can only hope God will forgive me when I stand before his throne for I have been truly penitent every day of my life since. I know you have always suspected the true nature of the events at that dreadful Christmas dinner.

I think I must have indeed been driven a bit mad at the idea that you would marry Patrick O'Hara, and the fact that he has been such a good provider and husband to you has proved me wrong many times over. I am not excusing myself, but it was something I would not have believed possible then.

I must now write the words, however painful. To say them to you would be worse.

I am responsible for the death of Sumner Cabot, and Patrick O'Hara was the man I wanted to kill. Bridget had been instructed to give the slice of pudding with the horseshoe charm to Mr. O'Hara—may God forgive me that too, seeking to make her the instrument of her own brother's end, although I did not know of their connection until that day. I mixed arsenic powder into the sugar to top that portion and you well know the outcome. I cannot bear to write any more of the details. It doesn't matter now.

The doctor here says I have but a few more days, perhaps only hours, on this earth. The cancer has spread.

Forgive me.
Mother

"Do you think Franny ever read this?" Faith said.

Marian shook her head. "It was never mailed, and you saw that it was on the bottom of the pile of

Franny's letters. Perhaps her mother hoped when they packed up her things after her death that her daughter would come across it, but you can see the bow appears to have been untied."

There was a slight catch in Marian's voice. "It was a terrible, no heinous, thing to do, but what that woman must have suffered."

"No more curse now, though," Faith said. "We know the truth."

Marian nodded and took her daughter-in-law's hand. "But still . . ."

Faith gave the hand in hers a squeeze. "I'll call James Holden, our associate minister. See if he can make it."

"I think that would be wise, dear," Marian said.

What reality TV cooking shows fail to depict is the true hell of being in a greenroom with the other contestants. Sure, there are close-ups of knitted brows and piercing glances filled with pure or assumed malice. And the cameras zoom in on spats so staged that only the most gullible viewer could believe in them. Voices are raised. Words are bleeped. It's Showtime! The reality is, in fact, very far from Reality.

Faith Fairchild was sitting in a greenroom now. It wasn't network TV, not really TV at all, despite the high school kid walking around taping the night's event for the local cable channel. The greenroom hell she was experiencing wasn't one created by knives drawn or pots hurled and would have made for exceptionally bad ratings. No, the room was filled with a total lack of overt drama and a complete absence of conversation. The air was as dead as a doornail. The chefs sat mostly hunched over, eyes on their Crocs, avoiding any semblance of interest in one another. Mind-numbing boredom seized Faith, along with something akin to panic—had she only been sitting here for fifteen minutes? How long before they started?

There was no way the night was going to be a pleasant one. Faith looked up, knowing all too well what she would see. Three other chefs, professionals like herself, dressed in their work clothes— except for the toques the event planner had insisted upon. Faith never wore one and was pretty certain the others didn't either. The others. She knew them all, disliked them—some intensely—and she suspected they her.

Faith had regretted saying yes to this fund-raiser almost from the start. Grave doubts had sprung up during the initial phone call from the planner hired by the organizers, but Faith's best friend and neighbor Pix Miller was on the committee and had asked her to participate. Pix almost never asked her for favors, and when she did, Faith knew it was

something near and dear to Pix's heart. Not that
raising money for breast cancer research wasn't
important to Faith, but the woman who had con-
tacted her had been extremely obnoxious, abruptly
ending the conversation with one of Faith's least favorite kiss-offs: "Our people will get in touch with
your people."

"I don't have 'people.' I am the people person,"
Faith had said, immediately wishing she could take
the words back. She'd sounded like a Dr Pepper
commercial. "I mean, I handle my own publicity.
If you send me all the information, I'll post it on
my company, Have Faith's, Web site, our Facebook
page, Twitter, and get a press release to the local
paper."

That had been four months ago. She needed
to needlepoint a pillow—first learning how to—
with OBJECTS IN MIRROR ARE CLOSER THAN THEY
APPEAR as she invariably accepted dates thinking
they were distant and then suddenly, there they
were on her doorstep. Tonight was a perfect ex-
ample. She'd thought she had plenty of time to
think about possible mystery ingredient combina-
tions that might be thrown at her, maybe watch a
few shows on the various food channels. Certainly
consult further with her assistant, Niki, who, when
she'd heard Faith was competing, had shaken her

head and told her, "Presentation and the clock. Of course try to do something more than edible, but the other two criteria will be what the judges go by most. How it looks and getting it all on the plate. Above all, don't leave an ingredient out or use it without modifying it." Niki obviously watched these shows a lot.

For this fund-raiser, four acclaimed New England chefs would battle it out for a Golden Toque, producing the three courses: appetizer, entrée, and dessert, from the stipulated ingredients plus a pantry of basics in front of an audience that was paying big bucks to watch while drinking champagne and nibbling from a lavish buffet. The event was being held in a regional technical high school with an extensive culinary arts program, so the kitchen had the requisite stoves, counter space, and equipment with a large dining area where students ran a café three days a week.

The four chefs had been given a quick tour before being ushered into seclusion. The only thing they had been allowed to bring were their knives. Faith's case was sitting by her side. She'd brought more than she'd probably need, but packing them made her feel prepared.

Why weren't they starting? The audience must all be here by now. Pix had assured her that there would be a brief pitch, but Faith knew these things always went on longer than planned and then there were drinks to be poured. Poured liberally, especially between the courses, when there would be auction items to view such as vacation homes, artwork, and a private dinner party prepared by the Golden Toque winner, which the organizers hoped would prove to be the biggest ticket item. The live auction would cap off the evening after the winner was selected.

After each round, students, dressed as the chefs they hoped to become, would clean up the stations for the next course. The competitors would once more sit it out in the greenroom having just heard the judges' verdict.

The judges. All Faith was told initially was that they would be "three professional food writers and critics." Pix had leaked the names to Faith as soon as she'd gotten them herself. Faith was very grateful, as for some reason—drama?—the planner thought it would be fun for the chefs to be kept in the dark until the night itself. When it became clear that they would read the press releases along with the rest of the public, she abandoned the idea two weeks later. Faith had been relieved to get the names earlier, though. The judges would not be a problem—or rather she hoped they wouldn't be.

Mandy Klein was a food blogger with an impressive following. She lived in Cambridge, and while Faith had met her, she didn't know her well but had read some of her posts and found they were entertaining, expertly written, and very informative. Ms. Klein was managing to appeal to many levels of proficiency at once, no mean feat.

Simon Lake was the restaurant critic for a newspaper syndicate covering Boston's western suburbs and the North Shore. Their paths had never crossed, but Faith liked his reviews. He knew food and how it should be presented—eye appeal and without the distraction, and annoyance, of poor service. He was famous for walking out of places the moment he or a fellow diner was told "This is how the chef prepares it." In other words, Lake always commented, "We're ignoramuses who are supposed to like it or lump it." Adding, "So, leg it."

The last judge was someone Faith *did* know well, as she was sure the other chefs did too. Pierre Jacques was a legend in the business, especially in New England. As a young man in France, he had survived the torturous training so perfectly described by Jacques Pepin in his autobiography, *The Apprentice,* starting as a *commis.* Long hours of sheer drudgery and often what amounted to abuse in restaurant kitchens, but one learned *la technique.* Pierre left France and came to Boston, where he first found work as a maître d', lending an air of authenticity to a French restaurant with owners and a chef who had never been there. Both their speech and food lacked the accent. The cooking was decent, but when Pierre began lending a hand, stirring the pots, raves rolled in. His personality—true Gallic wit—and good looks— Gerard Depardieu in his salad days (the ones before the too-many-baguette ones)—soon made Pierre Jacques a star outside the restaurant as well. He was the go-to *homme* for anything relating to all kinds of food, appearing with Julia on TV and off.

Armed with an introduction from a mutual friend, Faith had called Chef Jacques for advice when she was thinking of reopening the catering company she'd started in Manhattan before her marriage. They'd met for what was the first of many lunches, and he'd been an early supporter of Have Faith—word of mouth from Pierre couldn't be bought and was worth a fortune. Despite their friendship, she knew he would be as hard on her as the others and welcomed the chance to shine before him.

That was before she knew whom she'd be competing against. When she heard those names, what she had begun to regard as fun and challenging turned to ashes in her mouth.

If she had to sit here even one minute more, Faith thought she might scream. The greenroom, aka the teachers' lounge, had a restroom, so she couldn't use a sudden need to wash up as an excuse to leave. No one had told the chefs specifically not to wander around the school, but it had been implied with the instruction to "Make yourselves comfortable and we'll come get you." There was an attempt at a craft services table with bottles of water, juice, and soft drinks plus the kind of assortment of snacks sold at big-box stores—small packages of cookies, granola bars, chips. Not exactly cordon bleu. Faith had grabbed a bottle of water when she came in and realized that she'd finished it. Best not to drink another. And she wasn't hungry, even for a Frito, a guilty pleasure. There were bags of them on the table.

She sighed and hoped it hadn't been audible. The last thing she wanted to display in front of this group was a suggestion of weakness. They were going to be on her, trying to cut her from the herd, soon enough—no holds barred. Her eyes rested on the chef sitting nearest to the door. He wasn't fat, but he was large. Everything about him was super-

sized—well over six feet tall, hands like catchers'
mitts, head like a basketball, and shoulders so
broad one wondered whether he had to turn side-
ways to enter a room. His name was Billy Gold and
he had immediately told the others they might as
well "pack their knives and go," since he was going
to win the toque by virtue of his name—and skill.
A super-sized ego and, Faith gave a slight shudder,
a super-sized temper. He'd been her first boss back
in the day, before Have Faith and before marriage.
It was an experience she'd tried hard to forget. She
had heard he'd opened a restaurant at Mohegan
Sun in Connecticut, but what was he doing here?
This was a very small-potatoes event for him.

Fresh out of culinary school, Faith did remember how excited she had been when Chef Gold,
the man routinely referred to as the "Twenty-First
Century's Escoffier" hired her to assist the pantry
chef—or the *garde manger* in French. It was his job
to prepare all the cold dishes: salads, cold appetizers, pâtés. Mostly she'd be washing and chopping
vegetables. It was what she'd expected when she
took the job, eager to gain experience. Her first day
had been an eye-opener. The air was blue—blue
with smoke from something that had spilled on a
burner and blue with the stream of invective spew-

ing forth from the chef's mouth. The chef's anger had been directed at his long-suffering sous-chef, but she'd feared for the moment it would be aimed directly at her. Days passed and Chef Gold had yet to acknowledge her presence. "Morons, idiots, I am surrounded by them!" yelled at the entire staff was the closest she'd come. It actually meant he was calming down. No more four-letter words. She'd been somewhat shocked the first day. Not by the language, but by the frequency and volcanic quality of the chef's eruptions. When the *F this* and *F that*s became less numerous, the worst was over. By the end of the third day at the restaurant, she'd decided it was pure self-indulgence on Gold's part, and even counterproductive. Faith saw her coworkers, eager to avoid being the target, frantically covering up mistakes—even sending out food they knew wasn't right to stay on schedule and avoid the chef's wrath. She'd stuck to her station and kept her head down.

The following week a new pastry chef started. Things in the kitchen perked up; her expertise and delight in what she was doing had spread over them like chocolate sauce on a profiterole (and hers were amazing). The fly in the crème brûlée turned out to be the chef himself. He couldn't find fault with Elise, so he redoubled his critiques of everyone else's work, all the while circling around her, sticking a finger in her mousse, shoving a Madeleine in his mouth.

And he'd begun to notice Faith, making her redo her work not just once but often twice. Her fingers were sore from wielding the knives. One dice or julienne a millimeter off the others would cause him to explode. But Faith stuck it out; she wasn't a quitter, and she knew she was good. She was there to become even better.

But then he began to get personal, making very audible asides to the others about WASP dilettantes and even speculating with a leer in her direction about whether she was a real blonde. Nervous laughter from the other males had greeted this remark. No way did they want him to turn on them.

The fourth week he'd gone too far—too far for Elise. The pastry chef had been giving Faith reassuring looks of commiseration throughout and had even whispered to her that men like the chef who had to fill the room with testosterone were usually lacking it.

Faith had been preparing mushrooms—cèpes—to go into that night's featured appetizer, the pork-based Pâté Forestier, which would also include black truffles for added richness—and an increased price. Chef Gold had come up behind her and screamed that she was slicing the mushrooms like a peasant. He'd jostled her arm and the knife came down across her thumb. Blood spurted out.

His words still reverberated, starting with the C word that was anathema to all women. "You c—! Do you want the board of health to close us down? How many other dishes have you contaminated behind my back? Out, out of my kitchen! Go to your mommy's and bake brownies. You will never be a chef. No woman can be a real chef! Have you ever heard of a famous female? No! Now, out!" He'd clapped his enormous hands so close to her ears that for a moment she'd thought he was about to box them. His closeness and the certain knowledge of how he viewed women, professionally and sexually, had made her feel physically ill.

She'd stood, pressing the wound with her other thumb in a vain attempt to stop the flow of blood. "Move! Are you deaf as well as dumb!" He'd laughed uproariously as his own joke. "You're fired! Done! *Finito!* Now, get out of my sight!"

Elise had come over with a wet towel, handing it to Faith as she said, "If she goes, I go."

"You don't have to do this," Faith had said. "I'll be fine."

"I know that. I also know when something in a kitchen really stinks and this does to high heaven."

Billy Gold had turned purple with rage. She could still see the room. It went dead silent. The dishwashers, most of whom didn't speak English, had huddled together in a group, aware that something was terribly, terribly wrong and figuring there was safety in numbers.

"I'm out of here too, chef," André, the sous-chef, had then announced. "I've been turning down other offers for months now." He undid his apron and laid it on the counter. Two others had piled theirs on as well, including the pantry chef.

Gold had screamed, "Go, all of you! I can replace you with far better by standing out on the street. And you'd better believe there won't be any references, you shits!"

Now in this unlikely setting so many years later, Faith and Gold were in the same room for the first time since then. He hadn't been able to replace the staff with others of the same caliber, or perhaps it was a jinx. Whatever the reason, the restaurant went under several weeks later, and the word going around was that it was all Faith Sibley's fault, at least according to the chef—and his investors. Gold didn't continue to fail, however. Since then he'd gone on to even greater fame, and fortune, hiring a canny PR firm to spin his out-of-control temper and foul mouth into culinary performance art, which Gordon Ramsay would much later perfect. Faith was sure the audience tonight was eager to watch Chef Gold explode, and she planned to keep well away from him. The look he had given her when she entered the room made it clear he hadn't forgotten, or forgiven, a thing. She'd have to watch her back.

She hoped her station was far from his, but then she also hoped it wasn't next to her former employee Chef Claudia Westell, the second chef Faith saw upon entering the greenroom. The woman was as perky-looking as the day she'd arrived at the catering kitchen in answer to an ad for an assistant four years ago. Today, as then, she wore her signature glasses—ruby-red frames—and seemed to skip into the room, a trait that Faith had found increasingly obnoxious. At the time, Niki Constantine had been taking maternity leave at Faith's insistence—"It's not like someone has to go buy milk," Niki had protested. "I can nurse at work— the ultimate in fast food." But Faith remembered how exhausted she had been with both her children, the handiness of the feeding notwithstanding, and Niki had reluctantly given in. Claudia had professed herself thrilled with the opportunity to work with Faith, even on a short-term basis.

By the end of the first day, the obsequious fawning—continuous use of "Chef" despite Faith's reminders to simply call her "Faith"—had begun to more than pale. By the end of the second day, Faith realized she had a much bigger problem on her hands. The woman couldn't cook. She had talked the talk during the interview and her résumé was impressive—stints in a number of restaurants in her native California, particularly the Bay Area, as well as a culinary degree from City College in San Francisco. Faith had checked two of the references, and both had emphasized her willingness to work hard. "You never have to worry that Claudia won't show up," one had said. In the restaurant business this kind of employee was a treasure, but Faith soon had realized she should have asked more specifically about punctual Claudia's actual culinary prowess.

Preparing forty portions of panna cotta and the mixed berry coulis to go around each should have been a no-brainer. First Claudia had asked Faith for the recipe—"I know yours will be special!"—she'd enthused. Well, okay, maybe she'd thought Faith wanted something other than a basic one, tea or infused with cardamom or some other spice or made with Greek yogurt. Claudia's first pot boiled over onto the burner, leaving that horrible smell

only burned milk and cream can produce. She'd
cleaned it up and managed to produce a finished
product, but when Faith tasted one, it was gritty.
Claudia hadn't dissolved the sugar properly. Third
time lucky, but the waste of ingredients was costly.
("My fault completely! I don't know where my
head is today! Please deduct it from my pay.")

And so it went. The woman lurched from disaster to disaster until by the end of the week all
Faith could trust her to do was cut up vegetables,
and even those would never pass muster in any restaurant kitchen Faith knew. She'd called another of
the references and had her suspicions confirmed.
Claudia had been great, but she'd been in the front,
not in the kitchen. What Faith had hired was an
extremely outgoing, competent server. The City
College degree, if she actually had one, had to
have been in Hospitality. Niki would be back in
three weeks and Faith figured she could tough it
out, using Claudia to run errands, get supplies, and
clean up. Until Niki called her. She'd dropped by
late in the day with the baby. Seeing an unfamiliar
car parked outside—and not seeing Faith's—she'd
let herself in. Claudia was in the office using the
scanner.

"She had your master book of recipes!" Niki had
reported immediately. "And she was going through

them like crazy. Very nervy dame. Wanted to know who I was and how I had gotten in. I told her and she looked guilty as hell, started giving me a line about your telling her she could make copies."

Faith hadn't, and a very big part of her was happy to have an excuse to fire the woman. She swore to check references more carefully in the future—and only give the keys to work to trusted employees like Niki.

And she was facing the "nervy dame" again. Claudia had given Faith what was probably supposed to be a withering look when she saw her. Ms. Westell had taken some basic cooking classes somewhere along the line and parlayed her perky little puppy act into a popular local TV show where she showed viewers how to wow guests in thirty minutes. The wow factor all had to do with elaborate presentations, while the recipes themselves relied heavily on "shortcuts" like frozen piecrust and Minute Rice—"No one goes through your trash at a party," she was wont to say with a wink.

It had gotten back to Faith more than once that the woman had said Faith fired her because she was jealous of her skill—and her youthful good looks. Niki had come in fuming one day after hearing that Claudia had been badmouthing Faith as a "has-been" and saying that "some people don't know when it's time to quit." Faith had laughed it off, but it smarted.

And on to chef number three. Maybe the fiercest antagonist of all—Jake Barlow. Faith hadn't done anything overt to derail the other two, but there was no ducking the fact that she had with Jake. It had been in Maine, on Sanpere Island, where the Fairchilds had a summer cottage. Sanpere's population doubled by the end of August, and there were several seasonal restaurants, although the Fairchilds' favorite remained The Harbor Café, open year-round and noted for the "Seconds on Us" Friday fish fry.

That particular summer, though, Faith had been looking forward to a new restaurant. Friends of theirs, the Hortons, had made the transition from Summer People to Year-Rounders and had been working hard all winter to fulfill their dream— restoring an old farmhouse overlooking Penobscot Bay and opening a restaurant that would use local ingredients, especially those from the sea. They had hired a young culinary school graduate who had garnered every prize at graduation and was from Maine, although not from the island. Faith had barely unpacked before the phone rang with an invitation from Doreen Horton to come as guests and sample the menu. Doreen's voice had sounded slightly strained, but Faith chalked it up to the inevitable woes associated with running a restaurant. She had seen many dreams go up in a puff of applewood smoke and had never herself wanted to be anything but a caterer.

Faith and Tom had been seated by one of the front windows and their first impression was that the Hortons had a winner. The place was packed, and the work they'd done was exquisite. The dining room had all the charm of an old farmhouse, but none of the mustiness. Doreen had been scouring yard sales and auctions for years to find vintage china in good shape. She'd sensibly avoided flowers on the tables, opting instead for large arrangements of whatever was blooming outside in white ironstone pitchers, placed on the sideboards and next to the front door.

The first indication that things were not going well came almost immediately. Faith was deciding whether to order a glass of prosecco to start or the cocktail *maison*—vodka, blueberries, and cucumbers, sort of a Down East Pimm's Cup—when she suddenly smelled something like burning rubber. Fearing a mishap in the kitchen, she started to stand up when Tom pointed across the room at a server who had just taken what looked like an inverted fishbowl from a plank of wood, releasing the aroma. The guest appeared startled by the dish. Faith couldn't hear what was said, but the whole thing was immediately removed. She grabbed the menu, which she had not yet had a chance to peruse. "Planked Chanterelles and Scallops in a Mole Sauce Smoked at the Table," she read aloud to Tom. "Oh dear, it's all molecular gastronomy. What could they be thinking? When done well, sublime, but here where people are expecting things like lobster and Blueberry Buckle?—and a chef with not much experience."

She'd known then why Doreen had wanted them there immediately, but resolved to keep an open mind. Maybe this young man—she'd seen his name at the bottom of the menu, Jake Barlow—would be a prodigy and they'd be like some of those incredibly lucky diners who just happened by La Rive, a place in the Catskills, when a young man named Thomas Keller was starting out.

The *amuse-bouche* arrived. It appeared to be thin strips of peanut brittle stacked like Lincoln logs in a white porcelain clamshell. "Um, Pomegranate Kelp Brittle," the server announced. Faith recognized the girl; she was an Eaton. She looked perplexed. "Enjoy!" she added. The brittle was very brittle—Faith almost lost a tooth with the first nibble and decided to wait for it to warm up. The chef had obviously used the blast chiller. Aside from the normal high cost of equipping a restaurant kitchen, Faith feared the Hortons had been persuaded to make many more purchases by their cutting-edge chef. When warm enough to eat, the brittle was sticky—Turkish pomegranate molasses, she'd decided—and the seaweed left a somewhat celluloid aftertaste.

The other courses followed the same pattern. Much use of liquid nitrogen evident and little flavor. Tom had been intrigued by his mozzarella "balloon," but when it popped it was just a stringy mess on top of what otherwise would have been a lovely piece of halibut. And Faith's dessert was just silly—roasted balsam pine needles sprinkled on top of lobster ice cream. She'd ordered it sight unseen, or explained, after reading, "Our Signature Dessert—A Bite O' Maine."

Albert Horton caught up with them as they were getting into their car. He didn't mince words. "It's a disaster, isn't it? He would only take the job if we agreed to give him free rein and stupidly we agreed. It all sounded great."

"I liked that melon ball thing," Tom had said. Faith had given him a little jab. What had looked like melon was actually a frozen quail egg yolk with bacon foam. Tom loved anything that had the faintest whiff of bacon.

"What should we do?" Albert had asked.

Faith advised a serious heart-to-heart with the chef and said they'd be back—as paying guests—the following week.

The restaurant was the talk, and laughingstock, of the island, but business was good. Everyone wanted to see what was going on, and diners from as far away as Bar Harbor had been lured by the rumor that the next Ferran Adrià was cooking on Sanpere Island.

Faith and Tom had returned the following Thursday. Although it was six thirty—people, even the summer people, ate unfashionably early on the island—the dining room was half-empty, or half-full, Faith amended. Possibly the curiosity factor had played out.

The restaurant meant everything to the Hortons, and she had been prepared to love her meal. Doreen had called to say they had had a good talk with Jake and he had changed the menu. A glance proved that he had, but there was still too much smoke and too many mirrors, Faith had thought.

They started with oysters—there were no *amuse-bouches* of any sort this time—and they were fine. Tom had his with the traditional cocktail sauce—

it was how he liked shrimp too. Faith went with the "Chef's Own Mignonette." She wondered a bit about the wording. Who else's would it be? It was okay, but substituting white rum for champagne was a mistake. Hard to taste the delicate oyster under the overly liberal dose of the strong alcohol.

The chef was definitely showcasing local ingredients, and the salads—field greens, a little dulse, and edible flowers, mostly nasturtiums with a wild strawberry vinaigrette—were tasty if uninspired. This time their table was away from the windows and a bit close to that of a couple Faith didn't recognize. Sanpere was a very small island and she knew most of the residents, so they must be renting or from off island. Eavesdropping, Faith learned the two were as interested in food as were the Fairchilds, especially Faith—Tom still unaccountably leaned toward the boiled dinners of his childhood. Soon the couples were conversing. Faith mentioned their earlier experience and that she understood the menu had changed—for the better. The woman—dressed in vintage Marimekko and with a haircut not from Curl Up & Dye on the other side of the bridge—said she'd been underwhelmed so far.

The chef himself served their entrées. Faith had caught a glimpse of him the week before and thought him more Byron than Beard in appearance. He wore a red bandanna to keep his long dark locks from his face and the food. His eyes were so blue she suspected contacts; the smile he gave them as he described what they were about to eat was almost nonexistent. When he left, the two couples burst out laughing.

"A very serious young man," the woman said.

Faith cut into the wild duck she'd ordered. It wasn't the season for game, but she thought she should try more than the seafood on the menu. Tom was having butter-poached lobster and he was good about sharing.

The duck was almost raw. She put her knife down and touched the meat with a finger. Almost stone cold. Pink would have been fine. Overcooked duck was chewy and inedible, but underdone fowl of any sort posed a health risk.

She motioned to the server, noting that the staff seemed to have turned over. The little Eaton girl wasn't there, at least not tonight, and she didn't recognize any of the others.

"My duck is almost raw. You need to bring it back to the kitchen."

The girl looked alarmed. "Bring it back?"

"Yes, it shouldn't be served this way. I'm sure the chef made a mistake and will understand."

"Let me see." The woman at the next table leaned over. "Gruesome . . ."

The cut Faith had made was now oozing bright pink blood. The server picked up the plate and headed for the kitchen. Faith felt sorry for the poor girl, who was looking panic-stricken.

It seemed like only a second before she was back with Faith's plate. "The chef says this is the way he prepares this dish."

At that point, Doreen Horton—sensing something was wrong—came over, took one look at the plate, and disappeared with it.

Again, it seemed only a second before she was back, happily empty-handed. "Please select another entrée and the entire meal is of course on us."

Faith hastily chose crab cakes. They would be ready to sauté and she could be out of there soon.

It turned out that the catastrophe of the evening had nothing to do with the end of Barlow's stint at the Sanpere restaurant, which occurred that night, and everything to do with the couple at the next table. The woman wrote a regular column for *Bon Appétit* magazine and had planned to spotlight the rising new young chef from Maine. How Jake found out about it Faith never knew, but when he did he called her and the blast he delivered wasn't a chilly one. He blamed her, her "uneducated palate," and her obvious envy of an up-and-coming chef for the food writer's change of plan. Later that summer he disappeared from the food scene only to emerge two years later having lived in Asia and trained, he'd proclaimed, with "real" chefs. He'd opened a small restaurant in Jamaica Plain that he'd labeled "Pacific Rim Fusion Cuisine," and it took off. Like Billy Gold, he turned his brooding romanticism—some would say surliness—into an attribute. Unmarried, he soon had a bevy of foodie groupies. The small restaurant had morphed into a large one in Boston's South End where reservations could only be made a month in advance with a hefty cancellation fee. It was immediately the hottest one in town. The Fairchilds had avoided it.

Unlike the other two chefs, he'd lashed out at Faith the moment he'd walked through the door.

"I wouldn't have taken the gig if they'd told me you would be here. No, wait. I take that back. I wanted to whip your ass once, and now I will."

The event planner had been somewhat taken aback at his words but quickly realized they meant more drama for the fund-raiser. "Now, now . . ." she murmured unconvincingly.

It was going to be a fantastic night.

Minutes earlier Faith had been dying to get out of the greenroom, and now she was dying to go back. How on earth did those chefs on TV do this? There was no way she was going to be able to produce anything palatable and presentable in the time allotted for the appetizer round, only twenty minutes.

"The ingredients you must use are in the boxes in front of you: anchovies, baguettes, rainbow chard, and smoked Ghost Pepper flakes," the head of the culinary arts program at the school announced. "Your time starts now!"

The other three chefs raced from their stations to the pantry and the fridge. Students had been assigned to assist each, though they couldn't help with the actual cooking. They were there to whisk away dirty pots and utensils only. Before the competition started, the high school principal had introduced the group by name, her "Very Own Michelin Three Stars" and described the mentor program that paired students with local chefs for a semester. "Chef Gold was one of our first mentors and I'd like to thank him, as I'm sure Jennifer, his current intern, will." Cue Jennifer, a petite teen who appeared very nervous. She was darling, Faith thought, and wished her well in the culinary world, an extremely tough one for female chefs. She was also obviously extremely shy or extremely nervous about speaking in front of a group. Gold had patted his intern avuncularly on the shoulder—her whole body had been trembling, as was her voice, as she managed to stammer a thank-you to the chef. The students spread out to select chefs, but before Jennifer could follow her mentor to his station, a boy twice her height elbowed his way to the spot. Jennifer came over to Faith, who hoped the girl wasn't too disappointed at what was obviously a second choice; but Jennifer gave her a radiant smile. She really was very pretty. What would have been called a Pocket Venus in another era.

And then it all started. The audience was a lively one, clapping and cheering the chefs on. The judges were talking softly among themselves. Faith felt like the proverbial deer in the headlights—frozen. She had to get something on the plates. Snap out of it, Faith! she chided herself and began to whirl through the Rolodex of recipes she kept in her head, desperately searching for one with all four ingredients. Out of the corner of her eye she saw Claudia dip a teaspoon into the small jar of Ghost Pepper flakes and raise it toward her lips. No matter what she thought of the woman, Faith couldn't let her put that amount in her mouth. But before she could call out, Billy Gold beat her to it.

"Claudia! Don't eat that! Ghost Peppers—Bhut Jolokia—are just about the strongest on earth!"

"I knew that," Claudia snapped. "I was just smelling them to see whether they were smoked or not."

Of course she had had no idea what they were, Faith thought, and if she had tasted the spoonful, she'd be smoking herself and out of the competition. She looked over at Jake and realized he was thinking—and wishing—the same thing.

The ovens had been preheated to a time-saving 350 degrees, which was a relief. Faith would make a savory bread pudding. It worked as an appetizer and also as a brunch dish. The individual ramekins would take ten to fifteen minutes to cook. She didn't have a second to spare. She joined the others as they darted around the kitchen for ingredients and returned to her spot.

She needed to rinse the salt from the anchovies before sautéing them with a small amount of garlic, just a hint. The anchovies would melt and lose their "fishiness." But where were they? The tin, which had been there when she'd left, was gone. So that's how it was going to be. Fortunately she'd seen a stack of others on a pantry shelf. She grabbed one, got the sauté going, then beat her eggs, adding some cream and ground pepper, and, using a microplane, grated some Parmesan from a

chunk she'd found in the fridge into the mixture. It
didn't need salt. Cautiously she added a tiny pinch
of the Ghost Pepper.

More tricks. While she'd been racing around,
someone had removed a few of her knives, including the bread knife. She'd deal with finding the culprit later. Chef's knives were expensive; they didn't
come from a five-and-ten. All Faith's had her logo
on the handles, so they wouldn't get mixed up with
others when she was on a job. They'd be easy to
spot, although whoever took them probably would
have hidden them.

With speed she wouldn't have thought possible,
she tore the baguette into rough cubes and added
them to the liquid to soak. While the bread absorbed the liquid, she greased the ramekins and
removed the stems from the chard. They were
pretty, but there wasn't enough time to cook them
through. She shredded the leaves, dumped them
in, and finally added the anchovies. At the last
moment, she sprinkled some golden raisins from
the pantry into the mixture for some fruitiness.
The ramekins went in the oven and while they were
baking, she made small glasses of Virgin Marys to
indicate it could also be a brunch dish. Besides the
traditional ingredients—all in the pantry save the
alcohol—she used another pinch of pepper.

The puddings came out and miraculously they were done, even developing a nice golden crust. She put them on the plate, happy to see they were cooked through but moist, and stuck a small, bright pink or yellow chard leaf with stem in each shot glass (what were those doing in a high school kitchen?).

"Hands down!"

On TV this was the moment where the competitors high-fived each other, even hugged. That didn't happen tonight. The round was over and Faith realized she really, really hoped she would win.

Claudia had produced some pedestrian-looking bruschetta.

"I'm not sure I'm getting a chard flavor," Mandy Klein commented.

"I just used the stems for color, chef," Claudia answered.

"And unfortunately there is a little too much of the pepper," Mandy continued. "It's a tricky ingredient."

"*Mais, très bonne.*" Pierre Jacques beamed. He was such a darling, Faith thought.

Simon Lake didn't say anything. He was gasping and drinking water.

Billy had done a quichelike custard, and it was pronounced delicious, as was Jake's version of the Thai dish Tom Yum Gung. He'd topped the soup with croutons and incorporated all the other ingredients, adding fresh lime juice and sliced ginger. Both men had been judicious with the chili flakes.

Faith's bread pudding brought raves. All three judges consumed the entire dish, commending her on the transformation of the ingredients and her playful presentation.

The verdicts would be swift. No sweating it out in the greenroom, although all the chefs would wait there while the guests hit the buffet and got more drinks. The students would clean up the stations and prepare them for the next round.

Simon had his voice back. "I'm sorry, Claudia, but you have been 'Sliced,' " he said.

She bowed to the judges and in a slightly tremulous voice—meant to show how very, very moved she was—she thanked everyone for giving her this opportunity. Faith half expected her to go on to say she'd devote herself in the future to cooking for orphans or some such thing and prove herself worthy to return to cook another day.

Back in the greenroom Claudia wasn't as gracious, and after she vented, she started in on Faith, reminding her that bread pudding was her, Claudia's, signature dish, and hinting that Faith had stolen the idea. About to come back with something like

"I think Mrs. Beeton got there before you," Faith left the room instead. Again no one had told them they couldn't wander. She'd avoid the "stage." She didn't want to be accused of peeking.

In the corridor she remembered she hadn't mentioned her missing knives. She'd ask Jennifer where the school kept theirs. They would have to do and shouldn't be too bad. The program had an excellent reputation, and the equipment she'd used so far had been of the highest caliber.

Killing time, she let her thoughts wander as well as her restless body. At one point she found herself in the automotive wing. She turned back and wished she could just go home. Tom hadn't been able to be here tonight. One of his parishioners was close to death and Tom had gone to be with him. But it would have been very nice if her husband could have been here in the audience. It was an enthusiastic one, but she needed more than a friendly face. She needed one that loved her.

Chef Gold had played around with his temper in the first round, teasing the audience with mini eruptions followed by coy "Gotcha" smiles. But when the student assisting him dropped a heavy frying pan, luckily empty, on the chef's foot, there was nothing fake about the reaction. After a string of invectives, Gold limped around in an exaggerated manner until the clock started to tick down and he forgot his act. Emerging from the greenroom, Faith noticed the male student had been replaced by a female who looked even younger than Jennifer. Her name was Megan, Faith remembered from the introductions, and the unlucky boy was Josh. Megan was standing at Gold's station, as far away from the chef as she could, clearly hoping to avoid any mishaps while still being helpful. Billy Gold must have spoken to the planner, demanding the switch, when Faith was out of the room. She was happy that Jennifer was still with her. The girl was quick and professional.

"You may open your mystery ingredient boxes now! They contain chicken livers, frozen lemonade, Cheez Doodles, and peppermint hard candies. You have thirty minutes for this entrée round, and the time starts now!"

Once again Faith felt her brain freeze, or was it melting? Niki had warned her that these shows threw ingredients like candy and junk food at contestants. But Cheez Doodles—and peppermints? The other two chefs had already sped to the pantry. Claudia, in a front-row seat, was glowering at her. Clearly she thought she should be cooking and Faith should be sitting down.

The woman's angry stare galvanized Faith into action. Once again she flipped through her mental recipe cards. What did the list suggest? Picnic food. A southern picnic? No time to create a good barbecue sauce for the livers, but she could still do something delectable. She'd pulverize the Doodles—too bad they weren't Fritos so she could munch a few for courage—coat the livers, and deep-fry them. Corn bread—she'd seen cornmeal in the pantry—as one of the sides. There had to be chard left over from the appetizers, and she'd treat it like collards, chopped and barely wilted on high heat. Tom's voice whispered "bacon" and she veered toward the fridge, which was a walk-in down a corridor where she found some plus the other items she'd need, like butter. The chicken livers would take the least time, but she had to get the oil up to temperature and quickly started the pot going.

As for the candies and lemonade, the obvious thing was ice cream. She had no time to go with anything but the obvious. Besides, what was a picnic without homemade ice cream in the cooler? There were red-and-white-checked paper napkins among others on a shelf, and she'd use those when plating the livers, which she hoped would be crispy on the outside and still soft in the middle. She'd add some Old Bay or something similar to the coating to give it a slight zing.

Just as in the first round, the spirit of competition—particularly with these chefs as opponents—kicked in, and Faith wanted to win. A lot. The trophy was prominently displayed on the judges' table. It was tacky in the extreme and shouted Dollar Store, yet it looked like an Oscar to Faith, gleaming like real gold in the bright lights.

She cooked the bacon and mixed her corn bread batter, adding some of the drippings. The collards would have to be cooked near the end. She opened the oven door to put the corn bread pan in to cook.

There was only one problem. Her oven was stone cold. She'd never thought to check, and someone had turned it off between rounds. More sabotage.

She looked around wildly. No way would Jake or Billy give her oven space, and it would take too long to get her own up to temperature. Jennifer coughed; Faith turned in the girl's direction. She angled her head slightly, indicating the stove immediately to her left. Faith ran over with the corn bread. The oven was on. Jennifer had barely moved a muscle. She couldn't be accused of helping Faith.

"Problem with your stove, chef?" the culinary arts director asked.

"Yes. It seems to have gone off after the first

round, but fortunately I thought you might have
had one preheated in reserve and that one over
there"—she pointed—"was on."

"Ah, well yes, we did have a spare." Clearly he
was covering up for a detail he'd neglected and
clearly he didn't want to be caught out. The audience gave a collective sigh of relief. The school had
thought of everything!

Time to get her ice cream into the ice cream
maker and then fry the chicken livers. Niki had
told her that contestants always ran into trouble
making ice cream or sorbets, but Faith felt she was
on a roll, and she was. When it came time to plate,
she was happy with the results. Everything smelled
and looked delicious. She wouldn't mind digging
in herself.

She looked at the others' plates with a sinking
sensation. They looked terrific. Billy Gold had done
a quick pâté by sautéing the livers with chopped
onions in butter, adding some of the unconstituted
frozen lemonade and ground-up Doodles, and then
using the blast chiller to cool, but not chill, the
mixture. He'd also created what he called a palate
cleanser of peppermint sorbet. The presentation
was lovely. Using a baguette from round one, he
had toasted thin rounds, which he arranged like
a tepee over the slab of pâté with a jaunty sprig of

thyme, indicating one of the herbs he'd used, flying like a flag from the top.

Chef Barlow was still sticking to his signature Pacific Rim cuisine and presented a kind of poke, the Hawaiian dish, but instead of raw ahi or a similar fish he'd used thin slices of the liver sautéed *à point* and cooled to room temperature, then tossed with the frozen lemonade before he arranged them on a bed of chopped lettuce. Ingeniously, he had very briefly deep-fried the Cheez Doodles in grapeseed oil, garnishing the dish with them. Faith was nervous about her chances against these two until she saw the little round peppermint Chef Barlow had placed on each plate. Clearly he had forgotten the ingredient, and when it came time to present tried to bluster his way out of it by saying he had planned it as an "After Dinner Mint" so one's breath would be minty fresh.

The judges didn't buy it—Pierre playfully wagged a finger at him—and he was "Sliced." Faith and Chef Billy Gold would face off in round three.

Back in the greenroom it was Jake Barlow's turn to explode. "I'm outa here," he fumed, starting to strip off his chef's jacket. The event planner—Faith had finally remembered her name, Gloria—put up a hand, as if she were halting traffic. "You may, of course, leave now, but you won't get your check."

Check? She should have realized that Barlow and Gold wouldn't have participated out of the goodness of their shriveled little hearts, even for a good cause. It wasn't a large enough venue. They'd do charity events for nothing, but only if the event was covered widely enough, i.e., nationwide at the least. She didn't let on that she was donating her time—she would have refused payment from this organization anyway—but Claudia squeaked, "A check! You're getting paid!"

Gloria looked quite annoyed, the annoyance clearly directed at Jake for letting the cat out of the bag. "We assumed you were donating your expertise, Chef Westell. If we were mistaken, I'm sorry."

She didn't sound a bit sorry, and before Chef Westell could say anything more, Gloria left the room. Faith followed soon after—the atmosphere was more poisonous than ever. The night couldn't end soon enough for her. And she was determined to beat Billy Gold in the dessert round even if it was the last thing she ever did.

With both Jake and Claudia looking daggers from the front row, Faith willed herself to start thinking the moment the Pandora's box of ingredients for the final round was opened. Like the appetizer round, this one was only twenty minutes. From the noise level, Faith knew the audience was feeling no pain, which boded well for the auction bids.

The culinary arts director and the planner were talking to the judges. It looked like a huddle. Chef Gold was nowhere to be seen. He'd been onstage a few minutes ago, walking over to the buffet, where Faith saw him down a flute of champagne and a quick refill. He'd been imbibing all evening.

Gloria left, obviously going to remind the chef of the time. He must be in the restroom, Faith thought.

But she returned without the chef in tow and went back to the group at the judges' table. After another hasty huddle, the director came to the microphone and announced that the round would start despite Chef Gold's tardiness.

"The ingredients for the dessert round are: fresh chèvre, canned lychee nuts, Swedish Fish, and Vanilla Wafers. You have twenty minutes, and your time starts now!"

Barely registering that Billy Gold—too much bubbly?—was still not at his station, Faith went right into action this time. Compared to the other boxes, this was an easy one, and the organizers may have planned it that way, recognizing the fatigue factor for the chefs. She put the gummy fish candies in a pot with the liquid from the lychees on the stove to melt. She'd combine the syrup with the chèvre for a quick cheesecake with a buttery Vanilla Wafer crust, crumbing the cookies in the food processor and adding melted butter. She'd top the cakes with sliced lychees and rosettes of whipped cream. There was heavy cream in the fridge, and she went to get it. She'd need it for the filling as well. Faith was feeling better than she had all night. She could take this thing!

Out of sight of the audience, she ran even faster to the large fridge and quickly pulled open the heavy door. She could see the cream on the shelf.

She could also see Chef Gold. He was lying on his back with a kitchen knife sticking out from his chest.

One of Faith's knives.

She knelt and felt for a pulse. There was none. His skin was still warm. The murder must have occurred only minutes before. Minutes before she had been wandering around—alone. No witnesses. The prime suspect.

She stood up, envisioning what would come next after the 911 call. The fear, confusion, and all the chefs back in the greenroom—save one.

Billy Gold had been "Sliced."

She'd left the door open and she heard footsteps.
Someone was coming. Before anyone could enter,
Faith went out into the corridor quickly, blocking
the view.

It was Jennifer. She looked a little pale.

Faith thought the girl must be tired out. It had
been a hectic night, although her nervousness had
not shown itself after the earlier introductions.
Calm and efficient. Faith hoped she wouldn't take
the death of her mentor too hard.

"You mustn't come in. There's been"—Faith
paused, searching for words—"an accident."

The girl nodded. "I know." And then she paused,
as if searching for words as well. They came out
slowly—"Megan was his next intern."

Her voice grew louder, the next words faster. No
more calm. Just desperation—and a kind of relief
in her voice.

"I couldn't let him do it to her too. You can see
that, can't you?"

Faith could.

The Two Marys

The Christmas eve sky was filled with stars when Mary Bethany found a baby in her barn. They hadn't had a real snow yet; the island never got the kind of accumulation the mainland did, but it was cold. She had pulled an old woolen overcoat that had belonged to her father over her winter jacket and grabbed a shawl her mother had knitted, draping it around her head. Her small herd of goats was letting her know that it was milking time, holiday or no holiday.

Mary wasn't leaving a festive gathering. She wasn't leaving any gathering at all. Just a cup of hot cider, a slice of the fruitcake sent by her cousin Elizabeth, and a few cats for company and to keep the rodent population down. Walking the short distance from the old farmhouse to the small barn she'd built when the herd got too large for the shed, Mary had remembered the legend about animals being able to speak on Christmas eve. She'd allowed herself to speculate about what her goats would have to say. They were Nubians, pretty, long-eared goats that gave rich milk with the highest butterfat content and protein of any breed. Her pretty nannies. Her neurotic nannies. Temperamental, easily miffed divas, they let her know with resounding *blaats* when something was even the slightest bit wrong. She was afraid that given human voices, their conversation would be a litany of slights and sorrows. Or perhaps not, perhaps they would tell her how much they depended on her, how much they loved her. She had entered the warm barn smiling, and her smile grew broader when she saw the large basket with a big red bow nestled against a bale of hay. It must be a gift from a neighbor. She hadn't thought she would be getting any presents. Even her sister Martha's yearly Harry & David cheese log had not arrived. A tag hung from the bow: FOR MARY BETHANY. She ignored the goats for a moment and knelt down before the gift.

It was an afghan in soft pastel colors. That would be Arlene Marshall, who crocheted so beautifully.

The summer people always snapped up her work at the Sewing Circle's annual fair in August. How kind, Mary thought. It would be just the thing to throw across her lap at night when she sat up late reading. But so unexpected. She hadn't seen or spoken to the Marshalls since she'd brought some of her rose hip jelly over in early September. It had been a wonderful summer for the *Rosa rugosa* bushes that surrounded the house and had seeded in what passed for a lawn and beyond it, in the pasture. Mary had gathered the large bulbous, bright orange hips and put up jelly, made soup, even dried some for tea. Looking at the gleaming jars on the pantry shelf, she had decided to bring some to Arlene and Doug—her nearest neighbors, a mere six acres of fields and woods away.

But this was too much! It must have taken Arlene a long time to make, the stitch was intricate and the wool so fine. Then she heard a tiny sneeze. The merest whisper of a sneeze. She pulled back the blanket and uncovered—a baby! Eyes squeezed shut, a newborn—tiny—about the size of a kid. She rocked back on her heels in amazement, letting the cover drop from her hands. A baby?

The goats were crying louder, insistently. There was nothing human about their speech, but Mary knew what they were saying. She would have to milk them or they would wake the child. Whose child? And what was it doing here in her barn? Mary touched the baby's face gently. It was soft and warm. A beautiful child, rosy cheeks—*Rosa rugosa* cheeks—and shiny dark fine hair, like cormorant feathers, escaping from the hooded snowsuit. A blue snowsuit, new, not a hand-me-down. It must be a boy. His eyelids fluttered at her touch, but he slept on.

Mary stood up shakily. She would milk the goats, then take the baby inside. That was as far ahead as she could think at the moment. In all her forty-seven years, nothing remotely like this had ever happened. Nothing unusual at all, unless you thought an old maid who kept to herself, kept goats, and made cheese was unusual—or odd—as some did.

Automatically she milked the six goats and put out fresh water, more hay, and the grain mixture of oats, corn, and molasses she fed them. They voiced their irritation at her haste. "I don't have time to coddle you tonight," Mary told them, and something in her voice seemed to chasten them. At least, the noise level dropped. "Besides," she added, "if anyone should be upset, it should be me. It's Christmas eve. You're supposed to be able to tell me what happened here tonight."

She brought the baby into the house, setting the basket down by the woodstove in the kitchen, then ran back for the milk, which went into the shed in the second refrigerator. She'd had to buy it after she'd started making cheese.

When she closed the barn door and let the latch drop, Mary looked up into the night sky. It was clear and the stars seemed close enough to touch. There was a large one directly overhead. She blinked and it was gone. Turning at the back door for a last look before she went into the house, she saw the star was back.

In the kitchen, Mary took off her coat and jacket, wrapping the shawl around her shoulders. The baby was awake and making little mewing sounds like a kitten. He must be hungry, she thought, and reached in to pick him up. He settled into the crook of her arm, as if it had been carved just for him.

"You poor thing," she said aloud. "Who are you? And how could anyone bear to give you up?"

Holding him tight, she pulled the afghan out of the basket. Underneath it were an envelope with her name on it, some baby clothes, cloth diapers, two bottles, and a package wrapped in brown paper—not the kind you buy on a roll, but cut from a paper bag. The letter wasn't sealed; the flap was tucked in, easy to open with one hand. Mary knew then that the baby's mother had tried to think of everything, even this small detail—that Mary would be holding the baby when she read the letter. It was short and typewritten:

Dear Mary,
    Keep him safe and raise him to be a good man. His name is Christopher.

That was it. No signature. No further explanation. Mary picked up the package and peeled the tape from one end. A packet of bills fell out. She shook it, and more followed. Packets of hundred-dollar bills. A lot of hundred-dollar bills . . .

Faith Fairchild was watching her family. Nine-year-old Ben was in a corner, Lego Technic pieces spread out on the floor. His sister, first grader Amy, was equally involved, but she was at the kitchen counter, perched on a stool, drawing. The elaborate art pack—"Just like a real artist's, I bet"—that her grandparents had sent was reverently placed next to her. Faith drank some of her coffee. She'd made a fresh pot for breakfast—the first pot had disappeared quickly along with the slices of her cardamom raisin Christmas bread after the kids woke them at six o'clock to see what Santa had brought. Ben had managed to keep the secret of the jolly old fellow's true identity, whether out of real regard for his sister or to save as a weapon when she did something really outrageous such as entering his room without permission, Faith didn't care—just let Amy keep believing a while longer. Last night in a whisper before sleep, her daughter had confessed her fear that Santa might not know they were in Maine. He might think they were in their house in Aleford, Massachusetts, as usual. Faith had reassured her that Saint Nick knew all and would always find them.

Faith's attention strayed to her best present, always her best present—her husband, Tom, the Reverend Thomas P. Fairchild, stretched out on the couch reading Bill Bryson's *A Short History of Nearly Everything*. Tom caught her glance and blew her a kiss. She sent one back to him and wished they could reprise the early Christmas present they had enjoyed upstairs under the eiderdown quilt last night. Children were nature's most effective prophylactics she thought, looking at her two, who were awake, alert, and very much around.

They'd put a CD of Handel's *Messiah* on, and "We like sheep" filled the air. Faith and her younger sister, Hope, had taken the passage literally as children and created their own version, adding "and goats and chickens and cats and dogs too." She'd call Hope later, and they could sing a few bars together.

Tom still looked pale. Just after Thanksgiving, he'd had a series of stomachaches. He'd eat lightly, and they'd pass. Stress, they'd told each other. Early in their marriage they'd talked about how much they loved the Christmas season, starting with the lighting of the first Advent candle and continuing on to the joys of Christmas day with its messages of hope and peace. Loved it—and hated it. As a preacher's kid, albeit in a parish on Manhattan's Upper East Side, Faith knew all about the stress Christmas brought. It was not simply because of the increase in the number of church services—or the lack of private family time (a year-round dilemma for the Fairchilds particularly)—but the problems that surfaced as lonely people compared their lives to television specials, and harried parents tried to combine work and keeping their offspring calm at home under the barrage of holiday ads—the have-to-have Tickle Me Elmos.

Stress, they'd told each other. That was the trouble. They promised each other some time off in January. Tom swigged Maalox and crunched Tums. Then the pains moved to his back, and one bright winter morning complete with blue sky and a dusting of snow like confectioner's sugar, Faith got a call from Emerson Hospital. Her husband was in the emergency ward.

It was pancreatitis, and the sight of him hooked up to an IV, pale as Marley's ghost, was almost more than she could bear. He tried for a grin, but it turned into a grimace. Their doctor was reassuring in that oxymoronic way doctors employ. Lucky to have caught it—but. Sound metabolism—but. So long as he watched for symptoms, he'd be better than ever—probably. They'd have to keep him for a while, and he'd have to take it easy for a while. So, forget about work for at least a month. Just one of those things.

When he'd said that, Faith had had to stop herself from retorting, "Hey, we're not talking about a trip to the moon on gossamer wings! Is my husband going to be all right or not?"

Yes, Tom was the best present. She'd been stunned by his illness. Tom was the picture of health, one of those perennially big, hungry boys whose tall, rangy frame burned calories as fast as their woodstove consumed logs. At the thought, she got up to add a few more to the sturdy Vermont Castings Defiant model—she liked the name: "Take that, Cold!" They didn't really need it, since they'd put in a furnace when they'd remodeled the house several summers ago. But the crackling birch smelled heavenly and filled the room with the kind of warmth no furnace could duplicate. She'd been opposed to putting one in—why spend the money when they would never be on Sanpere Island in the wintertime? She'd suspected it was Tom's idea of the proverbial thin end of the wedge. He'd spend every vacation on Sanpere if he could. While Faith loved the island too, there were others called Saint Barts and Mustique that beckoned more seductively to her in cold weather.

But here they were. Thank God. It was, of course, where Tom wanted to recuperate, and it had been perfect. The days they'd been here and the days that stretched out ahead filled with nothing more taxing than the *New York Times* Saturday crossword puzzle and the Audubon Christmas Bird Count made her slightly giddy with relief. Tom would be fine, better than ever. The words had become a kind of mantra she repeated to herself whenever her husband looked tired or she thought there was a new crease on his forehead.

Outside, Christmas day was clear and cold. The tide was coming in. It would be high at noon. After stoking the fire, she walked over to the large floor-to-ceiling windows that stretched across the front of the room—living room and kitchen combined.

There were Christmas trees of all sizes growing outside on either side of the shore frontage. The rocks in the cove, exposed at low tide, were glistening like tinsel as the water lapped over them. Inside the house, a small, living tree stood in a tub. Twinkling with the tiny white lights they'd brought, it was trimmed with ornaments they'd made from pinecones and clam and mussel shells. The only thing Faith had brought from home was the exquisite Gladys Boalt Treetop Angel figure Tom had given her their first Christmas together. She always put it on the top of the tree even before they put the lights on—that tedious job. The angel had become a kind of talisman, and Faith promised herself that no tree they'd ever have would be without it. The angel's deftly painted smile looked enigmatic this morning—or perhaps it was Faith's interpretation.

Last year had been a particularly hectic one both at the parish and her catering company. Gazing out at the scene in front of her, she thought what a gift it was to know you could walk away. Turn everything over to someone else—her assistant, Niki Constantine; Tom's associate minister; the divinity school intern; and the vestry. She never wanted the reason for all this to happen again—she planned that Tom and she would go gently into that good night someday far in the future, preferably at the same time; she couldn't bear to think of life without him. But now that he was on the mend, she knew she would always treasure this time, and she was glad of it.

The Christmas season on Sanpere Island was similar only in the barest outlines to Christmas in Aleford, one of Boston's western suburbs, or New York City—the standard by which Faith gauged most things. Holiday decorations, the guy in the red suit, Jesus, Mary, and Joseph, and presents were accounted for in all three places. In Aleford, people put up wreaths, maybe strung a few lights on their bushes; but in Sanpere yards were filled with snowmen, reindeer, elves, and Santa, of course. Colored lights outlined every house, glowing "icicles" dripped from the roofs, and even more wattage lit up the trees. Faith knew there was a contest each year for "Best Holiday Display," but she'd never suspected the contestants would rival Rockefeller Center.

In Granville center, the merchants had given over their windows to the season. The photo studio, a fixture for at least two generations, always featured a gingerbread village made by the island's kindergarten class. A local artist had created a nativity scene in another store, and a life-size Santa stood on the roof of the bank. But the biggest difference was that Down East in Penobscot Bay, Santa arrived via lobster boat. Faith had taken the kids to the town pier in Granville to greet him along with most of the island—population 3,134 in the winter. They'd cheered Santa ashore and joined the crowd for cocoa and cookies in the Grange Hall. With no school the next day for the children and all the boats out of the water for the fishermen, the evening took on a leisurely character. It was only the women, Faith had noted, who had that "to-do list" look.

She turned away from the window and thought happily about hers—nonexistent.

"Something smells wonderful, darling," Tom said.

"It will be a while. I'm steaming a wild mushroom flan to go with the game hens. Why don't I heat up some of that potato leek soup from yesterday to tide you over?" Tom's meals had progressed from clear liquids to pureed solids to almost normal fare, but they weren't sitting down to a goose or any of the other Yuletide treats Faith usually made. Much too heavy for now.

"A cup of the soup sounds great," he said.

"Coming up. I'll have some too. Kids, Dad and I are having soup. Do you want some—or a sandwich?"

Ben's head came slowly up from the intricate directions. When he was younger, Faith had tried to help him with the more advanced Legos he'd received as gifts and quickly realized she'd have more luck trying to assemble a cyclotron from her kitchen implements.

"Sure, PB and J is fine. Thanks, Mom."

"I'll make my own." Amy slid off the stool and went toward the fridge. She had a more adventure-some palate than her brother—she'd eat oysters for instance—and Faith watched in amusement as the small, towheaded figure pulled out some sharp cheddar cheese and Major Grey's chutney.

Faith had just finished delivering lunch and was about to eat her own when the phone rang.

"It must be Granny and Grandpa!" Ben was up like a flash. Tom's parents would be the first to call. Hers would still be involved with church obligations.

"Just a minute," she heard him say. It must not be her in-laws. "I'll get her. Oh, Merry Christmas." Ben set the phone down and said, "It's for you, Mom." He hunched his shoulders and raised his arms. Not somebody whose voice he recognized.

"I'm so sorry to bother you. You must be in the midst of dinner, or getting it ready. It's Mary Bethany, Faith."

"We're not doing a thing, Mary." She wondered why Mary was calling. They weren't close friends. In fact, it was her impression that Mary didn't have many—or any—close friends. The older woman lived by herself on her family farm, raising goats and some vegetables and making superlative goat cheese. The cheese had been their point of contact. Tasting some at a friend's house, Faith had tracked Mary down. Over the last few summers, she'd helped Mary with some new recipes—herbed chèvre, in particular—and encouraged her to market her cheeses more widely. When they'd arrived last week, Faith had stopped by to get some of the plain chèvre for Tom, and Mary had been very sympathetic about his illness—and comforting. "One of the Sanfords had the very same thing and was back hauling traps before the season ended." She'd also pressed various rose hip concoctions on Faith, swearing that they could cure everything from "a sprained ankle to a broken heart." This was the way Mary spoke—slightly quirky and always direct. Mary was a reader. Books were stacked all over the parts of the house Faith had seen, and she was sure the rest looked the same. The two women often exchanged titles and sometimes the books themselves. Faith had become fond of Mary and wondered what her story was. Didn't she need something, or rather someone, besides her books and her goats? Had she had it and lost it? Faith realized that the woman was probably alone today and promptly invited her to join them.

"We're eating lightly, because of Tom, but we'd love to have you with us," she said.

"That's very sweet of you, but I'm afraid I can't get away."

"Oh, Mary, the goats will be all right for a few hours," Faith said. It suddenly seemed important that she join them. Faith didn't like the idea of Mary all by herself in that isolated house on Christmas. Mary had told Faith that Nubian goats were very needy and got upset if they were left for very long. It apparently affected their milk. "I should really have started with a Swiss breed, something like White Saanens, much more placid," she'd told Faith. "But my first two were Nubians and here I am."

"It's not the goats," Mary said. "It's, well, it's something else. Faith, I know this is a lot to ask, but is there any way you could come over here for a little while?"

Startled, Faith heard herself answer, "Of course. When would you like me?"

"As soon as possible," Mary said, hanging up.

Faith hung up too, thinking how human the

goat in the background had sounded. Almost like a baby crying.

Mary Bethany had not slept since she'd found Christopher in her barn. At first, she'd determinedly blocked out all thoughts of what to do except take care of his immediate needs. She changed his wet diaper and burst out laughing as he sprayed her before she could get the new one on. His skin was softer than any kid's fleece. Soft—everything about him was soft from the top of his head to the soles of his feet. How could finger- and toenails be so small, so perfect? He curled his fist around her finger and made that soft mewling sound again. So different from her demanding nannies. So different from the cries of enraged infants she'd occasionally heard in the aisles of the Harborside Market.

Lacking any alternative, she had filled one of the bottles with goat's milk, warmed it, and watched in delight as he greedily sucked it dry. Mary prided herself not only on her cheese but also on her milk. It was always sweet and fresh. Two lactose-intolerant customers swore they couldn't tell the difference from cow's milk, as if that were the standard. Cow's milk—Mary thought it should be the other way around. She would never have taken up with cows. Much too bovine. No personality.

It was only when Christopher had once again fallen asleep—as she rocked him gently in the chair her mother must have rocked her in—that Mary began to consider her alternatives. Happily, calling the authorities was not a choice. There were no authorities to call. There were no police on Sanpere, just occasional patrols by the county sheriff. She was happy about this for several reasons, first and foremost being an innate disinclination to "open up a can of worms." They'd bring in social workers and put Christopher in a foster home, everything his mother was clearly trying to avoid by leaving him in Mary's barn. Mary had no idea who the woman could possibly be, but she did know one thing: Christopher's mother had chosen Mary, and she had chosen her because she thought Christopher was in danger. The baby was a trust, a sacred trust, and Mary Bethany was not going to betray that. Let it be according to her wish.

But what to do? Even though she rarely saw other people—only at the bank, the market, or if she happened to be in the shed when they came to buy cheese or milk—there was no way she could pass the baby off as her own. Besides the lack of any physical evidence—Mary had always been as slender as a reed—the notion of Mary with a lover would be greeted with not only skepticism but derision. She could hear them now: "Mary Bethany pregnant? Maybe by one of her goats."

Mary had been born on the island, but the Bethanys were from away. Her parents had come to Sanpere when her father got a job at the shipyard as a welder after the war. Her mother's family had come from Italy and endowed Mary with the dark hair and Mediterranean features that she shared with others on Sanpere. But their looks had come down from the Italian stonecutters who had arrived in the late-nineteenth and early-twentieth centuries to work in the now abandoned granite quarries. Mary's grandparents had landed in New York and worked in the garment business—the wrong kind of Italians for Sanpere. True, Mary's father's family were Mainers, but from the north, Aroostock County—potato farmers. They weren't fishermen. Her father had learned his trade in the service, met her mother, Anne, at a USO dance, and when the war was over they'd ended up on Sanpere not for any particular reason, but because people have to end up somewhere.

Without the kinship network that was as essential and basic to Sanpere as the aquifer and ledges the entire island rested on, Mary and her older sister, Martha, were always viewed as outsiders. Martha, a bossy big sister, had left as soon as she turned sixteen, married at eighteen, and lived in New Hampshire with what was now a growing brood of grandchildren. Mary had stayed. Someone had had to take care of their elderly parents— the sisters had been late children. Maybe if she had been more outgoing, more self-confident like Martha, she would have fit into island life better—or had the guts to leave, parents or no parents. But she had been a shy child, preferring her animals to any human playmates and books to everything animate or inanimate. Her father had died first, but the farm was paid for by then and they'd had enough to get by, especially after Mary started running a small B and B during the summer months to pay the mounting shorefront taxes. Her mother had taken her father's death as a personal affront and after several years of intense anger joined him, presumably to give him what for. That had been ten years ago.

Mary was alone. There was no lover past, present, or future. When she considered the complications love presented—gleaned from her reading and from observing those around her—she was usually glad to have been spared the bother. But it did mean she couldn't pass the baby off as hers.

Gradually, as the sky lightened, she had come up with a plan. Easy enough to say that Christopher

was her grandnephew, that his mother wasn't well
and couldn't take care of him. Although Martha
hadn't been on the island since her mother's funeral, it was well known that she had had ten children herself and that those ten had been equally
fruitful and multiplied. Mary invented a rich tale
of a young niece with three children already, abandoned by her good-for-nothing cheater of a husband, driving through the night to leave the baby
after calling her aunt in desperation. She'd tell
her neighbor Arlene, asking her to pick up some
clothes and other things the next time she went off
island to Ellsworth. "She was so upset, I'm surprised she remembered to bring little Christopher,"
Mary rehearsed. Arlene had two grandchildren she
thought hung the moon. She brought them to play
with the goats when they visited every August.
Arlene would be a big help. And since she also had
a big mouth, Mary wouldn't have to tell the story
to anyone else.

    That settled, Mary had turned her thoughts to
the rest of the plan. And the rest of the plan had
meant calling Faith Fairchild. She watched the sun
come up and waited for the right time.

Faith knocked on Mary's back door. No one used
front doors on Sanpere—or anywhere else in New

England to Faith's knowledge. It was a mystery why they bothered putting them on houses at all. Using Mary's front door was also complicated by the tangle of lilac and rosebushes that had grown up over the granite stoop.

Mary opened the door and slipped out. Faith was puzzled. From the urgency in Mary's voice, she had expected to be ushered immediately in and told whatever Mary thought was important enough to pull someone away from hearth and home on Christmas day. The goats? It had to be the goats. Mary didn't have anything else to worry about. Or, Faith thought with sudden apprehension, it might be Mary herself. This must be it. She was ill. Cancer. She had cancer.

"Faith, I don't know how to put this any other way, but I want to tell you a secret."

Faith felt relief and anticipation in equal measure. She loved secrets.

"But I have to have your absolute word that you won't tell anyone else. Not even your husband."

Husbands were exempt from the not-telling-secrets rule, but maybe Mary didn't know that, not having one herself. "You know, Tom's a minister," she said. "He'd keep anything you tell me totally confidential. He has to or they take away his collar or robes or something."

Mary folded her arms across her chest. She was the kind of woman who looks so ordinary that you feel you must know her or at least have seen her before. The gesture and the current expression on her face transformed her. This was a woman you'd remember.

"No Tom. If you can't agree, I can't tell you." She paused. "And I'm sorry I called you out all this way for nothing." Mary's farm backed onto Eggemoggin Reach. By water, or as the gull flies, it wasn't far from the Fairchilds'. By land, it took a good fifteen minutes.

"It's not a crime or anything like that, is it? I mean of course you haven't murdered anyone." Faith thought she'd better ask. It was no never mind to her, but Tom tended to take a dim view of her involvement in these things.

"No crime has been committed to my knowledge," Mary said firmly. "But you don't have to agree. Go into the shed. There's some fresh cheese. Take one home with you for your trouble."

"Oh, Mary, of course I agree. You have my word." Instinctively Faith put out her hand, and Mary shook it, opening the door wider.

Faith stepped into the kitchen, thinking they should have mixed spit or pricked their fingers with a safety pin. But she didn't think for long; she simply reacted and was on her knees by the basket instantly. The baby was wide-awake; his dark eyes shone up at her and his mouth curved in what was definitely a smile. They weren't supposed to do this until they were older, but both of Faith's babies had smiled from birth—and recognized her face, despite what the experts said.

"Where on earth did this beautiful baby come from?"

"I found him in the barn last night when I went to do the milking. His name is Christopher."

"In the barn! Christopher! Was he in the manger? Any visits from angels lately?" It was too much.

Mary grinned. "And I'm a virgin too. You can hold him if you want. He's a hungry little fellow and I was just going to warm a bottle."

Faith was only too happy to comply. She adored babies, especially other people's at this point in her life.

"Sit down and I'll tell you everything I know, which is not much. And I'll tell you why I wanted you to come."

Faith called Tom and told him Mary's story— literally Mary's story—the one fabricated for public consumption. She wanted him to take the flan out of the oven and asked if he'd mind her staying for another thirty minutes or so. Since he was almost asleep, Ben still involved with his Legos, and Amy gathering more pinecones, Tom thought she could be spared.

Mary continued her explanation.

"I can't involve anyone on the island. It would be too dangerous for the baby. His mother obviously brought him here because she knew how isolated it is—still there is the bridge and word could spread to the mainland easy enough."

The Sanpere Bridge across Eggemoggin Reach connecting the island to the mainland had been a WPA project, a graceful suspension bridge that looked from a distance as if a particularly talented child had constructed it from an Erector set. For many on the island, it was still a bone of contention. (Joe Sanford, age ninety, had never been across. "Never had a reason. Everything I need is here.") But others found it pretty handy, especially before the Island Medical Center was built and the closest health care was in Blue Hill. A new generation of bridge haters had recently sprung up as wealthy off islanders began to build second homes similar to Newport's "cottages." These people wanted to preserve Sanpere in aspic, in other words, "the last person across always wants to pull up the bridge behind him."

Mary was right not to involve anyone on Sanpere, even with a blood oath. There were no secrets
on the island, and the bridge made sure they traveled.

"But I can't find his mother by myself. Aside
from taking care of him, I can't—"

Faith finished for her. "Leave the nannies. So,
very fortunately, I'm here for a while."

Mary looked a bit embarrassed. "I'd heard about
that business with the real estate man who was
found murdered by the lighthouse and how you figured out who did it." Several summers ago, Faith
had found a corpse while walking along the shore
near Sanpere's lighthouse. The death appeared to
be accidental, then more "accidents" occurred until
Faith untangled the threads leading to the killer.

"This isn't like that," Mary said, "but I thought
you might be able to help me find out who his
mother is and why she left him here."

Faith studied Mary's face. It was a plain, pleasant face, rather flat and with the look of one of
those antique Dutch wooden dolls. But not today.
Faith had never seen Mary look so excited. Not
even when one of her does had quintuplets the
spring before last.

"But why? Why do you want to find her? To give
the baby back?"

Mary was horrified. "Oh no, not to give him back."

"Then why don't you just keep him? Your little grandnephew."

Mary had been through this the night before many times. Just as she had debated back and forth whether to call Faith. She had changed her mind about the latter so many times that she still wasn't completely sure that it was the real Faith in front of her or the one she had conjured up and talked to during the wee hours.

"I think she's in trouble. She must be in trouble; otherwise she wouldn't have left him here. And I feel that I have to find her. It's hard to explain. It just doesn't seem fair to Christopher either, to have her simply disappear. What would I tell him when he was older? I'd have to tell him. Too horrible to find out when he's grown that everything he thought was real wasn't."

"Yes, you'd have to tell him and yes, we have to find her."

Faith had thought this was what Mary would say. It was what she herself would do. Besides, Mary would be in a precarious legal position. They hadn't mentioned it, but they both knew it. There hadn't been any birth certificate in the basket—or adoption papers.

What Faith didn't ask Mary—and wouldn't—was: How will you feel if she wants him back? She stood up abruptly. "Okay, what can we figure out from this stuff?" Faith had spread the contents of the baby's basket on the enamel-topped kitchen table. Mary's kitchen, circa 1949, was currently back in vogue. Unchanged, as if it had been transported intact like Julia Child's to the Smithsonian, it would cost more than all the goat cheese Mary could sell in her lifetime. Many, many more dollars than those stuck in the Hellmann's mayonnaise jar left so trustingly on top of the refrigerator in the shed.

The basket itself, although a roomy one, was unremarkable. You saw stacks of them at Pier 1—or rummage sales. Baskets and mugs—that was what future archaeologists would find in our middens, Faith thought.

Faith picked up the sleepers one at a time. There were three of them. Then she examined the snowsuit.

"Pretty generic. Not Baby Dior or Hanna Andersson—or even Baby Gap. Therefore, we're not talking money here, although"—Faith gestured to the stacks of bills—"there's certainly money here. The clothes are new, but not recognizable brands, so she could have picked them up anywhere. The only thing they tell us is that she didn't buy used baby clothes or get them passed down to her."

"So, no other children and no family involved. And she wanted brand-new clothes for Christopher."

Faith nodded. "She does have a computer, though—or access to one."

"How can you tell?" Mary asked curiously.

"The printing is a computer printout. Not typed on a typewriter. Much smoother."

"I thought the wording of the note might mean something," Mary said, picking it up. "Not the 'Keep him safe' part, although since she wrote that first I'm sure it means she thinks or knows he's in danger—but the 'Raise him to be a good man' part. Sounds like she hasn't had much luck there—or worse."

"Definitely worse," Faith agreed. "I'd guess Christopher's father is not her idea of a model father figure. Maybe not her own father either. Or it could be her father who is the ideal, but then why wouldn't she go to him for help, or her mother for that matter?"

"Maybe both passed away?" Mary picked up the note. "She didn't sign it. Just stopped writing. Do you think she was interrupted, or was it that she couldn't think of any way to finish it?"

"Either or neither," said Faith. "But she has to be

someone you know, Mary. Your name was on the basket and the letter. Plus she knew you had a barn and kept goats—knew your routine, that you'd be out to milk them at six. She wasn't taking any chances that the baby wouldn't be found quickly."

"I've been going through all this since I found him, believe me. And I can't think who she could be."

Faith put the clothes down.

"What else? The afghan—exquisitely hand-made. But it doesn't tell us anything except she's a good crocheter or went to some kind of fair."

"My neighbor Arlene could read it like a book. Tell us where the yarn came from, who does that kind of stitch—at least on the island. Maybe we can think of a way to show it to her without having her get suspicious."

"The cloth diapers suggest she's pretty green."

"You mean inexperienced?" Mary asked.

Faith laughed. "No, as in environmentally friendly, eco-aware. No disposables, but washable cloth diapers."

"A tree hugger. Well, I'm with her on that one. Easy enough to wash diapers."

"Wait and see. The jury's still out on whether you use more resources washing the cloth ones than those other diapers consume. And they do cut down on diaper rash. I know how much time you spend tending your herd, but babies are even more work than your nannies."

Noting Mary's skeptical expression, Faith gave a little smile and continued speculating. "Computer access, environmentalist, young—that's a logical presumption—and can't keep her baby. This all says 'student' to me."

Faith was feeling quite Holmesian and wished there had been a bit more evidence such as cigar ash or mud from a shoe, so she could say that the young woman had been in Morocco recently, purchasing smokes at a stall in the bazaar from a red-haired man with a limp named Abdul. Hair!

"Are there any strands of hair on the blanket—or on Christopher himself?"

"How stupid. There was one and I forgot to mention it. It's dark like mine, or like mine used to be." Mary was starting to go gray. "It's not mine, though, because it's long. Not Christopher's either, but the same color." Mary's hair was sensibly short. Faith knew she cut the bangs herself and exchanged cheese for a trim from one of her customers who worked over on the mainland at Hair Extraordinaire.

"Well, we've certainly narrowed it down. A young female student with long dark hair," Faith said dejectedly.

"It does seem impossible," Mary agreed.

But Faith was nowhere near giving up. "Don't say that. We've barely scratched the surface. What about the money? Where would a student come up with this kind of money? Have you counted it?"

Mary looked very serious. "There's fifty thousand dollars in one-hundred-dollar bills."

"Good Lord! That much? As soon as I leave, you have to hide it. You should have done it already."

Mary nodded in agreement. "I have the perfect place. I'm going to—"

"Don't tell me. I don't know why, but I think it's better if just one of us knows."

"A student," Mary mused. "Unless she comes from a very rich family with ready access to a trust fund—and then maybe she would have bought more expensive baby clothes—there's only one thing I can think of that brings in that kind of money for someone her age."

"Drugs?" Faith had been thinking the same thing since she'd first seen the stacks of bills.

"There's been a lot in the news about it, and I guess you've heard about all the break-ins on the island. They're pretty sure they're looking for stuff to sell for drugs. Plus it's not just marijuana, but heroin and prescription drugs."

Faith had heard about the break-ins. Thirty in

September alone, all during the daytime and all summer places closed for the winter. They'd used a crowbar to pry open doors, taking anything of value plus canned goods, clothing, and from one cottage, an iron. That had made her think a woman must be involved, either directly or indirectly—"Honey, could you pick up an iron; this one is on the fritz"—or an extremely anal-retentive male.

"This would explain why she wrote about keeping Christopher safe. If his mother is involved with drug dealers, they wouldn't want a baby around," Mary said.

Or his mother might be dealing herself, Faith thought.

"The paper bag is another clue," she said. "It's not from a Hannaford or any other chain. Must be a pretty small mom-and-pop operation. The name, 'Sammy's 24 Hour Store,' looks hand stamped. Get your phone books, Mary, and let's see if we can find it."

Mary put Christopher back in his basket and handed Faith the yellow pages for Hancock and Penobscot Counties, the only phone books she had. She also gave her the B and B register from last summer.

"I have to check on the goats. I've been so wrapped up in Christopher, I've been neglecting them and they're such social creatures. They just have me since my dog died last spring and the wild goose that had made a nest in their pen took off with her goslings once they were old enough to fly."

Faith had always been impressed by the way Mary cared for her herd, and other animals.

"I have to make sure no wind is getting through any chinks in the boards. The nannies don't mind lower temperatures or snow, but they sure hate drafts."

When she returned, Faith looked smug. "Bingo! Or I should say 'Orono.'"

"And," Mary said, "since that's where the big UMaine campus is, we're probably right about the student part."

"I wish I could stay longer," Faith said. "But call me if you find out anything more—or you need help with Christopher. I didn't look at the register, so maybe you can go over it and see if anything pops out at you."

After giving Christopher's chubby little cheeks one last kiss, Faith left. Back in the rocker, Mary had the baby in her arms again, swaddled tightly in a flannel blanket she'd made by cutting a larger one up. She looked so happy, Faith almost wept. There were other reasons for tears as well. She hoped Mary would hide the money right away, and not in her freezer or in her underwear drawer, because whoever it belonged to—and Faith had a strong feeling it wasn't the baby's mother—wouldn't waste any time looking for it. Looking for it all over the great state of Maine.

Miriam Carpenter sat staring at the blue book in front of her. Her professor had offered her the chance to come in and take the exam today, the day after Christmas, when Miriam had called her office and told her she was too sick to take it during the regular schedule. Having a baby was not an illness, but Miriam's labor pains had coincided with Anthropology 106's final exam. As she looked at the questions again, she wondered if Professor Greene had suspected anything. Miriam was tall and big boned. It had not been hard to conceal her condition under the many layers of clothing necessary in Maine as the days grew shorter—and colder. Yet, during the last few classes, the professor seemed to be eyeing Miriam in a speculative manner, and twice she had asked her how she was doing in what Miriam thought was a pointed way. But then she had always been a little paranoid. Or maybe it was only lately. But she was definitely a little—make that more than a little—paranoid now.

"You can take a makeup exam," Professor

Greene had said. "And if you could possibly do it before the first of the year, I won't even have to give you an incomplete. You've done so well this semester, it would be a shame to skip the exam and lower your grade. But you must be going away for the break, home for Christmas."

"No, I'm not going home for Christmas. I'm Jewish and, well, I'm not going home. I live off campus, so I'll be around," Miriam had told her. The professor had suggested the twenty-sixth, and here she was.

No, Miriam wasn't going home for the holidays, or any other days.

She stared at the first essay question. "Discuss the roots and implications of gender-motivated infanticide past and present. You may select one society or several upon which to focus."

Infanticide. That had never been an option. Male or female. As soon as she knew she was pregnant, she knew she would have the baby. Knew she would have it, because she was going to stop thinking about it. It wasn't that she was in denial so much as she was simply on a kind of all-encompassing autopilot.

Bruce hadn't found out until last week. They'd stopped having sex in August when he'd started bringing Tammy around. He was so high most of the time that even before, sex hadn't played a big part in their relationship. What had? The drugs to start with. She'd never felt so free, so happy. Even coming down, she'd never gotten depressed or angry the way Bruce did. But gradually, it was enough just to be around drugs and the people doing them. Mellow folks, good folks. Folks who smiled when they saw her. Folks who cared about her—at least when they were using. She found she didn't need the drugs, which was a good thing, because somebody had to keep house—and keep the money straight. Somebody had to let kids on campus know where they could go. Somebody had to deal with the suppliers when Bruce was too wasted. She had been the responsible one. ("Baby, I don't know what I'd do without you.") She hadn't needed drugs, just Bruce.

She'd come to a party at his apartment at the end of her freshman year and stayed. He looked like Kurt Cobain, or that's what somebody had said when he walked into the living room, leaving the group shooting up in the kitchen. He'd grinned that big, lazy grin and walked straight up to her. "Hey, pretty lady, where have you been all my life?"

It had been good. She was sure it had been good. Then one night he walked out of the kitchen into the living room and Tammy was there. Miriam heard him say the same words. She'd learned Bruce relied on a few stock phrases in life and this was one. Another was "If you're not part of the problem, you're an asshole."

Tammy took over the sex part, and Miriam was left to do everything else, which was mainly cleaning the apartment after the parties, because even though Bruce was trying to get straight and mostly succeeding, the parties never stopped. He was straight when she'd told him about the baby.

Her hand automatically went to her neck. She'd wound a long scarf over the turtleneck and would have added a cowl if she'd had one to be sure the necklace of bruise marks his fingers had left stayed hidden. She had thought he would choke her to death and struggled desperately, pulling at his hands, fighting for breath. They'd crashed to the floor, knocking over a lamp. The bulb had exploded and Tammy had come in. Would he have killed her if Tammy hadn't been there? She'd taken in the scene dreamily—she was always pretty wasted—and said, "Leave her alone. She's not worth it."

They'd left her on the floor. She hadn't moved from the protective fetal position she'd rolled into once he'd stood up. She'd assumed he would kick her, but he didn't.

"Get rid of it. If it's here when I get back I'll kill both of you."

He was leaving for Canada, a major score, and Tammy was going with him. They were going to spend Christmas there.

Miriam opened the blue book and started writing. China was the obvious choice, but she didn't want to be obvious.

"The cruel Arctic climate of the aboriginal Inuit reduced the male population significantly as they pursued their traditional hunting and fishing roles, forcing the . . ."

She wrote furiously for a while, and then paused. What if her parents had known the sex of the child they were going to have before she'd been born?

She wouldn't be here.

How old was she when she'd first heard her father say to her mother, "You're worthless. Completely worthless. You couldn't even give me a son," in that flat, cold voice he used before he would start the rest? Not caring that Miriam was in the doorway—was she six? Or seven?—and could see it all. Could hear it all—her mother's cries.

Miriam shook her head to force the thought to the back of her mind with the rest of the things she didn't want to think about. It was getting pretty crowded in there.

Her father had answered the phone when she'd called after the baby was born. It had been an easy delivery. She could have done it herself, she realized afterward, but she had been frightened at the thought of being alone and had gotten a name. The woman believed in home births and said she was a midwife. Maybe she was. But it had been all right. She'd insisted Miriam stay overnight and brought her cups of green tea. During the delivery she kept lighting fragrant candles and playing that waterfall kind of New Age music that Miriam's yoga teacher in high school had liked so much. It was something they were trying that year, letting students take yoga instead of field hockey or soccer. There were only three kids in the class. Three kids who didn't have to worry about peer pressure, because they didn't have any peers.

The midwife had given Miriam a beautiful baby blanket and Miriam had given her $1,000.

Her father was the only person she could think of to call. She'd just had a baby; shouldn't she call someone? She'd called him last year to tell him she was in school, and he had told her not to come to him for money. It had been a pretty short conversation. She'd heard her stepmother in the background talking rapidly, as usual. Brenda was a very high-maintenance lady. Daniel Carpenter made a good living selling real estate in the Portland area, but Brenda, who was some unspecified number of years younger, decorated their house and herself in extravagantly perfect taste—according to her—and went through money almost as fast as she talked.

"Hi, Dad, it's Miriam," she'd said.

"Yes?"

"Well, I just, I guess I just wanted to say hi and . . ."

She heard Brenda ask, "Who is it, Dan?"

"It's Miriam." Her father hadn't bothered to turn away from the receiver.

"What does she want?"

"I don't know yet. What do you want, Miriam?"

What she had wanted at that moment was to hang up, but she hadn't. She'd gotten mad. Why did her mother have to die the way she did, slipping determinedly into a half world of bourbon and despair before Miriam could grow up enough to take care of her—or live without her? And why did her father have to marry Brenda of all people, petite, a perfect size four? Even at age thirteen, Miriam had felt like one of Swift's Brobdingnagians whenever they were in the same room, which wasn't often.

"I don't want anything. I called to tell you you're a grandfather—a bouncing baby boy—and you can tell Brenda she's a grandmother." Miriam had added the last bit with calculated cruelty. Brenda would not like to be a grandmother.

"I assume your child is a bastard; like mother, like daughter," her father had said, then Miriam had heard Brenda's voice closer to the phone, "Child, what child? Miriam's had a baby? Boy or girl? Find out where she is."

It had been those last words that had caused a prickle of fear to run down Miriam's spine. Not the ones about her mother. She knew she was the reason for the marriage or, as her father called it, the entrapment. No, it was Brenda's sudden interest in Miriam's whereabouts that had made her feel more nauseated than her morning sickness ever had.

"Well, good-bye then. I've got to go."

"Wait. I need to know where—"

Miriam had hung up before he finished the sentence.

She had thought she'd keep Christopher with her until New Year's, which was when Bruce had said he'd be back. But she had been foolhardy to bring the baby back to the apartment—Bruce constantly changed his mind, and he could arrive any minute.

With her father's words echoing in her ears, she'd decided to head for the coast right then, the plan from the beginning. For some reason Brenda wanted the baby. They'd never had one of their own—was it because they couldn't? Miriam had always assumed they didn't want a child, but maybe they did. Or Brenda did. The ultimate soccer mom. Or a little one as the ultimate accessory, a step beyond a bichon frise? In a weird turn of events, she had to keep Christopher away from both his grandfather and his father—one because he wanted the baby, one because he didn't. And in their own way, each would murder the child.

Her essay came into focus and the phone conversation faded. Christopher was safe.

It was Boxing Day, and Faith was back in Mary's kitchen. Ben and Amy had been invited to spend the afternoon with friends they'd made at the island day camp they attended during the summer. Tom had urged Faith to go help Mary. He would enjoy the solitude—maybe do some writing—and when she returned they'd walk to The Point. Every day he felt stronger.

Mary had gone over her B and B register. "There were only three couples who could possibly fill the bill—and two mentioned their pregnancies," she said. "The only single women I had were a young woman from Norway who was 'seeing America' for the summer and a cousin of the Marshalls they didn't have room for. She was in her sixties, so we can cross her off the list. And it would seem unlikely that a Norwegian girl would come all this way to leave me her baby, although the whole thing is so unlikely perhaps we'd better not eliminate her."

"I think we can for now," Faith said. "But what about these couples, especially the two pregnant ones?"

"A first child for each. The Warrens live in Vermont—not that close—but the Tuttles were from Saco and up here vacationing. They're a possibility, although I can't see them giving their child up. They were looking forward to coming back next summer and every summer after that to watch little whoever play with the goats. The nannies are very sweet playmates, you know."

Faith did know. It occurred to Faith that someone looking for strong maternal instincts would only have had to watch Mary with her herd and listen to her talk about them to conclude she was a natural-born nurturer. Not only did Mary keep her goat house clean and dry—it looked like something from Carl Larsson's *A Farm*—but she also religiously tended to the nannies' every need from physical to psychological. All her goats had had their horn buds removed and Mary gently but firmly discouraged butting from the moment they were born.

She greeted each one by name starting with the queen, stroking and petting them several times a day. After the stress of breeding—and delivering— she read to them and even sang to them, as Faith discovered one day hearing a stirring rendition of "Seventy-Six Trombones" with accompanying bleats issuing from the barn. Their play yard was just that, with several cable spools courtesy of Bangor Hydro for the nannies to climb on. The pasture had a high electric fence, and Faith was pretty sure the Nubians were better fed than Mary, who seemed to exist on whey sweetened with honey (bartered for cheese), rose hips in various forms, and whatever vegetables the garden yielded fresh or put up. Maybe it wasn't such a bad diet; it was the thought of it that repelled Faith's taste buds.

Granted, her charges were ruminants, but if you were looking for "Mother of the Year," Mary was a contender.

"And the third couple? Who were they?"

"They were young. I started thinking about them right away last night when you said she might be a student. There was a University of Maine Black Bears bumper sticker on their truck. I don't know how they heard about me. You know I don't advertise, just that card at the market in the summer. They stayed a week, and he was gone all the time. Said he was helping a friend whose sternman was sick, but he didn't get up early enough for fishing and he came back late, six or seven o'clock. Then he'd take her off to get something to eat. She helped me with the goats and the garden. So much that I didn't want to charge them full price, but she insisted she'd just been having fun. That it was a vacation for her. Her name was Miriam. His was Bruce. She was the one who wrote in the book. Their last name was Singer and the address was in Calais. I've already checked directory information and there are no Miriam or Bruce Singers in Calais. No street by the name she listed either."

"How about Orono? Because of the bumper sticker—and the bag the money was in," Faith suggested.

"Thought of that too and same thing. And directory assistance didn't say the phone was unlisted."

"You don't ask for a phone number in the register?"

"No—I only started asking for a name and address this summer. Before, I'd leave a guest book for people to sign if they wanted to. I'd introduce myself when they got here and they would tell me who they were. Seemed enough. Nobody ever left without paying, but my cousin Elizabeth told me I should be keeping a record. That you never knew—and she was right, as usual."

"This is the one who lives out west? And gave you her goats when she moved?"

"That's Elizabeth. I was only a teenager. My sister was already gone and Elizabeth thought her two nannies would be company for me. Dora the First—this Dora is Dora the Second—lived to be twenty, but I lost the other one, Nora, when she was twelve."

Filing away the interesting notion of two Nubian goats as a substitute for human contact for further thought, Faith mentally thanked Elizabeth for the easier-to-grasp idea of a guest register and got back to work.

"All right. First let's see if we can eliminate the Tuttles from Saco. What could be more natural than for you to call and say you'd like to send some of that jelly of yours or whatever to congratulate them on the new baby? You know what I mean. Say how much you're looking forward to seeing them next summer."

"Do I have to? What if something went wrong with the pregnancy? I had a toxemic doe once. Oh, Faith, I don't think I could call up strangers, even strangers who have stayed here."

Mary was tough, but she was also shy. Faith sighed. "Give me the phone."

She dialed the number and a woman answered.

"Hello, may I speak to Mrs. Tuttle please?"

"Speaking."

"I'm a supporter of the Sanpere Chamber of Commerce and over the holidays we're trying to reach people who visited our island last summer to plan for next summer. Would you mind answering two quick questions?"

"Not at all. We had a lovely time and plan to return next summer."

"Well, that answers my first question, which was whether you had had a positive experience, and my second as well, would you return?"

Mrs. Tuttle laughed. "This is the easiest survey I've ever done."

"Could you tell me if you plan to return to the same accommodations as last year?"

"Why of course. It was ideal. Bethany Farm Bed and Breakfast. I really should have written to Mary. I'm glad you called. It's reminded me to get to it. We had a baby last month and she said to let her know. Little Cecilia will adore Mary's goats next summer."

"I'm sure she will. Thank you for your time."

Faith hung up. "Cross out the Tuttles."

"I don't know how you do it," Mary said.

After some baby feeding—and baby worship—Faith called the couple from Vermont just to be sure and reported that the Warren family now numbered four. Twins. She decided it wasn't necessary to call Norway and reassured Mary that since Faith hadn't actually said she was from the Chamber of Commerce, only a "supporter" of it, which she was—the Fairchilds contributed every year—no lies had been told or laws broken. Then she went back to her house.

Tom was ready for their walk, and Faith almost didn't answer the phone as they were leaving, but what with two small children of her own plus Mary and Christopher, there was no choice. It was Mary.

"I knew I was leaving something out! Miriam Singer had lovely, long dark hair, just like the strand on Christopher's blanket. She wore it in a braid down her back, but one day she washed it and sat out in the sun to let it dry. She looked, well, she looked like a Madonna."

I know you want to help Mary, sweetheart, but isn't there someone else who could go? Or why doesn't she leave the baby here and take our car? That old truck of hers barely makes it to Granville." The Reverend Fairchild was feeling better.

Emerging from the cocoon of his illness, he wanted to spread his wings—with his wife for company.

"There isn't anyone else. And unless she's taught one of the herd to drive, Mary won't go any farther than Blue Hill. I just want to get her the bare necessities—clothes, a Snugli to use when she's milking, diapers, bottles—you remember. The crib we borrowed from Pix for Amy and never gave back is still in the garage here and I want to take that over. I'll have to get some sheets, though. I want to do this for Mary. A belated Christmas present from us."

"Come here, gift o' mine," Tom said, reaching for his wife. Outside Ben and Amy were trying to make a snowman from the two inches of fluffy snow that had fallen early in the morning. Tom motioned toward the ceiling. "I thought this might be the perfect occasion for some quality adult time upstairs."

Faith hugged him hard. "What's that line about having 'world enough and time'? I know Marvell was addressing his coy mistress and I'm not being coy. There will be time—many times."

Tom kissed her, and in a voice suggesting slight regret but hope for Plan B, said, "Hey, why don't we all go? Maybe see a movie in Ellsworth?"

Faith had been deliberately vague about where

she was going. Orono was in a different direction from Ellsworth.

"You know you would hate it, and so would the kids. The after-Christmas sales bring out the beast in everyone and the stores will be packed, especially on a Saturday. I'll be back as soon as I can." She kissed him hard. A kiss full of promise. Promise of Plan A.

Tom held her closer. "I swear if I didn't know that Mary and her Nubian goats existed, I'd think you made the whole thing up so you could sneak out and meet your secret lover. Mary Bethany. Bethany— the village where that other Mary was born. A baby, Christopher, turning up at Christmas." He settled back, still with his arm around her. "I've always felt sorry for Mary—or rather Miriam, which is the Hebrew. She was as sorely tested as Job. Some sources put her age as young as thirteen when she became pregnant out of wedlock. The gospels don't tell us much about her, barely mentioning her by name, but it's not hard to imagine how the good people of Nazareth would have treated her."

Faith agreed. "I always thought it was a little mean of God to leave her on her own for so long while Joseph was off building houses. Here she is betrothed and all, picking out pottery patterns and getting more full with child by the day. She knew she was a virgin—but it took a while before it was all sorted out. I've always imagined her as a feisty lady. She had to be."

"Joseph stuck by her, though."

"Yes, I'll give him that—thanks to one of those convenient dreams people in the Bible always seem to have. But when it came time for the blessed event, why did it take so long for him to find someone to deliver the baby? Mary was on her own again in that stinky barn—or cave if you want to believe James—having the baby all by herself. But speaking of Marys, I have to go. The sooner I leave, the sooner I'll . . ."

"I know, I know. Say hi to your secret lover."

"Hi, lover."

Besides hitting the Bangor malls for baby things and driving to the 24 Hour Store in Orono, Faith didn't have a plan. If she found Miriam, she'd talk to the girl, make sure she knew what she was doing, and then what? Ask her where the fifty thousand dollars came from? Get her to sign some kind of papers, so Mary could adopt Christopher?

She decided to hit the malls first. Then with the car loaded, Faith headed north, away from Bangor to Orono. It wasn't far, and once there she only had to ask twice to find the convenience store.

As she had suspected, the store was a mom-and-pop operation, a cross between a market and a five-and-ten, only they were Dollar Stores now. Sammy's was located in a mixed residential/commercial area and had a little bit of everything from beef jerky to Rolex rip-offs and dusty plastic poinsettias, still on sale from last Christmas. There was no Sammy in evidence, unless the tired-looking older woman at the counter was named Samantha.

Faith picked up a slightly faded package of colored construction paper for Amy and an ancient balsa-wood model airplane kit for Ben. At the register, she added a Milky Way for Tom. She'd check the expiration date in the car. As the sale was rung up, she said, "I wonder if you might help me. I'm supposed to drop off a Christmas gift for a friend of mine. It's for her niece, who lives around here. I've misplaced the address, but the niece's name is Miriam. She's tall with long dark hair that she usually wears in a braid down her back. Do you by any chance know her?" Unless Miriam had stopped at the store on her way someplace else, she probably lived in the neighborhood.

"Sure, I know Miriam. Comes in here a lot. Always polite, not like some. She lives over there." The woman pointed across the street. "I saw her this morning, so she's probably home."

Faith's hunch had been correct. She looked through the window—obscured by HOLIDAY GREETINGS sprayed on by a liberal, but unsteady, hand—and saw a run-down house that had obviously been carved up into apartments for students fleeing dorm life—or just fleeing. She thanked the woman and walked slowly across the street.

The front door of the building swung open easily and she stepped onto a litter of junk mail. There were six mailboxes, each with several names. Some had been crossed out and new ones added above in tiny writing. Faith studied them as if they were the Rosetta Stone. She knew she wouldn't find "Miriam" or "Bruce Singer," but she wasn't finding anything remotely resembling them. No initials *M* or *B*. No *S*'s. When people put down false names, they usually stuck to their own initials. Or they chose a similar name, as in a similar occupation.

"Singer." No "Chanteuses" or "Vocalists"— what other synonyms were there? Preferably synonyms that made sense. She went back to the cards and searched again. And there it was. Apartment 4B. One word in minuscule writing: CARPENTER. The Carpenters. Karen Carpenter. "Singers." Miriam Singer; Miriam Carpenter. It was worth a try. Nothing else suggested itself. Maybe Miriam was into the 1970s—or tragic female singers. Faith pushed the buzzer. There was no answer. She pushed all the buzzers until someone let her in. After climbing the dark, narrow stairs, she knocked loudly on 4B's door for what seemed like ages before concluding that Christopher's mother wasn't home.

Miriam had turned in her exam, avoided Professor Greene's attempts to draw her into conversation, and spent the evening getting really, really drunk at a dive bar down the street. She hadn't had a drink since she'd discovered she was pregnant, and even before that all she had drunk were wine coolers and cold duck when Bruce was in a romantic mood. At least she was in her own bed in her own apartment, she thought when she woke up the next morning with a hangover the size of Texas. She stumbled across the street for some Diet Coke and aspirin. She planned to spend the day in bed. She was due. Somehow she had managed to take a full course load, finish all her papers, take a final, and have a baby in the last two weeks.

It wasn't until she was halfway into a *Buffy* rerun that the sickening thought hit her that of course her father knew where she was because he had caller ID. Getting a street address from a phone number was a piece of cake for a real estate agent like her father.

She had spoken to him when? Not yesterday. No, the night before. The twenty-fifth. But he hadn't shown up so far—or had he? Why had she let Bruce convince her to put the phone in her name? No, he hadn't convinced her. She had never questioned it. He had told her to do it, and she did.

Groaning, she pulled her jeans back on and went to the apartment across the hall. Ellen the Airhead opened the door. From the way she looked, her night had been even worse than Miriam's. They called her the "Airhead" not because she was spaced-out on drugs, but because she was very, very stupid. She *was* usually spaced-out on drugs too, though.

"Ellen, think hard. Did a man come looking for me recently? An older man. Tall with dark hair."

"Dark hair," Ellen repeated obediently.

Resisting the urge to shake her even sillier, Miriam said, "How about some coffee? Why don't I make us some coffee?"

"Sure." Ellen looked around her apartment, as if unsure where the kitchen was. Miriam pushed her in the right direction.

With a mug of instant she had no intention of drinking, Miriam led Ellen back over the previous few days and was rewarded for her patience with a flash of almost total recall on Ellen's part.

"He said he was your father." She hesitated.

"He is my father. It's okay. Then what did he say?"

"He was, like, looking for you and I go, I don't know where she is. Not Canada. Maybe on Sanpere Island with that goat lady."

"What!" Miriam screamed. "How do you know about Sanpere!"

"You told me." Ellen stuck out her lower lip. "You didn't say it was a big fuckin' secret. You told me all about the nice lady with the goats on Sanpere that you and Bruce stayed with last summer. Hey, you didn't drink your coffee?"

He had more than twenty-four hours on her, Miriam figured as she frantically tried to find someone with a car she could borrow. It had been easy Christmas eve. She had gone to a party on the other side of town and taken the keys from the drunkest person there.

She debated whether to call Mary Bethany, but she didn't want to alarm her. For all she knew, Mary might call the police, the county sheriff's office. There weren't any police on Sanpere, which was one of the reasons Miriam had picked it. That and Mary. Mary would take care of the baby. She'd raise him to be a good man. Miriam didn't care whether her son went to college, made money, or did anything other than raise goats. All she cared about was that he be as honest and kind as Mary Bethany was.

Miriam finally located a car and arranged to go get it from her friend Cindy. They'd met Miriam's first week of school. It seemed a long time ago and definitely another life.

Hastily, she threw some things in a knapsack. She was pretty sure Mary wouldn't be fooled by whatever story her father cooked up, but she needed to give her some sort of letter that would say Christopher was hers. That she was surrendering her parental rights to Mary. That would keep her father away. Mary could use some of the money for a lawyer if she had to.

Stupid, stupid, stupid. She blew a stray strand of hair out of her eyes angrily. How could she ever have called her father!

She was ready to go. Bruce hadn't been back. There was no beer in the fridge—or empties on the counter. Suddenly she looked at where she had been living for over a year—the stained and sagging couch, a few beanbag chairs, a coffee table scrounged from the trash. It was covered with white rings and cigarette burns. The place stank of stale air and more. The doorknob was greasy. She turned it and pulled the door open. Pulled it open and stepped back into the room.

"Hello, Miss Miriam. Glad to see you're finally home. We've been looking for you."

"For you—and the money."

Duane and Ralph, Bruce's local suppliers. Miriam let the knapsack slip from her shoulder. She let her whole body sag. Then she sprinted past them, slamming the door behind her, and ran out of the house into the street as fast as she could.

I'm sorry, but I don't operate my bed-and-breakfast during the off-season. They should have told you that at the market."

Mary had been startled by the sudden appearance of a big fancy car coming up the long dirt drive that led to her house from the main road, but not so startled that she hadn't quickly erased all evidence that a baby was living in the house. It wasn't hard. She had prepared herself for the possibility—the eventuality. She took Christopher himself out through the shed and across into the barn, placing him in one of the mangers well away from the goats. He was such a good baby, but he might cry, and if he did, the nannies would more than drown him out.

"I must have misunderstood. My name is Dan Carpenter, by the way. I own a real estate agency down in Portland and I'm up here to check out a property."

Mary's eyes narrowed. Skunks, that's what they were. The local agents had given up on her long ago, but there were new ones all the time. Telling her what she could get for waterfront on Eggemoggin Reach, what a genuine Down East saltwater farm would fetch. She knew what it would fetch. More skunks. Skunks who would have the farmhouse down in two minutes and put up some sort of hotel-looking place with a tennis court.

"I am not interested in selling my property, Mr. Carpenter. Good day." Mary started to close the door.

"No, wait. Please. I'm sorry. You've misunderstood me. I'm not interested in your property. I mean of course I'm always interested in property, but that's not why I'm here. I simply need a place to stay for the night."

"They should have sent you to Granville. There's a motel that stays open year-round there and I can't imagine they'd be full, even with the holidays." Mary started to close the door again.

But Dan Carpenter was very good at what he did. He was used to people trying to close doors in his face—and equally used to getting his foot in them. Finding Mary had been simple. He'd stopped at the market, bought a snack, and asked about a woman who ran a bed-and-breakfast at her goat farm. "That would be Mary Bethany," offered the teenager with a singularly repulsive Goth look who was minding the till. Dan had been in luck. Anyone older from the island would have either asked him what his business was that meant he had to stay the night or more likely, simply grunted, rung up his purchases, and taken his money.

"She won't let you stay, though. Isn't open now. Better go to the motel in Granville." The boy was a veritable hydrant of information.

But Dan had gone to Mary's after looking her address up in the phone book thoughtfully offered for free by the local island newspaper.

Dan Carpenter had cracked tougher nuts than Mary. "Please, I'm sorry to have troubled you, but could I call the motel? I don't want to drive all the way down there and find they haven't any room at the inn." He gave a little chuckle, presumably to show how very, very harmless and how very, very charming he was.

Mary opened the door grudgingly. "I'll call Patty and see. You sit here." She pointed to one of the kitchen chairs and turned to the phone on the wall.

"Did I hear a baby crying? Are your grandchildren visiting for the holidays?"

Instantly Mary swung around. "Those are my goats, mister. I don't have any grandchildren and there are no babies in this house. Now, why don't you take yourself down to Granville? I don't think I care to call Patty after all."

Dan Carpenter started walking toward Mary. She grabbed the phone again and he stopped.

"Look, I know Miriam is here with the baby. You are going to be in major trouble for hiding them if you don't get them right now!" He glared at Mary and, raising his voice, shouted, "Miriam, come here this instant!" There was no answer.

He broke the silence. "My daughter, Miriam, is mentally unstable. I don't know what kind of story she's told you, but she's not fit to raise a child. She's a thief, a drug addict, and an alcoholic, just like her mother. A pathological liar too. I'm only thinking of the baby. My grandson."

Mary had listened and watched impassively, her hand still on the phone.

"I don't know anything about your daughter," she said calmly. "She is not here. And, as I told you before, there are no babies in this house. I'd say you were welcome to search the premises, but then I'd be the liar. You're not welcome at all. You came into my home under false pretenses and now I want you out." She was dialing as she spoke the last words. When it answered, she said into the phone, "Earl, I have a man here bothering me. Could you come over right away? And, Earl, bring your gun."

Ralph and Duane. How could they have connected her to the missing money? Bruce was in Canada and couldn't have known it was missing from the storage container. And when he did find out, he wouldn't connect her with it. He didn't think she knew about the one down in Brewer.

Miriam had hidden behind the Dumpster in the parking lot of the convenience store across from the apartment until she'd seen the two thugs leave. They had only been to the apartment once before. Mostly Bruce met them down in Bucksport or in Bangor. He didn't want them at the apartment. Too risky.

She watched them go to the end of the block in either direction and circle the house. Ralph screamed, "Bitch, we know you're out here, so listen up. We will find you!" Duane took out his cell phone but put it back in his pocket right away. Miriam assumed he was trying to call Bruce wherever he was, and she blessed Maine's erratic cell service.

Her mind was racing. Bruce must have come back, gone to Brewer to stash the prescription drugs he'd brought across the border—that very long border impossible to patrol, just as Maine's very long coast was in better weather. By land or by sea, Maine had always been a smuggler's dream and a law enforcement nightmare. He must have found out that the money was missing sooner than she thought he would—she hadn't taken it all—and sent Duane and Ralph to grab it, and her.

The two got in their pickup and roared off. It was tricked out with flames airbrushed on the sides. Perennial adolescents: totally amoral, psychopathic ones. But she couldn't think about them—or Bruce—now. She had to get down to Sanpere and make sure her father hadn't taken the baby away.

It didn't take long to walk to Cindy's apartment and pick up her car keys. Cindy was living with her boyfriend and using Miriam's address for her parents. She stopped by to pick up the mail every week and score some dope. Miriam figured Cindy owed her. Her parents never called, because dutiful daughter that she was, Cindy had arranged a weekly time when she would call them, saving them the cell phone minutes, since "I'd probably be in the library anyway and you'd just get my roommate, Miriam." Cindy had had Bruce take a pic-

ture of Miriam and her on the couch with a stack
of books on the coffee table, so she could send it
to her parents. They lived in Duluth, and it was
highly unlikely that they'd be dropping by unan-
nounced. Miriam had been impressed by Cindy's
thoroughness, but college students in general were
a pretty crafty bunch, she'd noticed—or maybe it
was that parents just wanted to believe.

Miriam was passing through Orrington when she
saw her father's car pass. It wasn't hard to miss.
There weren't too many silver Mercedes S500s
(have to have a killer car to impress the buyers and
sellers) around at this time of year. The summer
people were going for the SUV version in the
absurd belief that they were blending in rural-wise.
To really blend in, they'd have to drive an at-least-
ten-year-old pickup with vanity plates that combined your name with your wife's or one of your
kids'.

Miriam thought fast. Her father had obviously
been down to Sanpere if he was coming this way.
He might or might not have Christopher. Suddenly
she was furious. She pulled into the deli Freshies'
parking lot, did a quick U-turn, and followed him.
He wouldn't know Cindy's car, or any other car
Miriam might be driving. Her hopes for one as a

high school graduation gift—even a used one—
had been dashed when neither her father nor stepmother turned up for the ceremony. Returning
home, she'd found a note on the front door telling her to pack her things and be gone by the time
they came back from their weekend. There had
been a fifty-dollar bill inside. She'd supplemented
the money with Brenda's jewelry, some of which
had been Miriam's mother's. Because she didn't
consider herself a thief, but thought of the whole
thing as making up for a lot of years of gifts like
tube socks, Miriam saved her mother's, pawned
the rest, and put the tickets in an envelope, which
she left in Brenda's jewelry box before leaving for
good herself.

It was easy to keep the big silver car in sight.
If her father didn't have Christopher that would
mean the baby was still safe with Mary. If he did,
she would take the baby back, and when he re-
sisted, as she was sure he would, she'd either grab
Christopher and run or—failing that—make a
scene and get somebody to call the police. Christopher was her baby, not his.

She was surprised when he didn't turn south
toward Portland. What was going on? Where was
he going? He was speeding up too. Well, so would
she. Except she'd have to stop for gas. Damn. She

followed for a couple more miles and saw him turn. Okay. She was sure she knew where he was going now. But why?

The car loaded with baby things, Faith Fairchild passed both Daniel and Miriam Carpenter. She took note of the Mercedes. It was so unusual to see one out of tourist season, but the man driving it meant nothing to her. And Miriam's borrowed Toyota didn't even register. Faith was thinking of how pleased Mary would be. Now they knew the baby's mother's name and address. They'd be in touch with her by phone, meet her—and find out what was going on.

The afternoon light was fading fast. Faith speeded up. She hated driving at night in Maine. Even in the summer the dark was very dark. She wanted to get home before night fell and even your high beams couldn't pick out the twists and turns in front of you.

Mary Bethany had been sure her words would get Dan Carpenter out of the house. Bullies were usually cowards. She was eager to tell Faith what had happened and especially looking forward to telling her all about the call she had put through to the small Granville library, knowing it was closed,

and not Lieutenant Earl Dickinson. Earl *did* patrol
the island, in fact he lived here, but Mary hadn't
wanted him around any more than she had wanted
Daniel Carpenter.

She went to the barn and decided to stay there
until dark, when it would be easy to see headlights, although she wasn't expecting anyone. But
she hadn't been expecting Miriam's father either.
Better to err on the side of caution. She'd told Faith
to wait until tomorrow to bring the baby things
over. The poor woman hadn't had hardly any time
with her family these last few days. This meant
that any lights Mary saw would not be welcome
ones.

Christopher was sleeping so soundly, a warm
little bundle against the straw in the manger, that
she didn't want to disturb him by moving him
to the basket. The nannies were content for once
and continued to greet her cheerfully. Christopher
didn't move a muscle, so Mary turned her full attention to the herd, starting with Dora, her oldest
goat—the queen. Then she spent time with each of
the others in order of age. You had to do it this way
or they got upset and confused. It was the same order for milking, grooming, everything. Each goat
knew her place. No one tried to squeeze ahead.
They all got along together and with her. Faith was

going to bring her some baby books, which would be a help, but Mary thought raising goats and raising children were much the same. Of course she wouldn't have to make ear splints for Christopher. Sometimes Nubians were born with folded ears and they had to be splinted for a few days, otherwise they'll stay that way. She looked at the herd with pride, shining coats and straight ears.

Christopher weighed about as much as a newborn kid too from the heft of him. Could be he was even a little more. She'd made a kind of sling from her shawl and carried the baby close to her body when he wasn't in the basket. Mary had had to do that for one of her kids once after the kid had opened up her muzzle on a nail she'd worried loose. Goats are very curious, and childproofing a house would be child's play—Mary smiled to herself—compared to goat proofing the barn and pasture. And the nannies were social creatures, like people—except me, she thought ruefully, and the enormity of what she was contemplating struck her.

She continued to sit and reflect on the last forty-eight hours, stroking the youngest goat, Sheba, who had a particularly appealing face. Trusting, innocent. Yes, it was in the Bible, but Mary never could understand the Almighty's choice of a goat to bear the sins of the world, abandoning it with all that wickedness in the wilderness—the scapegoat. Why not a scapeox or a scapesheep? Those were around back then too.

Christopher gave another of those sweet little baby sneezes and Mary decided it was time to get moving, although the barn was warm as toast and she hated to leave it. Besides the coziness, it was the way the place smelled. Nannies didn't stink the way bucks did, just gave off a kind of living-things aroma.

The second milking done and goats fed, Mary went back into the house with the baby. She would have to make cheese tomorrow. The nannies were giving more milk than usual, and even with Christopher's consumption, she had too much.

Mary loved making cheese. Anne Bossi at Sunset Acres Farm over in South Brooksville had given her the recipe years ago, and Mary had taught herself, soon turning out a soft, spreadable chèvre. Every time she added the rennet and returned the next day to her curds and whey, she was as pleased at the way nature worked as she had been the first time. Faith had been the one to suggest adding herbs besides salt and eventually sun-dried tomatoes and mixed peppercorns for two more varieties.

In the kitchen she stoked the woodstove and settled back in the rocker to feed the baby. The house seemed very quiet. The creaking of the rocker on the old linoleum began to get on her nerves, as it never had before. She got up and went into the parlor to finish the feeding, turning on the small television she'd bought for her B and B guests. The early news was on, and she settled into the sofa to watch while the baby drank. His mother must have bottle-fed him, Mary realized. He wasn't missing her teat.

She hadn't watched the news in a while and had forgotten how tedious it could be. First they tantalized you with the weather, not actually telling you what was predicted lest you turn to another station or, heaven forbid, switch the set off. It was going to be—something. Then there was more about Afghanistan. Mary thought about a twenty-year-old Christopher going off to fight some war and prayed that by that time the world could come to some sort of truce. Not like each other—that was impossible. Just a truce.

"This just in. Police are investigating a homicide in Orono and we are live at the scene. Steve, are you there?"

Mary sat up straight, unmindful of the baby on her lap for the moment. A reporter was standing in front of a shabby-looking multifamily dwelling, the sidewalk cordoned off with those yellow crime scene plastic ribbons. Yellow ribbons for hope; yellow ribbons for despair. She'd never thought about it before.

"Yes, I'm here, Rosemary. Police are not releasing the name of the victim pending notification of next of kin, but according to our sources here, he was a Caucasian male in his twenties who lived in the building behind me in an apartment on the top floor with several other people. Again, the police have not released any information other than they are treating the death as an apparent homicide."

"Do we know anything about how and why this might have happened?"

"Our preliminary sources have indicated that the cause of death was a stab wound in the chest, but police are neither confirming or denying that. We have also been told that drug paraphernalia and a large quantity of heroin were found in the apartment."

"Thank you, Steve." The picture shifted back to the studio, and the anchor, face carefully composed in a serious expression of regret—and condemnation—said, "A homicide in Orono. We're at the scene and will keep you informed. Now, how about those Bruins, Larry?"

Mary reached for the remote and muted the sound. It wasn't just that it was in Orono, it was what she had seen as the camera panned past the flashing blue lights and knots of curious—or prurient—onlookers to a small block of stores. Sammy's 24 Hour Store was right on the corner.

She had to call Faith.

Had she waited for the weather report, Mary would not have been surprised at the way the wind picked up an hour later, nor at the snow that began falling in horizontal sheets shortly after. She gathered flashlights, candles, and blankets, setting up camp in the kitchen. There was plenty of stove wood. The house's wiring hadn't been replaced—in her lifetime anyway—and she often lost power in just a stiff breeze, so the possibility was not alarming. Possibility became probability as the howls from the heavens increased their ferocity.

The phone rang and it was Faith. Mary had left a message with Tom for her to call, and Tom, who had heard the weather report, was very worried about his wife.

"How could it take her so long to go to Ellsworth and back?" he'd said when Mary had called.

"I don't know," Mary had replied honestly.

"This could be a big storm, Mary. I'm going to come and get you and your nephew. We're bound to lose power and you could be snowed in for days."

Confused momentarily by the reference to her nephew and quickly realizing he meant Christopher, Mary had told Tom, "It's happened before. We'll be fine. Besides, I don't think you have room for the two of us and six goats."

Tom conceded the fact and said he'd have Faith call as soon as she got in, which better be soon or he was calling the state police.

Fortunately Faith had arrived home safe and sound a few minutes later. She called Mary immediately. "I know you can't leave the goats, but do you want me to come get the baby? There's so much to tell you. I found out his mother's name is—"

"Miriam Carpenter and I guess I'll keep Christopher here."

"How on earth did you find this out? Is she there?"

That was the only logical explanation and Faith was momentarily miffed. She had been so clever at putting two and two together, or in this case, many more numbers. And why was it "two and two," anyway? In her experience, things came in double or even triple digits.

Mary told her about Dan Carpenter's visit.

"He wants Christopher—that's obvious—but from the terrible things he said about her, it seems he doesn't want his daughter. I'm sure she wouldn't

have wanted me to give him the baby. I didn't lie
but took a page from your book and left a lot out.
But, Faith, he scared me. I'll never let Christopher go to him. When Miriam was saying a 'good
man,' I know she wasn't thinking of her father.
But I haven't told you what was on the news just
now. There's been a murder in Orono and I could
see that convenience store—Sammy's—when the
camera was filming the neighborhood around the
house where the police found the body."

"Who was killed?" Faith asked anxiously. Could
it have been Miriam? She calmed down. If it had
been, Mary would have mentioned it right away.

"They're not releasing the name yet, but he was
white and in his twenties—and there were drugs in
the apartment."

"Can you describe the building?"

Mary did. Faith could have described it herself.
It was Miriam's building and Faith was pretty sure
it was Miriam's apartment. The top floor.

Miriam hadn't been killed, but was she the killer?

Power went out all over the island at 9:45 P.M.
Since a good many people were already in bed, this
posed no hardship for most. Keeping the fire going
and trips to the bathroom would be nippy, but this
was what winter Down East was all about.

With the storm raging outside, Mary felt a deep

sense of peace. She wondered if Christopher was an unusually good baby. He got hungry about every four hours and let her know by slightly increasing the frequency of the little noises he made—noises somewhere between a cry and a bleat to her ears. Sometimes he hiccupped and it was real comical. He was sleeping now and she thought she would nap in the big armchair her father had moved into the kitchen one day, taking the door off to do so. Some summer person was getting rid of it. Mary had slip-covered it with a bright floral chintz that she'd found at the Take It Or Leave It at the dump. There wasn't quite enough, so she'd used some plain blue cotton from the Variety Store for the back. She checked the fire, kissed the baby, and curled up in the chair.

At first she thought the knocking at the door was a dream. She struggled to pull herself awake. Conscious, she realized the storm must have torn a branch loose and it was knocking against a window. She hoped the glass wouldn't break.

But it wasn't a dream or a branch. It was real knocking at her kitchen door. She jumped up to look out the window, then quickly pulled the door open. A woman was standing in the snow that was piling up on the top step and all but fell into Mary's arms.

"It's all right, Miriam. I've been expecting you," Mary said.

The driving hadn't been too bad until she turned off the main road at Orland, and even then Miriam got lucky. The town plow was lumbering along ahead of her. She could barely see through the windshield but kept following the truck's taillights. Her heater was working all right, but the radio had conked out. She was thankful she'd taken the time to fill the gas tank. Once she'd figured out where her father was heading, there was no rush, so she took the time to fill it up.

She wasn't in a hurry after all. Just the opposite. She needed to think. He wouldn't have been heading north unless he had been going to her apartment, and that meant he didn't have Christopher. She wished Ralph and Duane had stuck around as a welcoming committee. Torn between her disinclination to return to the apartment ever again and her desire to have it out with her father once and for all, Miriam had found herself driving north too. She had to make him understand that there was no way he could take her child. He'd taken her childhood. That was enough.

The wiper blades kept freezing. How many hours had passed since she'd seen his car parked on her street, quickly parked herself outside Sammy's and run upstairs to the apartment? It seemed like days, even weeks, but it was hours. Only a few hours.

She was tired. More tired than after the baby had been born. More tired than she'd ever been in her whole life. By the time the plow truck turned toward Castine and left her without a guide, Miriam wasn't sure she could make it to Sanpere. But she had no choice. No choice at all.

Don't think about it, she told herself. Don't go there. It never happened. You were never in that apartment. You didn't do a thing.

She made it as far as Sedgwick, getting out every few miles to clear the ice from the blades. Then, seeing headlights behind her, she pulled off the road and flagged the 4x4 with its plow up that was barreling along behind her.

"Pretty rugged night to be out," the teenager commented when she slid into the cab.

"Yeah, well, my mom's sick and I have to get down to Sanpere."

"I don't want to get stuck on the bridge. I'll take you as close as I can."

Miriam closed her eyes. The warmth of the truck enveloped her like a quilt. The radio was working and tuned to an oldies station:

If I were a carpenter and you were a lady
Would you marry me anyway
Would you have my baby

But she was the Carpenter, she was the lady, and she had had the baby. Miriam had heard the song before; she knew the refrain, ending with: "Give me your tomorrow."

Still she cried, and the hot tears ran down her cheeks. Cried silently, looking out the side window into the darkness, her eyes wide open. Exhausted as she was, if she shut them, it would all come back. The room. The blood. No tomorrow.

"Stay with me. I can't let you out here. It's freezing. You'll never make it!" The boy grabbed her arm. He'd slowed near the bridge and now he'd changed his mind. She pulled her arm away.

"I'm not going to mess with you," he said. "Nothing like that. I'll drop you off at my cousin's. She'll be glad to give you a place to stay. You can't get to Sanpere tonight in this storm."

Miriam was tugging at the door. "I'll be fine. I have really good boots and this parka is supposed to be what those guys who live down in Antarctica wear. I got it at the L.L.Bean outlet. Don't worry—and thanks a lot."

He wasn't ready to give up. He was only a few

years younger than she was. The hood of the gray sweatshirt he was wearing under his jacket was pulled up. He smelled like cigarettes and WD-40, like a million other guys his age in Maine.

"You won't help your mother much if you turn up dead yourself."

She had the door open. He was forced to slow down almost to a stop.

"It's okay. Really. And thanks for the lift."

She was out and away from his headlights before he could say another word. It would have been impossible to explain to him that she didn't care whether she made it through the night or not. She only cared about getting to Mary's.

Getting across the bridge was surprisingly easy. The high winds had kept the snow from piling up and there was no danger that Miriam would be blown into the frigid waters below. Unlike other suspension bridges that allowed for a scenic view, the island bridge had solid five-foot-high walls and was all-business. At the apex, it was hard to keep from sliding down the other side; the road-bed under the snowfall was treacherously slick. The wind blew the falling snow into her face. It felt like grains of sand, sharp and painful. Tiny knifepoints. She ducked her head down against

her chest and pulled her hood more tightly closed.
Knives. She couldn't think about knives.

Back on land, Miriam was sorely tempted to
stop at the first house. It was dark, no lights at the
window. She'd expected the island, like the mainland, would have lost power. Yet she knew a house
was near. She could smell wood burning. A woodstove or a fireplace, maybe both. The pungent
aroma meant there would be warmth—a warm
room, warm clothes, something warm to drink.
But how to explain herself? What was she doing
out on a night that wasn't fit for man or beast? And
tomorrow, when power was restored and the news
came on, what then? She trudged past the smell
and all the others that beckoned until she came to
Mary's road, perpendicular to the Reach, parallel
to the bridge. It wasn't snowing as hard now and
thankfully she'd recognized the turnoff. Once Miriam started down it, there wouldn't be any more
houses. She'd make it—or not.

First we have to get those wet things off. It's all
right. Your baby is safe. Hush, don't try to talk."

Mary ran upstairs and pulled a flannel nightgown, sweaters, and socks from her bureau. She'd
eased Miriam into the big chair, dragging it closer

to the stove. The girl was barely conscious. As she stripped her wet clothes off, Mary was relieved to see Miriam's skin was pale, but not dead white. No frostbite. She rubbed the girl's feet and put on several pairs of socks, then wrapped her in a blanket before undoing the frozen braid that hung like a poker down her back and dried her hair with a towel. The girl had not tried to say another word, but Mary could feel Miriam's eyes following Mary's every move. She heated some whey and honey on the stove, then fed it to the young mother with a soupspoon. After she'd consumed half the cup, Miriam took it herself and drank.

"More," she whispered.

After she finished the second helping, she slept.

Mary had moved Christopher's basket next to Miriam where she could see him. Now she stationed herself in the old rocker and kept watch on them both through the long, dark night.

The Fairchilds were enjoying the power outage. Two full propane tanks at the back of the house had meant hot chocolate and hot water for baths. Now the kids were snuggled in sleeping bags in front of the woodstove; Tom and Faith claimed the couches. The house was almost too well insulated and Faith had tossed off her down comforter. Tom was reading Norma Farber's poem "The Queens Came Late" out loud as they always did on December twenty-seventh. It was a tradition they'd started when Ben was two.

> "The Queens came late, but the Queens
>   were there
> With gifts in their hands and crowns on
>   their hair.
> They'd come, these three like the Kings,
>   from far,
> following, yes, that guiding star.
> They'd left their ladles, linens, looms,
> their children playing in nursery rooms
> And told their sitters: 'Take charge! For this
> Is a marvelous sight we must not miss!'
> The Queens came late, but not too late
> To see the animals small and great,
> Feathered and furred, domestic and wild . . ."

This mention caused Faith's thoughts to drift to Mary's goats. Mary's small, furred, domestic animals—and from there to Christopher, the baby who had appeared on Christmas eve. In the poem the Queens bring useful gifts—chicken soup, "a homespun gown of blue," and a cradle-song to sing. Faith's car was loaded with useful gifts, and she'd already brought the baby a few necessities yesterday. She had gently explained to Mary that unlike baby kids, kid babies needed more nutrients than goat's milk—superb in every other way—could provide and Christopher would have to have formula. The Harborside Market had enough in stock to feed him for a while and Faith had planned to lay in a larger supply on her trip off island. And diapers. "Just as a backup, Mary. You can't keep washing what you have on hand." With the power out, Faith knew Mary must be relieved to have the bag of Huggies. They fit little Christopher better too. The cloth diaper had enveloped him almost to his chin.

> *"The Queens came late and stayed not long,*
> *for their thoughts already were straining far—*
> *past manger and mother and guiding star*
> *and child a-glow as a morning sun—*
> *toward home and children and chores undone."*

"Read it again, Daddy," Amy begged.

"Absolutely," Tom said. He usually read it at least three times, occasionally four, and they'd be reciting it altogether by then.

The storm was winding down. Faith was sure that Mary was doing fine. She pictured her in the kitchen with Christopher in her arms, next to the woodstove. It wasn't their well-being due to the weather she was worried about. What worried her was the news report Mary had relayed. Faith had heard it for herself on the transistor radio they'd turned on earlier to listen for the latest on the snowstorm. There had been little more about what had happened in Orono other than what Mary had described, except for one detail—the name of the murder victim: Bruce Judd. Miriam and Bruce Singer in the B and B register. That Bruce? And was he Christopher's father?

Faith willed the snow to stop. Their car had four-wheel drive, but it would still be hard to get out in the morning if there was much accumulation. And she had to get to Mary's.

She'd had to wait for John Robbins to plow them out, so it was close to noon before Faith could leave for Bethany Farm. If Tom was puzzled by the intensity of his wife's need to get the baby things over to Mary, he didn't say so. Faith felt slightly guilty at keeping so much from Tom. It wasn't what they did—wasn't what their marriage was about. But she didn't want to upset him when he was coming along so well—or so she rationalized. She felt an almost painful surge of love for him, the kind of feeling you don't have until you're faced with an illness, or worse.

There was no way she was going to drag Tom into this.

The main roads were clear, but when she reached the Bethany Farm road, Faith saw to her dismay that it wasn't. She'd have to walk in, carrying a few things, but leaving most behind. She pulled off the road and started out. It was a bright sunny day—warm enough so the snow that clung to the trees was starting to fall in clumps to the ground. The weighted branches relieved of their burden sprang up like jack-in-the-boxes. Ben and Amy had barely stopped for breakfast before racing out to make a fort, or maybe an igloo, or maybe both with snow-men to stand guard.

By the time she got to Mary's door, Faith had peeled off her outer layer and imagined her children virtually naked from their exertions. It was hard to get them to wear jackets even when it was actually freezing. Mary opened the door immediately and Faith walked into a storybook picture—Jessie Will-cox Smith or Tasha Tudor. A young woman Faith assumed must be Miriam was sitting in Mary's big chintz easy chair, Christopher cradled in her arms while she fed him. Her long shining dark hair tum-bled over her shoulders, tumbled over the soft blue sweater she was wearing. She glanced up at Faith but finished singing to the baby, "You'll still be the sweetest little baby in town" before saying "Hi." It was as soft and melodic as her singing had been.

"Faith, this is Miriam Carpenter; Miriam, Faith Fairchild," Mary said, adding to Faith, "She knows all about you."

But I don't know all about you, Faith said to herself as she greeted Miriam.

The room was glowing—with the heat from the stove, the smiles of the three women, and the radiant baby. Faith felt enormously relieved. Miriam was here, safe with Mary and Christopher. She wasn't in Orono, couldn't have been in Orono at the time in question and made it down to the island in the storm.

"I have a lot more stuff in the car, but it will have to wait until you're plowed out. If I try to drive in, I'll get stuck for sure," Faith said. She put down the bags containing more sleepers, baby towels, more formula, bottles, and a Snugli. She'd viewed this as a necessity, so Mary could tend the goats with Christopher securely strapped to her chest. She hadn't bought any baby wipes—Mary got them by the carton to keep the goat's udders clean. She had plenty of Bag Balm too. Mary's hands were as soft as the finest French leather gloves. Faith had never milked Mary's goats, but she imagined they felt the same. Christopher's pelt would never suffer.

"I can walk back with you and make another trip," Mary offered.

"No, I'll go," Miriam said.

Mary shook her head firmly. "You're not to stir from where you are. You need to rest up. Besides, Christopher hasn't finished his bottle."

Mary grabbed her jacket and the two women walked out into the sunlight. The air was fresh after the closeness of the kitchen, and Faith felt inexplicably happy.

The snow was so soft that small, sparkling eddies swirled about their feet as they made their way back to Faith's car. The surface caught the afternoon light, turning Mary's pasture into a field of diamonds.

"Have you listened to any more news?" Faith asked.

Mary shook her head. "I don't have that kind of radio. Even if I had I wouldn't have turned it on and upset Miriam. She doesn't know about it."

"I heard the victim's name last night and again this morning. It was Bruce Judd."

Mary stopped walking. "I thought that might be who it was right from the beginning. I haven't asked her any questions—and she hasn't said much.

There's no need to push her." She reached down and shook the snow from a bayberry bush, freeing its branches from the ground.

"I think we do have to tell her about what we've heard," Faith said. "But I'm sure she's not involved. She wouldn't have made it all the way here in the storm unless she'd left Orono early."

Mary started walking slowly. "I don't know when she left. It was almost three this morning when she turned up here."

"Oh," said Faith.

"Yes," said Mary. They reached Faith's car, loaded up, and started back to the farmhouse.

Christopher was in his basket and Miriam was looking at the things Faith had brought when they returned through the kitchen door. Faith started to take off her boots and put them next to Miriam's on the boot tray. Miriam's boots were wet. Not still wet from last night, but newly wet. There was a coating of fresh snow on the right toe. Faith stopped what she was doing. Enough was enough. What had Miriam been doing outside? What possible reason could she have had to go to the barn—the only destination? It was time for the girl to start answering some questions.

"Miriam, your boots, they're—"

Miriam cut her off, shouting: "It's Duane and

Ralph! Look!" She pointed out the window. A pick-up was slowly making its way toward the house, the snow impeding, but not stopping, its progress.

"They'll kill us! Me, anyway! They want the money!"

Mary didn't waste any time. "Get your boots on and wrap the baby under your jacket. Go straight through the woods to the Marshalls. Faith knows the way. Go by the shore, just in case you have to use the canoe. The Reach isn't frozen solid. The canoe's under a blue tarp." As she spoke she was dialing.

"I can't let you do this!" Miriam said.

"Don't waste time, just get out of here! You've got to get Christopher away from them!"

Miriam seemed immobilized. Faith pushed her toward her things. "Hurry!"

"You take the baby," Miriam said, pulling on her parka and calling over her shoulder, "give them the money! Let them have it. Tell them where it is right away! You don't know what they can do!"

As she followed Miriam out the door, Faith could hear Mary telling Sanpere's volunteer fire department—the number you called if anything at all was wrong—"It's Mary at Bethany Farm. Send the truck, an ambulance, and call the police as fast as possible!"

Things with sirens. Faith only hoped they would get there in time.

Outside, the sun was almost blinding. Faith and Miriam with their precious bundle ran across the old pasture behind the house toward the woods. The pickup had stopped and discharged its cargo. The two men were coming around to the back door following the footprints Mary and Faith had made earlier.

"She's getting away! Both of them!" yelled Ralph, spotting the women. He started to run. "Come on!"

"There's someone in the house," Duane said. "I saw the curtains move. She may be trying to trick us." He pointed toward the two figures almost to the trees. "You go after them—I'm going in the house!" He started kicking at the door. "Open up, bitch. We know you're there!"

Inside, Mary knew the longer she could keep them out, the farther ahead the others would get. Ralph had stopped running while he waited to see who was in the house.

The door was solid oak and Mary had hopes it would last until help arrived.

"Sonofabitch!" Duane hopped on one foot, rubbing the toe of his boot, then went back to the truck for something stronger. "What are you waiting for? I told you to follow them, asshole."

Ralph took off again; the two figures were still in plain sight but nearing the woods. Duane shook his head and smacked the side of the truck with his hand before he reached into the bed to get a crowbar. He didn't know what was going on. Mostly his life was pretty simple. He got what people wanted, gave it to people to sell, and they handed over a lot more money than he had paid in the first place. No, he didn't like not knowing what was going on. He felt better thinking about what he was going to do to Miriam when he got her—and he would get her.

Lyle Sanford got out of the cab of the pickup. He'd been watching the scene with detached interest. That was some awesome weed these dudes had was his main thought. He'd been at the register at the market when they'd come in looking for "some old lady who has goats." Lyle had paused before answering, a pause Duane and Ralph mistook for reluctance to divulge information. In fact, Lyle was wondering why so many guys were looking for Mary Bethany, who was like older than his mother, and wondering even more where the two in front of him had gotten their cool tats. Before he'd had a chance to tell them what they wanted to know, they'd offered him some weed and more if he would take them to Mary's farm. Would he! But he had to

wait until Darlene came on, so Ralph and Duane
helped themselves to some Doritos, pork rinds, and
a couple of beers and sat in the truck.

Who are they?" Faith managed to gasp as she ran
toward the woods and safety.

"Drug dealers. They think I stole some money
from them."

There was no mistaking the sound that split
the air.

"Oh shit," said Miriam. "Ralph's got a gun."

As soon as Mary saw Duane approach her door
with the crowbar, she opened it.

"There's no need to damage my property. What
do you want? And what on earth are you doing
here, Lyle?" Mary had seen the boy from the window but hadn't recognized him at that distance.
She hadn't seen him at the market for a while, so
the transformation from white tee shirts to black
and the addition of several pieces of metal stuck
through various parts of his face was new to her.

"Not sure, ma'am," he mumbled.

"Fer sure we're not here for a fuckin' cup of
coffee. Now get Miriam and get the money."

"I don't know what you're talking about," Mary
said.

Duane started toward her, fists clenched.

"That won't work," Lyle said with surprising clarity. "You got to get her goats." He pointed toward the barn.

"No!" Mary cried. "Don't you dare go in there. I'll give you the money. Miriam isn't here. You could see that."

"Well now, this is much better." Duane lowered his arms. "Ralph will take care of Miriam. Okay, Grandma, let's get the cash—and it had better all be there."

"You stay here; I'll bring it to you." Where was the fire truck? Why hadn't at least one volunteer arrived yet?

"No, I think we'll all stick together."

"It's in the barn." Mary hated to bring him anywhere near her nannies. They'd be upset for days. But there was no choice. Lyle tagged along, and as predicted, the goats bleated in panic. Mary tried to calm them, but Duane—after giving the goats a startled look; he was apparently a city boy—told her to hand over the money and hand it over fast.

She walked over to a pile of small square bales of hay—she bought it like this rather than in the rolls because it was easier for her to handle. Easy to handle the other day when she'd hollowed out the middle of one and replaced the straw with the money.

"Here." She shoved the packet at him. "Now get out."

Duane opened it up. "Looks like it's all here, but I think I'll just count it to make sure. Could be you wanted to use some of it for a new billy goat." He laughed. It wasn't a pleasant sound. Mary didn't correct him as to the gender of her nannies. The longer he took the better. She was straining to hear the sirens, but the only sound in the barn was her goats' piteous racket, louder than ten fire engines.

"Now, now, what's this?" Duane snarled, grabbing Mary's arm. "There's two thousand dollars missing!"

"I don't know anything about that," Mary said firmly, pulling free. "I haven't touched that money since I put it there."

"So I guess you musta taken it out before then." He reached into his pocket and took out a Buck knife, flicking it open. "Hey, Lyle, get that little goat over there. He needs a haircut."

Faith knew they were close to the shore. There had been a couple more shots, but since Ralph had to look down to follow their tracks, they'd been able to keep ahead of him. Mary's canoe was under a blue tarp. You could find just about anything under a blue tarp in Maine. Miriam tugged at it, freed the canoe, and dragged it to the shore. Mary had been right. The water in the Reach wasn't frozen the way it was in the smaller coves. There were chunks of ice, but they'd be able to get the canoe in, and then what? Faith certainly hoped Miriam knew how to paddle, because otherwise they were sunk.

"Get in! Grab a paddle and go! I'll push us off!"

"I don't know how!" Faith said. There hadn't been much opportunity for canoeing growing up in the Big Apple and she'd managed to avoid the activity since.

"You'll learn fast! Now go!"

Christopher had started to cry. Faith felt like crying herself but saved it for later. The canoe teetered in the water. She didn't even want to think about what would happen if they capsized. A minute, two minutes in water this temperature before they were gone?

Miriam was moving them along with strong, swift strokes. Faith tried to match the rhythm, but gave up and concentrated on calming the baby.

A bullet hit the water just behind them. Ralph was yelling at them from the shore. He emptied the gun as they pulled farther and farther out of range.

Around the corner of one of the points of land that extended like gnarled fingers into the current, Faith could see the Marshalls' dock. They were safe. And some of the volunteer firemen must have arrived at the farm by now. Mary was safe too.

Mary was fine, but Duane was suffering from a nasty bite on the hand from Dora, who had been very curious about the bright shiny object in his hand. She'd slid through the gate from the stall that Lyle hadn't closed properly, and lunged to explore the blade, encountering instead Duane's very fleshy palm. Before he could do more than just shove at the 180-pound pride of Mary's herd, the fire department, ambulance corps, and an officer from the sheriff's department all poured through Mary's barn door. He arrested Duane and Lyle immediately and sat down to wait for Ralph to return in the custody of the men who'd gone after him. One of the volunteers took pity on Duane and poured more than enough iodine on his open wound before bandaging it.

We can call the farm from the Marshalls' and as soon as we speak with Mary, they'll drive us back." Faith was nuzzling Christopher's tiny head, which seemed to be keeping him quiet.

Miriam maneuvered the canoe toward the dock, and Faith grabbed a line tied to the end of it, pulling them in alongside.

"Maybe we should put the canoe on the dock. No, it won't be here for long. We can moor it and someone will take it back to Bethany Farm." She stepped out and reached to help Miriam. The expression on the girl's face troubled her. They were safe. All of them. Why did Miriam look so sad?

"Look, Faith, this is where I get off. Or rather you get off," she said with a sigh.

"What!" Faith exclaimed.

"I'm not like you or Mary. I'm not a good girl. And I certainly wouldn't be a good mother."

"It's Bruce, isn't it?" Faith said. The cold dread she'd felt since hearing about the murder gave way to cold certainty.

"Kind of. I didn't kill him, though, if that's what you mean."

"Then who did? Those men? Duane and Ralph?"

"Pretty much. They got their licks in first. But, believe me, you don't need to know about this. Tell Mary that Christopher is hers. I left a letter in the drawer where she keeps her dishtowels. If that's not enough to convince the state, I'll sign whatever they want. Help her get a lawyer. She's got plenty of money. It was mine; don't let the cops have it.

It's Christopher's inheritance from his father and all he will ever get, thank God.

"I thought this was going to be a whole lot easier." She sighed. "I decided last summer that I wanted Mary to be the baby's mother. When he was born, I wanted to give him to her even more. She's the best person I ever met. Tell her that. And also that the week I spent with her was the happiest in my life."

"Then why go?" From the moment Faith had seen the three of them together in Mary's kitchen, she had been picturing a perfect happily ever after. Mary and Miriam—the two Marys—raising Christopher, goats, and vegetables together on into the sunset.

"I'm only twenty-one years old. Even if I was a good person, that's too young to have a child—at least for me. And I have to figure some things out, a lot of things out."

"What about your family? Your father?"

"There isn't any family now, never was much of one. But don't worry, Daniel Carpenter isn't going to try to get Christopher as a trinket for Brenda—that's my stepmother, or rather, his wife—or a male to continue the sainted Carpenter line. Be sure Mary changes his name to hers."

Faith had so many questions, but Miriam was already untying the line.

"How can you be sure that he won't take legal action to get his grandson?"

Miriam hesitated for a moment, then said, "Because, good, kind Mrs. Fairchild, Daddy finished what Duane and Ralph started. I got there just in time to see him go nuts when Bruce managed to pull a knife on him. The knife ended up in Bruce. Self-defense? Helps to have a witness for that."

She started to pull away from the dock. The shadows were lengthening; darkness was falling on the picture in Faith's mind as well. Then Miriam remembered something else.

"I took two thousand dollars from the money I'd left with the baby. Mary stashed it all in a bale of hay in the barn. She told me last night. I think she knew what I'd do. But I'll pay it back. Be sure to tell her."

Miriam had a lot of things she wanted to be sure Mary knew, Faith thought. This wasn't the right ending, but it was the ending.

"I told you that you could get in touch with me if you need to," Miriam said. "The island newspaper is online now. In July we joked about how high-tech the island was becoming and that Mary would be selling cheese on the Internet soon. We'll use the Personals, you know where people put ads saying happy anniversary or thanks for the cards when they were in the hospital. I'll call you if I read, 'Mother Mary come to me.'" She pulled away from the dock, gliding toward the open water in the Reach.

Faith held Christopher up so Miriam could see him. She waved and left them, heading for the bridge, which was not far away—and a ride to somewhere.

Let it be.

A Few Tastes

FROM

Small Plates

Cardamom Raisin Bread

FROM "THE TWO MARYS"

1 quart milk

1 ½ cups sugar

½ cup butter

1 tablespoon cardamom, ground

2 cakes compressed yeast or two packages of yeast granules

1 teaspoon salt

1 package (approx. 2 cups) seedless raisins

1 package (approx. 2 cups) golden or Muscat raisins

2 eggs, beaten

12 cups flour (approx.)

Topping:

1 egg yolk

1 teaspoon vanilla

1 tablespoon sugar

Heat the milk and sugar, then add the butter and cardamom. When the butter has melted, cool the mixture to lukewarm. Add and dissolve the yeast.

Add the salt, raisins, and beaten eggs. Work together well and add enough flour to make a firm but elastic dough. Cover the dough and let stand in a warm place until doubled in bulk. Knead well until you have a smooth, elastic dough and form into two round loaves—or four standard-size bread loaves. Place the loaves in greased pie tins or loaf pans, and let rise until doubled again.

Bake at 350° for 1 hour. Meanwhile mix together the egg yolk, vanilla, and 1 tablespoon sugar. Brush the loaves with egg-and-vanilla mixture when they come out of the oven.

After you've made it once, you'll get the knack of it for the next time. It needs to rise for a long time and you also have to watch that the top doesn't get too brown or burn in the oven. You may have to cover it with foil near the end. You can also make the dough in a braid. The Fairchilds eat it Christmas morning, but it can be an all-year-round treat for every occasion.

Mussels with Pasta
FROM "DEATH IN THE DUNES"

3 pounds fresh mussels, washed and bearded

3 tablespoons unsalted butter

3 large garlic cloves, finely chopped

½ cup fresh parsley, finely chopped, plus 2 tablespoons for garnish

1 sprig fresh thyme (or 1 pinch dried thyme)

1 cup dry white wine

8 ounces thin spaghetti or linguine

If your mussels are farmed or from a fish market where they have already been cleaned, your job is easier. Just be sure that they are bearded and rinsed thoroughly, and discard any mussels that are not closed. While you are doing this, bring the water to a boil for the pasta.

Melt the butter in a pot with a lid, large enough to hold the mussels, leaving some room at the top—the mussels will take up roughly two-thirds of the pot. Add the garlic, parsley, and thyme to the butter, and sauté briefly. Be careful not to let the garlic brown.

Add the mussels and pour the wine on top. Cover immediately.

Cook the pasta. You want it all to come out at the same time as the mussels—around 7 minutes.

Drain the pasta and divide it among four large heated soup bowls. Spoon the mussels on top of each portion. Make sure all of the mussels have steamed open. When you have finished, ladle the broth over each bowl. Some cooks strain the broth, but I like the bits of garlic and the parsley. Sprinkle each dish with the remaining parsley and serve with a side salad and crusty bread.

You can do all sorts of things with this basic recipe: add lemon zest, fresh chopped tomato, and/ or chopped sausage—chorizo or linguica—to the pot before you put in the mussels and sauté. I also like to use whole wheat pasta, which stands up well to the hearty mussel and garlic flavors.

Serves 4.

St. Germain Cocktail
FROM "ACROSS THE POND"

Ice cubes

1.5 ounces St. Germain brand or other elderflower liqueur

2 ounces dry white wine

Club soda

Lemon twist

Fill a Collins glass (a 10–14 fluid ounce narrow tumbler) with ice cubes, about three-quarters full.

Add the liqueur and wine. (The liqueur is very sweet, so this is why you want a dry white wine, such as a pinot grigio or sauvignon blanc.) Stir and top off the glass with the club soda. Add the twist of lemon.

For special occasions, use champagne, eliminating the dry white wine and club soda.

You can also prepare the drink in a cocktail shaker filled with ice cubes, then strain the liquid into a chilled martini glass and garnish with a twist of lemon or lime.